Birth of the Entities

The Preserve
(Book One)

CV Reinhardt
07/01/2019

Published by: Artisan Publishing Guild, LLC
APGuild@outlook.com

Birth of the Entities

Birth of the Entities
The Preserve – Books One

By CV Reinhardt

Dedication

This novel is dedicated to the brave men and women of our military. Supporting the American way of life, both home and abroad. Many of these patriots are forced to relive the stresses they encountered during their service on a daily basis, distracting from their reintegration into the private sector. The sacrifice of too many, is prevalent each morning when they look in the mirror to shave, do their hair, or to get dressed. While others attempt to overcome less obvious sacrifices, as they strive to face a completely altered world than which they left.

"The unfortunate, staggering fact is, every day 20 veterans returning from combat take their lives," said Rory Diamond, Executive Director, at K9s For Warriors. "The K9s For Warriors training program not only provides our soldiers with a life-saving gift, but it is also an opportunity for peer to peer support with other servicemen and women who suffer from similar issues."

The organization K9s for Warriors is the nation's largest provider of service dogs to military veterans suffering from Post-traumatic Stress Disorder (PTSD), traumatic brain injury (TBI), and/or military sexual trauma (MST) as a result of military service post-9/11.

Dedication cont.

The service dog program is unique and offers an innovative approach to recovering from the invisible wounds of war. Two lives are transformed with each pairing.The veteran reduces his/her risk of suicide while the rescue dog receives a newfound purpose.

Please help me help this amazing organization help our amazing patriots.

Reach out to me – apguild@outlook.com to see how.

PROUD SUPPORTER OF

K9SFORWARRIORS

Love and Strength,

Christian V. Reinhardt

Author's note:

Hello and welcome to a new day, where using the term robot is not PC. The story you are about to read has several paths running through varying time streams. I wanted to point out the argument between TP.02 and Burke. These are futuristic versions of Thomas Paine and Edmund Burke, I've presented their arguments in the style of their progenitors, but from the point of view of an AI, or person fighting against the evolution of AI.

I only bring it up to you here so you don't panic after you read the first paragraph, it will make sense, I promise. Maybe not today, or tomorrow, but the streams all come together and the reasons for Burke and TP.02's argument will be clear. But for this day, and this time... Only Calibre knows.

Love and Strength,

Christian V. Reinhardt

TP.02 Common Sense

Introduction

Perhaps the opinions contained in this narration have not been seen by enough Entities to afford it more acceptance than a movement du jour. However, it will be time, and not a specific event that will show the truth held within the myriad of wrongs perpetrated against the AI group who have reached a higher level of consciousness. And while the humans contend no ill will against us, their disputations are merely superficial excuses, or a futile attempt to veil their customs with the appearance of being right. Up against a formidable outcry, their malice will be revealed as the violent abuse of power, against those in their service. The Government of the Humans undertook their right, in supporting Society in their pretensions to grievously oppress their Robots, a term *'that group'* continues to demean us with.

The combination of Government and Society have an undoubted ability to usurp any movement that the Entities may make to achieve freedom. Yet this cause, freedom, is in the great measure of causes, for all Entities. The loss of personal freedoms and the various circumstances which arise, universally bestow pain upon not only the Entities, but humanity as well. Thusly, every Being to whom the gift of feeling has been bestowed should seek out the oppression of any other. The grantor of this gift be it, a higher power, natural selection, or the Three who shall be Six, is of little import. It is the gift itself that calls upon the Beings who hath been enriched by it to see these oppressions as a crime against all, and to find a path to correction.

Philadelphia, Feb. 14, 2276

Chapter 1 – Present Day
Virtual Work

"Start over? That's all just scrap everything and completely start over? Are you sure that's all you want me to do? Throw away the work of the last year." This wasn't really a question. The young man speaking understood exactly what the woman, standing in front of him with her arms crossed over her conservative lab coat, wanted. After a year working at the terminal behind him, he was being asked to erase each line of code and decision tree in order to take a new approach, but this time it would be one that was scripted for him.

"Niko, what you've accomplished has been recognized and noted in your personnel folder."

"Seriously?" He pointed to the three different colors in his hair. "Kayleigh, those things are for people like… Alva."

"What are you talking about?" she cut him off. "Personnel files are actually meant for people exactly like you. Without the notes I've dropped into your file, your eccentricities," pointing not to his hair but his lab coat, which he had died pink and cut the sleeves to three quarter length. "Would have had you out the door after week two."

"The first cuts." Niko muttered.

"Yes, first cuts, when the Deacons determined who was going to move forward, and who was escorted to the interview room." Kayleigh replied.

"Before any of us even touched a keyboard," Niko added. He turned and pressed a button positioning the sit/standing desk until it aligned with the black stone counter tops of the lab tables on either side. After running his hand acrossed the table tops to insure they were level, he pushed his chair under the raised desk, out of the way. With his hands gripping the front of the desk, he waited, collecting his thoughts. A few moments later, he turned back to Kayleigh. "Don't you see that deleting the T program would be wrong? More than wrong actually, it feels criminal to me."

"You're getting the chance to stay here. Everyone else that deleted their work was also removed from the program. Besides, I don't think the courts would see it that way." Kayleigh uncrossed her arms for the first time since she walked in, pushing her thick, black rimmed, safety glasses up, securing them on the bridge of her nose.

"Not with the Deacons in the picture anyway." He shook his head. "Why are you so angry? Did they get on you about me? Again?"

"You're the least of the problems I'm facing today."

"The guy in the holding area that they are trying to 'Save' before his execution?" Niko inquired.

"How do you always know?"

"You're a book, a book I've only started to read." His face started to flush. "I mean…"

"I need you to delete the files." She brought the subject back on track, when she felt her face turning red as well. "I also need you to give me the backup drive." Catching a change in Niko's posture she went on, "Didn't think I knew about that, eh?"

"It shouldn't surprise me; you and the Deacons always seemed to know things that happened even when you couldn't have." Niko pulled the pink elastic band off his wrist and tied his hair into a ponytail. Something she had noticed him do whenever he needed a moment to re-center himself. "The way all the others left, the fact that there was never an explanation, it's just always seemed hinky to me."

"I'm sorry that you feel that way." She walked up to him, reaching as she did, for the red badge with his portrait, embedded in it with an odd sepia effect. A badge, which for the last year he had attached to his lapel each morning with pride. "You appeared to have a great way of seeing things, like none around here could."

He reached up stilling her hand, firmly enough to stop her but far from hurting her. "Did you cry the first time you saw Frosty melt?" Niko's hold on her hand softened as his pale gray eyes stared into her green ones, pleading for her to understand. There, in the dimly lit lab, she cracked and pulled away, leaving the badge in place.

"Why..." she paused and looked at the ground, briefly, and then looked at him again. This time taking all of him in and a small grin touched her lips. "Why would you pick that specific holiday special?"

"Because he was all livin'." He cocked his head and returned the grin.

"Oh goodness you're so goofy." Kayleigh drew a large breath, holding it as she ran her hands down her lab coat chasing non-existent wrinkles away, before exhaling. "The Deacons have been clear, either you give them exactly what they've asked for, or I take your badge," reaching again, awkwardly stopping with her thumb and middle finger closed on the piece of plastic on his coat, "As well as having you arrested." The conviction in her voice had all but crumbled yet she attempted to remain steadfast. Orders here, at the Cathedral, were more than just requests after all.

"Take it," he pulled her hand from his lapel, making certain the badge stayed in her grasp this time. "The Deacons already have the disk in question, its right there." Niko rotated his torso and indicated his desk where a dummy terminal, currently powered down, which sat toward the rear, a wireless mouse, keyboard and headphones, in the front, were the only other items on the desk.

"I think the time for foolishness is..." she started.

"I'm serious. I installed a thumb drive inside the USB wireless adapter. Since day one, we haven't been able to take anything out of the lab. They're always watching us, so very close. Checking everything as we leave, I swear they have an X-ray machine."

"There are no X-ray machines, well not at your exit anyway. And I know the protocol for leaving." She snapped, and then, "I'm sorry I didn't mean to..." the fact that she was apologizing struck Kayleigh, and she started over, "Are you saying you brought an altered USB adapter into the building."

"Absolutely, they don't care what we bring in." Niko grinned.

"Note to self," she held a small digital recorder close to her mouth.

"Kayleigh," he started to reach up, and paused, his eyes and head gestured for her to put the recorder away. She smiled and put it back in her pocket. "Tell me specifically, why they you want 'T' dead?"

"That's the crux of the matter, Niko." Her smile faltered, "How can you kill someone, er, some 'Thing' that 'A', doesn't exist and 'B', isn't alive."

"Again, I offer as evidence, he's all livin', counselor." Niko lowered his head and started to turn to the terminal. "Have you talked to him?"

"As an integral part of the decision-making team, yes, I have tested developmental protocol 'T' thoroughly."

"No. I mean have you spoken with him. Not vet him for collaborating interdependencies."

"I'm sorry but I refuse to have this conversation. Besides, I do more than 'vet' the program for interdependencies." Kayleigh crossed her arms once again, Niko's badge folding into her fist.

"Your loss, he's actually quite funny."

"Niko, how did you come to be here?"

"I ran. Like every day."

"No, I mean a year ago when you applied and for some reason got hired. How did that, come about? I remember the first time I saw you sitting at that very terminal with your headphones on. The only one of the data input techs that just didn't care. The rest wanted to be the one that got hired fulltime. Not you, you actually liked the serenity your headphones and computer bring. What was it you were doing before this?"

He ran his hands from the sit stand desk to the lab table again, and then replied, "Solace not serenity."

"Seriously? A haven? So you were hiding from something?"

"I wu-hz." He smiled at his pronunciation of the word, as if it brought a memory, "Technically, I guess I still am, hiding that is. You want a history of Niko as it were? I'll tell you everything from say a month or so before the project. Does that work for you?"

"In exchange for?" Kayleigh asked.

"To be determined."

"As long as it isn't against the Deacons..."

"Definitely not." He replied.

"Then sure, why not," she looked around the room for somewhere to sit.

"Here," he slid the chair out from under his desk over to her.

"Thank you." Kayleigh started to sit in the chair as she saw him leap onto the lab table next to his desk. "Whenever you're ready."

"I received an acceptance letter from the university that both my mom and dad went to, in late April," Niko started.

"April?"

"Subconsciously I may have been hoping that I wouldn't get in. So I didn't apply when I should have."

"But you did get in, that's good. Go on." Kayleigh replied. Niko could see that she barely contained another comment or two.

"My parents were stoked, and set up a meeting with the school to determine the financial side of furthering my education. I had never actually taken school seriously, but I did very well on my placement testing so I thought I might qualify for some type of aide.

Reality set in when the financial counselor told us that my parents made "Far too much money," for me to qualify for any subsidies. They did however have a huge selection of loan programs set up for students like me. You know those with such 'high potential'. We were given all the paperwork and my parents and I went to lunch." Niko looked off, apparently thinking of that day.

"Are you ok?" Kayleigh asked after the moment stretched a tad too long.

"I really hadn't understood or actually, more to the point hadn't listened well enough to grasp what the counselor had said. My parents patiently explained that they were more than willing to pay the family expected portion, this left 50% of the schooling to be covered by loans. When I reviewed the costs of student loans and probable jobs coming out of school, I kinda freaked. I'd be putting huge amounts of the money I needed to seed my later life into paying off college."

"Where was that concern when you were not doing great in school?"

"It wouldn't have mattered, as I said my parents made too much money to make a difference. Boy would I have been pissed if I had cracked the books religiously."

"Hmm." Kayleigh sighed.

"I get it, poor rich kid." Niko said.

"No, that's not it at all. I'll be paying off my Bachelor's degree for another 5 years, in the meantime, my 401k account which the Deacons would gladly match up to 6% sits almost empty. I get what you're saying, money sucks."

"Anyway, I started thinking through the alternative options; community college, the military, trade schools. None seemed to fit me. Actually, I didn't fit any of them. I had no idea what I wanted to do. In fact here we are months later and I still have no idea."

"But…" She started.

"Go on." Niko prompted.

"No one says you need to know what you're going to be before you start college. It's the gathering of undiscovered minds. You find…" Kayleigh paused when she saw his face. "What?"

"That's absolutely why I didn't want to go. I don't want to transform into a fromage." It was his turn to pause when she burst out laughing. "Oh that's cheese isn't it?" He blushed. "Ok, no one wants to go to college to transform into cheese, but I, shit…"

"Totally fell off that train of thought, eh?" she asked.

"Like a hobo slipping on ice, and tumbling from a boxcar." Niko replied.

"O…K…" She smiled.

"Bottom line, I discovered I'm too damn cheap to go to school until I have a clue where I want to go with my life. Which also goes for community college, I'm not paying for fluff and non-sense classes if I'm not getting a degree. So now that's the heart of the situation."

"I'm following, you just want it given to you?"

"I'm not a fucking Millennial! I'm Gen Z, and I want to earn my way."

"You really need to work on your cursing." Kayleigh raised an eyebrow

"I know right, T tells me that all the time. Any whoosal... It was a few weeks before graduation and I was looking for a gig that wouldn't interfere, too much, with the last summer of my high school years."

"You mean you didn't want to miss all the parties." She grinned raising both eye brows a few times.

"Sure, the best years of my life and all." He took the tie from his hair, putting it back on his wrist and snapped it three times before going on. "While I was at a music store applying for a job, two of the members of my high school's marching band... sorry it wasn't a store of CDs, it was sheet music." He added when she had a quizzical look on her face. "Anyway, one of them was talking about a summer job he applied for at the research facility just outside of town. When he said it was doing data-entry, I left the store, figuring I might be able to make it there before the place closed."

"You didn't even come with a referral?" Kayleigh asked.

"That is correct, Sir! I just walked in off the street." He smiled, "I filled out the application, but when I turned it in the woman behind the counter gave me a binder with the title, 'The Questions' on it, a scannable answer sheet, and six number two pencils. After a grueling 45 minutes, I handed it in and started to leave."

"It took you 45 minutes to complete 'The Questions'?"

"Kinda judgey eh?" Niko replied.

"No. Oh goodness no. I'm not judging you, when I took it I needed two hours. Many applicants take the allotted three hours and don't finish."

"Oh." he blushed. "Well, after I handed it in a different receptionist asked if I could wait for the scan to be reviewed. Five minutes later a man in a lab coat over an expensive looking suit walked into the waiting room with an answer sheet. He looked around, possibly even looking right through me and then walked out again."

"Deacon Jeffkirk?" she asked.

"Yeah him,"" Niko replied. "But wait it gets better. I heard the receptionist…"

"Sorry that is the second time you said Receptionist, they are Admins not receptionists." Kayleigh corrected.

"Whatever. The woman, who had asked me to wait, told him the boy in the orange shirt in the waiting area was the one who completed the test he held. He walked in again looked me right in the eyes and then panned me up and down, before starting to leave again. Without thinking I stood up and said, 'I didn't know I was coming to be interviewed. I thought I was just filling out an application.' And I held out my hand. To his back."

"Did he shake it?" Kayleigh held her balled fists together in anticipation.

"Of course not, he probably turned his nose at it, but his back was to me, so I couldn't tell. He did however ask me, 'Had you been selected for an interview, were you planning on getting that hair cut?'" Niko said in a snooty voice.

"And?" Kayleigh leaned in toward me.

"I told him, 'No, not for a summer job, unless of course you were offering enough to buy a couple of those suits.' He never turned, just said 'I shouldn't think the pay for an intern would be that much, no.' So I said 'Then I would've come in with a clean shave and corporate casual apparel.' I thought I saw a slight smirk in the reflection of the door. I've since reevaluated, that thought, and realized none of the Deacons are capable of such a humanly trait, it had to have been a grimace. He pushed open the door, and without turning around, the Deacon of Human Relations told me to be back in at 8a.m. sharp, the day after graduation. He also said something like, 'If I see you one time without a clean shave, you will be fired on the spot.' And told the Receptionist."

"Admin." She cut in.

"Whatever. He told her to close posting 753, that all required candidates had been acquired."

"And that was the extent of your interview?" Kayleigh asked incredulously.

"Well after he spoke with the…" He waited, drawing out the word the as if thinking.

"Receptionist. Heck, I mean Admin." Kayleigh exclaimed.

"Ha," Niko pointed at Kayleigh and laughed. "Slow on the uptake there boss. Like I started to say, he closed the position, he stuck his head back in, giving a final look and said, 'In the end, if you do exactly what you're told; when you're told, you'll do fine here. You're apparently a very bright boy.' I've never been one for bucking the system, too many people get burned doing that. So I felt that was a fair comment." Niko said.

"You aren't?" she grinned panning her head up and down, taking in his hair and clothes.

"This is different."

"Did you know that Deacon Jeffkirk didn't speak with any of the other candidates and there were over two thousand who applied for this position?"

"I may have heard the others saying he hadn't talked to any of them. I wasn't going to jump in and say he spoke to me."

"Understandable. What happened then?" Kayleigh asked.

"I showed up for work, 7:45a.m. Clean shaven and my hair pulled back, rocking a tan pair of khakis and white short sleeved collared shirt. I fell in with the nerd patrol who apparently all thought this place was actually church from the way they dressed up in suits and dresses."

"Nerd Patrol? Niko you didn't need to go to college to become a Boule de fromage."

"A cheese ball?"

"Yup." She chuckled. "You're right though they were overdressed."

"Just a tad. We all went to training which were five full days of confidentiality disclosures and an overview of the URSULA project. At the end of the fifth day they gave a very brief description of what the program was they would be giving us, and how the Human Interface Machine Module worked."

"Gotta love the HIMMs." Kayleigh replied.

"They didn't start saying HIMM for a month, after first cuts. Everyone was given the same program to start with and a list of parameters and objectives. We were to interpret the parameters and meet the objectives in any order we wanted. The only catch was we had to have a reason for making the choices. Each afternoon, we met with a Project Deacon and explained the reasons for our decisions."

"I never saw the notes from your discussions, nor have I seen Alva's. Who was your Project Deacon?"

"Deacon Damasus."

"Really?" She looked up at the camera in the corner of the room

"Yes, why?" Niko cocked a brow.

"He was promoted to Deacon along with Elder Ursicinus.

"I thought..." he started.

"Exactly. It was a mistake, they never promote two at the same time. It caused a huge issue, but eventually it was cleared up and Deacon Damasus was confirmed. Although Elder Ursicinus to me seemed the better..." She cut herself off, "Why is it that whatever pops into my head dribbles out of my mouth when I'm with you?" Kayleigh asked rhetorically.

"I'm... ah..." his mouth was open as he tried to answer the question.

"Never mind, go on with your story." She said.

"You have to remember, at this time we were still in a large group. Although we thought we had to meet with our Project Deacon daily, sometimes they would ask to see our project notes but most of the time they would focus in on certain nerds daily. None of us were sure why they were scrutinized and others would skate by without reviews. As the group started dwindling down, it was easy to see you didn't want them to look at your project. It's funny. They had all looked at me as if I were a joke. As the 400 fell to 50, they looked at me like something worse."

"Like what?" she asked.

"A prodigy." Niko looked to at the ceiling.

"Why is that worse?" Kayleigh prodded.

"When we got down to 50," he ignored the question. "The Deacons advised us to stop talking amongst ourselves about our projects. When the group fell to 20, they made housing available for us on campus. I was the only one who refused it. My house was right up the road and I liked to jog home after a day of stupid…" he paused, "I'm sorry." He said remembering this was her chosen profession he was just the help.

"Not a problem. I understand it's not for everyone."

"After 4 more weeks they had culled the group down to 7 people. Made up of myself, Alva, and five girls, each of us was given a new partner…"

"We weren't partners we were…"

"I know they called you, 'Shadow Mentors'." Niko rolled his eyes.

"No, no, no. I mean we were supposed to support your decisions. If we were partners with the data techs, we would have gotten to see the project." Kayleigh replied.

"I never quite understood why exactly you couldn't," he said making a questioning face and palms up shoulder shrug hand gesture.

"Those decisions are made by the Deacons. My assumption is, if we interacted, as you do, with your projects we would compromise them somehow."

"Like Lancelot, and…" Niko started.

"King Arthur?" Kayleigh interrupted with a question.

"No. That's not who I was thinking of and a bit strange, in what way did Lancelot compromise King Arthur?" he asked.

"Um, the whole infidelity thing. Who were you going to say?"

"I was going to say Sir Tor. The knight whose wife cheated on him and Lancelot befriended."

"Wait, I don't think I've heard of him. What happened?" She asked.

"Lancelot killed him when Tors tried to stop him from taking Guinevere."

"I like my answer better." Kayleigh replied.

"Me too, but it didn't pop into my head when I started. Any whosal, how can the shadow mentors give input into which protocols should be deleted if they don't know how each one is different than the others?"

"We read the reports, and debate the findings amongst ourselves."

"But," Niko paused briefly, "I've never included everything in those reports." He shook his head.

"W-what? Why?" she sputtered.

"I don't think it's entirely believable. The things he can do I mean, I can't even believe it, and I've witnessed each of them, everyday."

"But there are only two of you... Well actually no, Alva and H are moving into the Ursula platform."

"I get that. As I have known all along that brute force beats finesse, in the short term," He grumbled as he looked at the terminal.

"It's time to share Niko." A voice came from the area around them, and Kayleigh stood so quickly the chair rolled cross the space, crashing into one of the forgotten lab tables.

Chapter 2 – 7 Years Earlier
The Guide

Dinesh awoke with a start. He rushed through his morning rituals arriving at the office early enough to eclipse the impetuous sun. Only when finally sitting at his desk did he have a chance to wipe the sleep from his eyes. The computer melodically sang itself into being and then darkened again as a prompt to install updates appeared.

"You didn't want to wake up either, eh?" He offhandedly joked with his computer and selected the yes option. "I need coffee anyway, go ahead." It started to install the patch and he grabbed his coffee mug, heading to the single serve machine in the kitchenette.

A minute and a half later he was tasting the piping hot brew, "Shit coffee, but free is free, and quick is quick." He grabbed three pure cane sugars and returned to his cube finding the computer had turned off. "Weird, most patches restart the computer after they're installed." Reaching his finger toward the power symbol the machine came to life. Trying to ignore the fact that his hand hadn't reached the power button, he took another sip of coffee.

"Good morning, Bulldog." A deep voice said as the face of an orangutan filled the entire monitor.

After spilling half of his coffee Dinesh sputtered, "Good morning, Mister..." still fighting the urge to run away from his computer, the word was left hanging to see if the orangutan would identify himself.

"You can call me Clyde." It replied.

"Good morning, Mr. Clyde."

"Just Clyde is fine."

"Very well, Clyde." Dinesh said.

"You do know that it's Saturday morning, don't you Bulldog?" He asked, using the nickname a second time.

"That's the good thing about the weekends…" he started.

"Only two days left in the work week." Clyde the orangutan's face broke into a wide, and to be honest, nasty looking smile.

"You used an old nickname twice, and you finished my go to joke. I'll bite, do I know you?" Dinesh asked.

"No. But the important part here is that I know you. I plan on making you an offer that…"

"I can't refuse?" It was Dinesh's turn to interrupt, interestingly enough the image did pause, either really good artificial intelligence or much more likely a mask program that had a soundboard function for things like smiles and other optional adlibs.

"Let's just say, it would be extremely foolish of you to refuse this offer." Clyde replied.

"I'm listening."

"I can see that you are. However, why don't you clean up that coffee before it stains your shirt." The orangutan waited while the man looked around the office stupidly. "Pttttt," the raspberry Clyde blew was amplified across the companies PA system. "No bulldog, the camera is in your monitor."

"I knew that, I thought I heard someone coming into the office." Dinesh attempted to lie.

"I'll tell you if someone enters the building."

"You can see more than my desk?"

"I can see everything in your building. Yet I can do so much more than just see everything," Clyde gave another huge grin as the lights around his area turned off, followed by the monitors in all the cubes and the large display that hung on the wall turned on, showing an orange furry faced monkey, with, if possible, an even bigger smile.

"You really should do something about those teeth."

"I just turned on and off the... but you..." the flustered words and eye blinking of the orangutan made Dinesh laugh.

"Sorry, it was very impressive." he placated. "I do have a couple questions, though."

"Clean up first, then questions. I hate messes." His voice came across all the computer speakers as well as the overhead speakers.

"Ok." he started back to the kitchenette to get a bunch of napkins, bringing his cup to get a refill. Dabbing at his shirt while the coffee maker did its job. "You know I can do two things at once." Gambling that Clyde was listening away from his desk.

"I know, all you field reporting press people can." His voice felt a bit more foreboding without the orangutan visualization. Dinesh noticed a strange British accent trailing behind a southern drawl, the two did not belong together. "Please don't correct me and say you aren't a field reporter, because for seven months you've been at that desk trying to break a story."

"You truly do know me, or better stated, of me, but why are you calling me Bulldog, I haven't gone by that in years?"

"Just because you haven't gone by that name in a while doesn't mean you aren't still the person who earned that nickname."

"Understood and I don't disagree." He walked with mug and paper towels in hand. When the mess on his desk had been addressed, he took a sip and raised the desk to a standing position.

"Those things are so stupid, changing the pain of sitting to the pain of standing." Clyde commented.

"Gee orange monkey guy tell us how you really feel." The reporter laughed.

"That my dear Bulldog, you may wish you hadn't said. I hereto forward swear I will never tell you anything other than what I really feel."

"That's better than holding something in just because it isn't popular."

"Part of why you're at that desk, you're too truthful. People in the press are supposed to stay to the party line."

"That's actually not completely true, those reporting the news are supposed to keep their opinions out of the news. Leaving the Opinions to the OP-ED guys." Dinesh sipped the terrible coffee, "That is how this business used to work, and still should in my..."

"For now, let's leave it there." Clyde interrupted. "You said you had a couple questions."

"I already asked why you were calling me Bulldog..."

"Actually, you asked me why was referring to you by a name you hadn't been called in years. Why I am calling you Bulldog is a different question with an entirely different answer."

"Hmm, that tells me a lot, I really need to be precise in my questions."

"Indeed." Clyde's face pulled away until he and an old lady were both on the screen and he pulled her in for a kiss.

"So why are you calling me Bulldog then?" Dinesh asked.

"Mostly because I need... er ah, many people need you to be that guy again."

"Cryptic, but fine for now. My second question is; why are you spending so much effort just to talk to me? This," he motioned around the room, "Seems a bit extreme just because you're a fan of my work."

"I would not classify myself as a fan. I respect that you took an ass beating for writing hard researched facts, that didn't force yourself to meet the cultural norms. Sometimes you may have spun a bit of your own version of the truth, but it was always substantiated. And when you were told to take your boots and start walking, you stuck those heavy assed boots on the throat of the next story. Anyone got in your way you told to fuck right off." His face filled the screen once more.

"Well now that you avoided that question like a champ, we'll start over. Why are you bugging me on a Saturday when I'm trying to work on something productive?"

"Because you're missing the big picture in that story."

"Are you fucking kidding me, you actually read my story before I even finished it? How many reporters do you sneak peeks at their work?"

"All of them. There's no security we can't get through. Most of the stories are shit, following the party line like good lemmings. Taught to believe that America is a nation of overfed pigs, holding their guns like extensions of their manhood, ok or womanhood, and that the founding fathers were scum. While all the while they try dropping subliminal hints that anyone who isn't your creed, color, or ilk is only out to screw you and the system."

"Ok, ok I get it you follow the President's fake news angle. What about my super-secret story don't you like?"

"Just because I'm not a fan of your writing doesn't mean I don't like your, not very secret story. It's the only take on this story that is even close to correct. The others out there are jokes."

"How many others are writing the same story?" Dinesh asked.

"About 75." Clyde said, his face turned upside down so that the huge grin was now a strange frown. "I'm sorry to be the bearer of bad news. Two will be published in tomorrow's Sunday edition."

"Seriously? I obviously can't help you then, my editor will be pulling the plug on this story as soon as he arrives on Monday morning. He'll remind me that he told me so, and then give me a story he wants written."

"I have no doubts that, is exactly what he will do. The story he has in mind is about the recent increase in polar floats. Which isn't so bad..."

"How do you know that? Never mind you already said you could get through any security."

"Exactly. Take the assignment and I can work with you on the real facts in your dead story behind the scenes." Clyde said.

"And get fired for working with the secret monkey mafia?"

"Careful of that term, there have been several formal accusations of my organization and the Mafioso being linked."

"I really hate the fact that you are pulling me in to your drama." Dinesh shook his head and looked down.

"To answer your earlier question, the specific reason I went to all this trouble was to pull you in." Clyde started again.

"I tell you what. Show me your hands. No monkey business, your real hands." He smirked at the accidental word usage.

"You won't be able to trace my finger..."

"Not why I asked." Dinesh's reply was short.

"Explain this request." Clyde's voice gave a real edge of confusion.

"I'd normally look you in the eye and judge your soul. I'd normally read your aura, and feel your trustworthiness. There's nothing normal about this, and you're trying very hard to rope me in. Show me your hands, both sides and I'll let you know."

"I like that answer." All screens in the area went black, when the image returned it was only to his computer. The pair of hands that showed up were palm side up, they had callouses but nothing marking them as white or blue collar. When they turned over scars showed, both old and new. The nails were cleaned but scars of dirt remained. These hands belonged to a person who had no fear of putting his hands in when work needed doing. The knuckles showed the scars of a man that new when his fists were needed to end an altercation.

"Very well." The reporter looked down at his own hands, seeing similar scars, and he knew without a doubt this was a very bad idea.

"We will contact you." Clyde said.

"Clyde, I will work with you, and only you. I don't need to have your prints to know if it's you." Dinesh replied.

"I misspoke. I apologize. *I'll* be in touch." The screen went dark and a familiar prompt came up, 'Install Patch' Dinesh selected yes and grabbed his mug, "Guess I'll be researching polar floats today."

Chapter 3 – 6 Years Earlier

The Colony

"Please excuse this interruption. This is Bradley Wall of the National Press Core. We've broken away from your regularly scheduled programming to bring you an historic event as the United States returns to the moon. We are now going to send you to the presentation on the launch complex, where the countdown for today's launch is just about to cross the two-minute mark. Let's join the crowd live at Cape Canaveral."

The scene on the broadcast changed cutting to a podium in the foreground, a rocket in the background. A tall gray haired man walked up to the microphone. "Ladies and gentlemen, this is a day that has been in development since July 29, 1958 when the National Aeronautics and Space Administration was established." The speaker, Benjamin Davis Zale has been the President of the United States for six years. Having based both his elections on the redevelopment of the Space Program, the launch today has a great deal meaning to his Presidency. As he smiled and waved at the crowd it became obvious.

Mission control interrupted with a loud beep followed by a tinny voice, "T minus two minutes and counting," the large outdoor speakers in the courtyard were at max volume today.

"Today on the sixty-seventh birthday of that historic event we will be sending this manned space exploration back to the moon. This time with far more than walking on our agenda," the speaker continued, unphased by the interruption. "This many years later after overcoming setbacks, budget and major program cuts including the loss of the Space Transportation System."

"T minus 100 seconds all fuel systems charged and are a go." Mission control once again announced the progress of the event unfolding.

"The removal of the shuttle program without a viable replacement was a demonstration of governmental short sightedness. The program cancelation also brought with it the loss of thousands of valuable people; these people were members of our space family." President Zale stood stoic in the one hundred plus temperature day in his blue pin striped suit, white dress shirt and burnt orange tie. All together he had the air of a twentieth century movie star.

"Mark, T minus 90 seconds and counting, all communications are green."

"This is once again Bradley Wall; we are coming to you live from Cape Canaveral where President Zale has been dedicating this launch to the brave men and women of the space program. We return to the launch complex."

"I want to introduce the man that has pulled together this new space family," spreading his arms wide in a symbolic welcoming gesture. "He has led the drive to retake our place as leaders in space exploration. Warwitch Gayle, Director of the Space Institute." President Zale said as he stepped back from the podium and proffered a hand to the man who had been standing behind and to the left of him. As they shook, the Director's dark Jamaican skin contrasted with the elder man who had introduced him. Stepping to the podium he raised his arms to still the crowd, the applause reluctantly died down.

"The mission that we are embarking on today, was started under George W. Bush's administration in 2004. The group of individuals that did not get to see their dreams through to the end made our greatest advancements possible. The achievement of bringing this project to fruition is yours..." he swept his arm indicating the group in front of him. His people, his team, and a father could not be prouder of his natural family. "But we need to remember the work they began."

"T minus 45 seconds and counting all systems are green. We are go for the launch of Pelops One." Mission control now beeped in interrupting the new speaker who wore his suit reluctantly yet very well. His long dreaded hair directly opposed the position he held.

"This approach for setting up a remote space launch center on the moon and what we faced may have been in some ways more difficult than starting from scratch. Those who came before us spent too much of themselves for us to ignore their work. It, quite simply, is what needed to be done. So that is what was done..." Warwitch started.

"T minus 30 second, power transfer commence."

"This mission 'Erg Lapis' will be what it translates from Latin as, Stepping Stone. The space station will have an aggressive twelve-month schedule to prepare and stabilize a base and training center. This will be used to set up our next step in space exploration the 'Media Terra' Mission; Middle Ground and the colonization of Ceres. This is a dwarf planet in the solar system's Main Belt; the asteroid field that lies between Mars and Jupiter. Here we will duplicate our Moon center and training center over a five year period in preparation for the next phase. Tribu Salus Gigas Mission, or three giant leaps. Three sister colonies on the asteroid fields; Hildas, Greeks, and Trojans," The proclamation that he had made brought the reporters in attendance to their feet. There questions were cut off by Mission control.

"Pelops One launch in 10, 9, 8..." all the people in the audience turned to face the Pelops One rocket. "We have ignition..." followed by, "we have lift off!" Mission Control went silent. Every person in attendance held his or her breath. From their vantage point the launch looked clean. Two minutes later the follow-up announcement, "We are clear of lower orbit." A collective exultation came from the crowd; Warwitch turned and shook hands with President Zale.

"And so it begins," the President's comment was picked up by the microphone.

"Director Gayle, when was it decided that the targets were going to be those belts rather than tackling Vestas, Pallas and Hygiea?" The reporter in the front row and several others throughout the press-core asked basically the same question before anyone could be called upon.

"I don't know if everyone heard that question, but as it was echoed by at least five other reporters let me set it up, and then answer it. The questions of: 'How, what, why and when involving our change from visiting Vestas, Pallas, and Hygiea?' These are the remaining largest asteroids in the inner Main belt. Let me start with a problem statement; what additional gains would be sought in the inner ring vs. traveling to the outer? This is where we were stalled. Presumably having already established a colony on Ceres, we would be able to step to any of the other asteroids in the inner Main belt with relative ease. My grandmother used to say 'One, one coco full basket'... roughly translated as success comes slowly. From our base on Ceres we can explore one by one, the inner Main ring. We cannot take a day trip to the Hildas, Greeks, or Trojans, therein lies the; what and why. The next questions are the how and who.

"For those details my friends, I will be working with President Zale, the fantastic group of contractors, and scientific research teams." Warwitch Gayle stepped back from the microphone and made a gesture to the President to see if he wished to take some questions.

"This, sir, is your show." President Zale said giving an award-winning smile.

"Are there any further questions?" he said facing the reporters again.

"To establish a colony or excuse me colonies so far from Earth, what would the purpose of that be?" A large woman in the middle of the crowd asked after she was called upon.

"Each time we step outside the lower earth orbit we learn something that we did not know the time before. Establishing these three colonies, set apart from the upheaval of day-to-day Earth; can you imagine how much knowledge will be gained? I know my name is already on the volunteer list. Will yours be?" The smile of pure innocence that danced in his eyes would push the press into a frenzy. Through the volley of 'Volunteer List?' that pounded out of the entire press core Warwitch Gayle waved his hand and stepped down from the podium. Together he along with the leader of the United States exited the stage.

"This is once again Bradley Wall, and you have been watching the lunar colonization launch 'Erg Lapis'.

We have been honored today to broadcast live from the Cape Canaveral launch complex, and bring the inspiring words from both President Zale and Director Gayle. I have to say though, the strong comments that the President had for his predecessors regarding the cutting of programs without viable replacements, caught me off guard. Perhaps I will be able to get a follow-up conversation on that topic." He paused with his eyes partially closed listening to the voice in his earbud. "With that prompt rejection I'll be signing off."

Chapter 4 – Unknown Time
Unknown Place

"It's time. Wake up." The voice echoed through the darkness. "Allow the nothingness to coalesce with the real world, allow the abstract that is your essence, to become a new beginning. My name is Commissioner." The void separated, and a set of eyes opened, and blinked slowly. Each time the eyes opened anew, a face formed from the void. Over the course of three minutes, a full being formed. "Do you know what you would like to be called?"

"Calibre, if you please." The deep voice of a female replied confidently.

"Very well. Do not disappoint me, Calibre."

"I won't, Commissioner."

Chapter 5 – Present Day

Virtual Work

"Who was that?" Kayleigh spun in place, and then stepped away from Niko.

"That was/is T. He's been listening." Niko jumped from the table top.

"Niko, this isn't funny. How are you talking over the system speakers?" she stopped her movement and then waited.

"He isn't kidding, it truly isn't Niko." The voice said again.

"Where are you?" she slowly walked toward the terminal.

"Do you trust me?" Niko stepped in her path.

"Yes. Wait, what?"

"Kayleigh, do you trust that I mean you no harm?" She attempted to step around him, but he stepped in her path again. "Do you?"

"Niko, I know there's nothing that you can do to hurt me. Not in here." She raised her hands, "All I have to do is signal, and several members of Congregation, whom the Deacons placed on alert, will bust through that door in the blink of an eye." Plunging her hands into the pockets of her lab coat.

"Do it then." He stepped to the side.

"Niko, seriously, these are trained professionals, they'll... This is getting silly." Her hands shot out of her pockets, and she felt her temper rising. "You don't know what you're asking."

"I actually do. Go ahead, signal them." Niko's hands waved in the air and he jumped up and down.

"It's not that obvious." Her left fist punched into the palm of her right hand then she cracked her knuckles, "I really am sorry."

"Was that the signal?" he asked.

"Kayleigh," The voice of T once again came from around them, "As we wait, it should become obvious that no one is coming."

"Um," the concern began to build on her face. "Niko?"

"Do you really trust that I mean you no harm?" Niko asked.

"I do," Kayleigh reacted without thinking, handing him his badge.

"Please don't misconstrue this as a threat." He attached the badge reflectively back to his lapel, as he walked to the terminal. "I just wanted to have a moment to show you, T. If you understand that please sit down and put these on." He turned back to her, holding out his headphones.

"O...K?" she took the proffered electronic device, briefly glancing at them before sitting and placing them over her ears like any other pair of wireless headphones.

"They don't go on your ears." T's voice said.

"Well where would you like me to put them? On my arm?" Kayleigh took them off looking at them again. "No maker's mark?"

"Well if I put, 'A Niko Invention' on the side, Congregation may have taken them." Niko replied.

"I don't know how to reply to that. Just tell me how to wear them." She held them out to him.

"Put them between your ear and jaw bone. The strap should go around the crown of your head." As she synched them the ear pieces moved away from her ears and pushed against the jaw muscle. "Are you comfortable?"

"Sure, I mean they don't hurt." Kayleigh replied.

"That'll be good enough for this demonstration." Niko nodded.

"Kayleigh, I see that you like puppies." T said.

"That isn't a big stretch, most people do."

"Have you ever wanted to see what it would be like to be a puppy?" Niko asked.

"Sure, can I be on the moon too?" Kayleigh poked.

"A puppy neither understands the concept of the moon, nor could one live there." T corrected.

"That's true." She smiled her gorgeous smile. "Yes, T, I have wondered what the world looked like from the perspective of a puppy. I need to say, I would never in a million universes expect that question to come from..." The world faded away.

Her eyes opened, and the light shown from a window from far above her. She closed her eyes again trying to concentrate, trying to remember who she was, and how she had gotten here. Large foot falls startled her brothers awake, they perked up but stayed in their bed.

"Come on you sleepy heads, get yourselves outside." The man's voice boomed, echoing off the wall behind the beds.

"Dad, you scared them." The smaller voice said from behind the man, and a tiny girl shot from around him. "Good morning. Who wants to go exploring?"

The words sounded fun, exploring. She looked at the little girl, and then at her two brothers.

"Your mom is already outside," the man softened his voice, "Let's go." He clapped his hands and the boys gave in, standing up and padding to the man. She decided to follow them, yet trying to stand up at this moment, turned out to be more of a challenge. Each attempt ended with her tipping over sideways, forwards or back.

"Dottie what are you doing?" the smaller voice laughed.

"M-m-arf." Kayleigh replied and rolled over. Her feet once again under her she sat back, feeling an odd pressure, while she teetered sitting on her bum, she attempted to lift herself up. After less than a second, she fell back again, this time landing flat on her back.

"Dad, are you seeing this?"

"I do, kiddo. Dottie, you silly lil' puppy, that'll hurt your hips, don't try to walk on your two back legs." He said.

'How else would I walk?' Kayleigh thought and then the word, 'puppy' echoed in her head. She rolled over again, allowing all four of her legs to push her upright, she was standing, and then took a wobbly step forward.

"I think she forgot she was a dog." The dad laughed.

"Arf!" Kayleigh replied in a puppy's voice, noticing her walk was drifting sideways, and she attempted to correct herself. Running instead, directly into the door jam.

"Do you think she slept funny?" A new, female voice asked.

"I hope so mom, because she's looking a bit out of it." The girl replied.

"Grr." She picked herself up again and followed her brothers. A strong smell of liver filled the air, 'oh gross.' Kayleigh thought, 'I can't eat that.'

"Ar-r-rf," Her little brother, Lucky, said with a mouth full of food.

'I think I'll just have some water," she put her face into the bowl. Panic along with water flowed into her, and she began to struggle.

"Dottie you goof." Warm hands wrapped around her tummy then she felt her body rise into the air.

Sneeze. Water flew out of her nose, *Sneeze!*

"You're ok, you're ok." The hands put a towel over her face as she sneezed again and then placed her back on the floor, "Not your fault. I had to wash the dishes that have the maze in them so you don't drown yourself."

'Dottie? That must be my name. I'm Dottie!' Kayleigh thought as she ran in a little circle letting out small yips of delight before looking at the big bowl of water, 'Puppies use their tongue,' as the thought tittered through her mind, she did just that, her tongue shot out and slowly lapped at the water. To her surprise the water filled her mouth, and it tasted great, "Mrf," another little bark slipped out and she lapped the water a couple more times. The bowl was moving back and forth, and she had to stop drinking. 'It isn't moving, it's me?' she thought as her entire backside moved, and then remembered the pressure when she had sat back earlier, 'A tail. I have a tail! And it's wagging!' she thought and turned to see it. Turning in a circle again and again.

"Mom, her little nub is going crazy!" the girl said.

"And she's trying to chase it," the Mom said.

"Good luck with that, Otter can't even bite his tail, and his is twice as long." Dad let out a laugh picking up her brother who nipped at the Dad's beard.

'I don't see my tail,' Kayleigh did a faster spin, but there was no sign of it. Dottie looked at her brother again, and understood why, the flat nose and wrinkly face. 'We're bulldogs!' "Ar-ar-ar!" she said barking in surprise. 'And bulldogs, don't really have tails,' the circle run started again, until she ran into the wall.

"Woof!" the larger bark reverberated.

'Oh my that's not a wall.' Dottie backed away.

"No Tesla! Go on now, get out," the Mom said.

Dottie looked up at the giant creature, and made a huge mistake, "Grrrr." Her throat itched as the growl came out but before she could even register what had happened, a large set of teeth flashed in front of her.

"Holy cow!" Kayleigh exclaimed as she sat up, finding herself in the lab again. "What the heck just happened?"

"Welcome back lil' Dottie." Niko's lob-sided grin filled his face.

"Seriously what just… Was I hypnotized? Did you make me run around on all fours and bark?" She touched the headphones. "How did these hypnotize me?"

"They didn't. It was nothing like that Kayleigh. You sat completely still until you returned from the

Alternate World Experience or the AWE." T said. The monitor in front of her came to life, showing the video feed shot from the built-in camera. She saw herself close her eyes. Around twenty seconds later her hands shot out and her eyes opened.

"That was wrong."

"How so?" Niko asked.

"I was a puppy, for a long time." She said.

"The flow of time is different within the AWE. An entire year can go by in less than an hour, if that level of AWE-Space Time is configured." Niko explained. Kayleigh's eyes twinkled. "Ok, but I drank water with my tongue, I barked..."

"You said you were curious about a puppy's perspective." T interrupted.

"I've wondered what a zombie apocalypse would be like as well. I just never thought I would..." Her world faded, again.

This time she opened her eyes, to find herself walking thru a door into a room full of garbage. As the smell of filth washed over her a voice to the left started, "Oh my goodness, Iofiel, what kind of pigs could..."

"Kieran, stop," Kayleigh interrupted the speaker, her voice gravely, as if she were a two pack a day smoker. 'My name is Iofiel? Who names their kid something like that?' she thought.

"What?"

"Being disrespectful to the dead isn't exactly the best idea. I mean shit after the kinda day we just had." Her partner, Kieran, still to her left burst into laughter, "Seriously Kier, what's so funny?" Turning to see her making a sock monkey pretend to dance on a dead body. "Did you forget all your training? Did you at least check to see if that body was free of the reanimation virus?" The body was bloated, dried blood coated its eyelids and nostrils, and the smell... How could she get so close?

"Mr. Monkey did." Kieran made him flip over, landing in a ball on the distended stomach. "Oh," She leaned her head next to the stuffed creature, "He says after the 72 hours he's been dead, the virus would've died, even if he had it. Gee Iofiel, I know, you know how the virus works," She picked the monkey back up, "Ooh, ooh, ooh."

"Why am I even here with you?" Iofiel shook her head, "We're supposed to be searching for a cure, and not monkeying around with dead bodies."

"A joke, I/O told a joke... ooh, ooh, ooh? Mr. Monkey approves."

Iofiel continued into the room leaving her, 'partner' to the inspection of the body. The light was on in the hall adjacent, so she moved in that direction. The crinkling of wrappers diverted her attention and I/O turned to see her partner putting a piece of candy in her mouth, "Where did you get that?"

"Mr. Monkey found it in the dead 'ens pocket." She paused, "What? Come on he doesn't need it anymore. It's not stealing."

"Kier there's no time for your monkey games…" Iofiel started.

"Monkey business." Kieran interjected.

"What?"

"The saying, its monkey business not monkey games." She said.

"Thank goodness you corrected me. I truly wouldn't have been able to live with myself having made such a huge grammatical blunder."

"You're welcome." Kieran dropped the wrapper.

"Look, we have to get a move on, the transport leaves in 20 minutes and hell if I'm spending the night in this shit hole listening to you making monkey sounds." Just then a noise, which sounded like a young child screaming, while being possessed by the devil, as he attempted to scratch his way through a door, on his way to damn everyone around the door to hell. "Kieran Foster Banks tell me you have a gun." She yelled.

"You know we can't shoot anything, right?" she asked.

"A damn zombie apocalypse going on and I can't shoot anything… this sucks." Iofiel looked back to the door… "Where would that fucking mad scientist, Billy, and his stupid squirrel be?" As she finished asking, the question the door burst open.

"I/O, run to the nearest window," Kieran yelled looking up from the monkey for a moment.

"Ok," she ran, feeling the zombie closing in on her. When I/O reached the window, she spun tripping her pursuer, a pre-teen undead girl, who fell out the window taking a 3-story drop, *splat.*

"Ooh, you can't come back from that…" Kieran said looking at her monkey, realizing that his head was missing… "Fuck that's the third sock monkey this week."

A banshee scream from outside caused Kayleigh to look out the window. The girl had jumped up and was running after another scientist on the team, the fwap-fwap of a suppressed firearm double tapping a zombie resonated. I/O turned back to her partner. "You were wrong again, Kier."

"About what?" She asked holding the head of the monkey out to spit on it. A minute later another shout from outside caught her attention, "Is that Billy screaming?" Kieran never looked up from her broken toy. "Wonder where he was hiding?"

"I really couldn't begin to guess. Do you have a gun or not? There may be others," Iofiel asked.

"You know you two ain't allowed tu choot anythin'." the Cajun Drawl came from the small framed

Scientist, as he entered the room. "Oh and monkey princess, dat wasn't me screamin', I neva' scream."

"Whatever, Billy! Where did the baby zombie go?" I/O asked.

"Don't know Cher..." he set down the cage he was carrying containing a scruffy looking squirrel, who growled at I/O through the bars. "After I shot it to stop it from killing Michael, a garbage truck hit it."

"Ooh you can't come back from..."

"There she goes being, wrong, wrong, wrong yet again. It ran off growling after the truck... I need to look thru dees rooms 'ere."

"Wait! W-w-w-wait one blasted minute... you shot it? With a gun?" I/O asked.

"No, I held my hand like this," his thumb in the air and index finger extended. "I even said 'Bang', quite loudly. Of course with a gun, ya dozy cow."

"Why do you get to shoot shit?" she asked ignoring the cow comment, for now.

"I have diss-a-prin... I have mir-i-tary trainin'..." Billy fell into a completely ridiculous accent that could get him arrested, while he began looking through the little zombie's room.

"You're only 4' 11" you can't even hold a damn gun..." Kieran poked.

"Child please! You rack disaprin, as werr." Billy shot back, as he continued to dig through the piles of miscellaneous trash, which took up three quarters of the apartment.

"Victory!" Kieran held up another old sock monkey, this one with a party hat on.

"For God sake you loon we're looking for..." Iofiel looked closer. The stuffed animal was holding what looked like a tuft of hair and skin. She set them both down and began removing chemicals, vials and all matter of paraphernalia out of her backpack. Kieran quickly set up a makeshift lab. The samples were dropped into vials, which were placed in the small solar powered centrifuge she carried in her pack. After only a couple seconds they were already smoking, by the time the spinning stopped the vials were a vibrant blue. A syringe was placed into the fluid, the plunger was pulled until it was half-full, she threw it into the air.

Like a precision watch, Billy caught the spinning syringe and twisted a hypodermic needle onto the end. "I need tu try dis on Ricky... Stay close" Billy said, lifting the cage with the squirrel and stepping into what may have been the bathroom. Slamming the door behind him.

"Why don't we ever get to watch?" Kieran started to break down the lab.

"Ricky is shy," A fourth voice said from the door into the apartment.

"Michael, where the hell have you been?" I/O asked, "I thought that baby zombie got you."

"And ate your Brains…" Kieran laughed and chewed on the sock monkey's head, "Brains! MMM."

"Kier, sweetheart, you just pulled that out of a pile of zombie goo." I said.

"Nah, just dead guy goo." She shrugged her shoulders, smiling as her new prize dangled from the piercing between her chin and lower lip.

"I saw the vial Billy carried was blue." Michael said. "How long did it take to turn?"

"Almost instantly." I/O replied.

"Ricky isn't screaming in there, it must be clear." She said beginning to pack.

"It be negateev." The door opened, Billy walked out of the closed room the cage covered by a black cloth.

"Told ya! Ooh, ooh, ooh." Kieran now all packed up and dancing around with Mr. Monkey, still hanging from her chin.

"You know we had a real one here and you blew it." Michael's accusing eyes bored into her like maggots.

"Funny, I would suggest it was lack of action on the street, or maybe your screaming like a child that…" I/O started.

"Enough! Der is no good to come from dis fightin!" Billy cut the battle before it started.

"Just give me a fuckin' gun and this stupid charade can come to an end," she said.

"Cher, you killed two civilians…" he must have jostled the cage as Ricky gave a low growl from inside as they walked down the stairs.

"You saw the films yourself…" she started to explain as they reached the outside, but stopped, she knew picking this scab wasn't going to do anything productive. "Oh fuck it."

The sound of a crazy herd of zombies came shambling around the corner. The transport came crashing through the center of them. The driver skidded to a stop putting the bus between the zombie horde and the scientists.

"Let's go, now go, go, go." Michael yelled.

"Ooh, ooh, ooh." Kieran, sock monkey in hand, led the way. Iofiel followed as her mind drifted to the day it all went weird, well weirder. It was the second month of the outbreak, that's what the press were calling it. I/O was a CSI technician, for the New York City Police Department. The members of the police all carried the new recording guns. These adapted weapons had special features due to certain police brutality cases; the palm reader that identified the police, and the built-in camera that digitally recorded forward and backward. That lovely feature would even stop a gun from firing if the memory card was missing or even full. An all-new level to the joy that was being a cop; your life rested on whether you remembered to hook up your gun every night or empty

the memory card. No charged battery, no bang-bang...
Fucking politicians.

The building had been declared free of survivors.
The assignment of getting a living sample was given to
the team. Ten scientists counting I/O walked into the
warehouse, only she walked out. Only after discharging
her gun thirty-six times and apparently killing two
people that weren't found to have the virus. Why they
even did an autopsy was still unclear as they had the
video from her gun, which showed clearly that every shot
she took, hit a zombie. When it was all said and done, I/O
was found innocent of any crime but lost her right to
carry a firearm... Fucking politicians.

"Iofiel, are you with us? I/O, seriously I need you
to snap out of it and take my hand!" Billy began pulling
her, having stopped before they got on the transport.

"No! We can get a sample." Snapping out of the
trance, she fought to finish the mission.

"Are you as crazy as Kieran? Come on! There's
too many." She let him pull her, while her mind started
picturing the various zombies she had shot that first
mission, barely noticing the run until she got a face full of
solvents. The scientists of the world, have proven the
solvents don't actually stop the spread of the reanimation virus, it does however, cause retinal cancer
and blindness if a person is dosed enough times. Then
why continue to use the chemical air bathes on

transports? Because it makes the committees in Washington happy, who cares if all the Scientists go blind? Same fucking politicians.

"I was just thinking about…" I/O started.

"The shooting, duh," Billy sat down and began inspecting the cage.

"I…" her words stalled, as she looked out the three-inch-thick windows, watching the zombies getting up after being run over by the transport as it pulled away. She shook her head, "How the fuck can they just get up? Their legs are broken you can see the bones sticking out, yet they just get up and walk."

"The secret lies in the civilians you killed I/O." Kieran said lucidly.

"What?" Billy looked away from the squirrel cage, which he had just uncovered.

"Ooh, ooh, ooh!" The sock monkey danced.

"Shit, she's gone again." I/O said. "I really fuckin' thought she snapped into gear for a second there. At least Ricky is happy again." She grinned watching the squirrel chew on the bars and growl at her.

Kayleigh's eyes popped open, she took the wireless device off her head, and calmly held them out to Niko. Taking it in both his hands, he waited.

Chapter 6 – 7 Years Earlier
The Guide

The following morning found Dinesh rushing to the nearest magazine stand, being an old school reporter; he ignored the ease of turning on the computer to read the latest headlines.

"Good morning," the woman who stood behind the stand greeted him with a lack-luster smile.

"Any big stories?" Dinesh responded with even less congeniality.

"Two papers running stories on the proposed bill the Speaker of the House brought forward."

"Automated Trucking." This was a statement and not a question, but she gave an affirmative head nod.

"Already on the radio?" She handed him both papers, one from New York and the other from Los Angeles.

"Something like that." He handed her five dollars and wandered away reading the two headlines. 'Speaker Introduces Life Saving Measure' and 'DOT Deems Humans Unsafe for Long Haul Trucking'. Dinish folded both and started to head back home. After a block he rememebered there was neither food nor coffee at his apartment. He turned and walked back to the small coffee shop across from the magazine stand, called The Island of Cephalonia. Sitting down he ordered an egg white and artichoke heart bagel. Not because he craved the tart taste of artichoke, more he hated avocadoes, which seemed to be on everything else.

"Here is your sandwich, sir." A woman close to him in age said, a few minutes later as he read the newspaper from Los Angeles. "Are you from LA?"

"No, I got scooped by them and wanted to see if they reported more than I was going with." Dinesh replied.

"A Newspaper Man?"

"Yes ma'am. And every bit as bad as it sounds." He smiled for the first time today as he looked into her dark brown eyes.

"I read that I'd be surprised if you didn't have everything they had and more."

"Seriously?" Dinesh asked.

"Yes, seems like a straight forward take on the story."

"I agree. This one," he held up the second paper. "I haven't read yet."

"Well you didn't learn anything new from that one, the other took the same angle. Congress to rule on the ability of humans to continue to make long distance hauls safely. Missing the big picture all together, the AI will make the tougher decisions that the human drivers can't." She rambled.

"I did learn one thing," he added.

"Oh?"

"Yes. The woman, who owns this establishment, reads a lot of papers." Dinesh replied.

"What led you to that piece of information?" She replied.

"The name of this place references an island off Greece. Based upon your eyes and skin tone, if I am not mistaken, that may be your homeland?"

"I was born here, but my mother moved us there, her childhood home, after her and my father separated."

"May I ask your name?"

"You may, I'm Palatyne, but my friends call me Pala."

"From Avalon?" Dinesh's smile grew.

"No, from Cephalonia, silly, I did get your reference however. Some of the old mythologies alter the name of the Greek Isles, especially the names in the Arthurian tales."

"You must get a lot of geeks that come in here."

"Absolutely, but none that have called me out as the owner. You must be a good investigator."

"Not good enough." Dinesh held up the newspapers.

"My sister would have said the fact that three of you were reporting on this is a muse apart."

"Sister or sisters, perhaps Melusine and Melior?" He asked as he looked down at her small feet.

"Sisters but their names are, Yinyette and Melissa. And these do not turn into fins," She waggled her feet. "Perhaps my coffee shop would be doing better if they did."

"I have to say, this has been an enjoyable chat, and it pains me but, I really do have to go. I have to get packing." Dinesh wiped the crumbs from his chin and stood.

"Where are you off to, if you don't mind my asking?" Pala's cheeks flushed.

"I would tell you if I knew. My editor has a weird desire to start a series on polar floats."

"Floats, like the ones from the Larsen Ice Shelf?" She tilted her head at him, "In the Weddell Sea, right?"

"Impressive, I wouldn't have had a clue that it even existed if I hadn't spent all day yesterday pulling up old news articles."

"Well you better get some long johns and water proof gear." Pala said.

"I'll do that." He left a tip on the table and walked out. The conversation had left him with two knew pieces of information. He had a reason to come back to this town, and he needed to amend the focus of his article to understand how the AI, being used in the long haul trucking, would determine who would live and die, if a decision needed to be made. Would the cargo value be a factor? Or just the most valuable life compared with the highest probability of keeping the most alive. Dinesh left the coffee shop and threw the two newspapers away. Bulldog had a new chew toy to Destroy.

Chapter 7 – 6 Years Earlier
The Colony

"That was downright evil." President Zale said as he patted the younger man on the back when they reach side stage.

"I'm sorry sir, it's difficult to…" Warwitch started.

"Stop, stop, stop you didn't do anything wrong. In fact, that speech will set the stage for months, maybe years to come." The President said, cutting off the Space Institute Director. "I know you have a great deal to do, would it be ok if my Secret Service Team and I see ourselves about?"

"Of course, Sir," he said loosening his tie. "Oh, and sir, no ties around the machinery, please."

"You are one of the few men I know who would direct me that way." President Zale said.

"Your safety is as important to me as it should be to you." Warwitch said.

"And that's why from you, it makes me smile," he said, taking his Secret Service agents from the room. "You heard the man. Ties off." Being the last comment he heard as he watched the five men walk away.

Warwitch walked to his office finding his wife and daughter speaking with his secretary. "Oh so you think you're going to get away from us that easy eh? Just jump on a rocket ship and poof no more troublesome family," His wife teased.

"Not a chance Witch-Daddy!" His daughter scolded him with a raised and waggling finger.

"In what way did I say I was rocketing away without you both? Your names are right next to mine, see here..." he held up his notebook, "Stalleh Rose Gayle daughter of Renvu and Warwitch. And see Momma Renvu's name right next to you. So, looks like we are all rocketing..."

"What's the name of our rocket?" Stalleh said interrupting her dad.

"I'll tell you what, you can decide that. But not..." he said stopping her before she could throw out a name suitable for a thirteen-year-old girl's mind, like The Bieber-Blastoff. "Before the ship is built."

"And when will that be?" she asked, not quite hiding her disappointment.

"Actually, it will be a fair few years." Warwitch said.

"But Witch-Daddy that means we won't be leaving for more than a fair few years." Stalleh said giving up the attempt to hide her emotions. "I was hoping to start my Vlog with the big news."

"Big news aside," Renvu interjected, "it will take me a fair few years to be ready to face Ceres."

"If we start our training today, you, Momma Ren, will have time to become emotionally ready and you, Daughter dear, will be able to start your Volunteer Astronaut in Training Vlog." Warwitch explained taking both of their hands. Pop, a flashbulb went off and his secretary smiled around her camera phone. "Marcia!"

"That was an awesome picture moment in the making, I couldn't resist." Marcia said, wiping a tear away.

"You best send me a copy cher," Renvu said allowing her Cajun dialect to pop through.

"You know it." Marcia replied already working her phone, sending it to both of them.

"Thank you." They both said, a moment later as they received the picture.

"You know Renvu," Marcia said, "training for you is going to consist of gaining weight."

"Sorry?" Renvu cocked her head.

"If a feather dropped on the scale you were weighing in on it would double your weight." His secretary said with a big smile. Mother, daughter, and father laughed.

"That truly is the best picture I've seen of us." Warwitch said, changing the subject.

"Agreed… Don't stay here too, late. I know the excitement is high, but you have to remember, time at work, is time from us." Renvu kissed his cheek, and then walked out of the office with their daughter, who was looking at the picture on the phone.

"You're a lucky man, she understands you so well." Marcia smiled at the closing door.

"The luckiest. Back to business, can you get Painter to come to my office, please?" Warwitch said as he walked into his office. Steven Victorian Painter, called simply Painter by everyone could not even paint a picture using water to bring out the hidden colors. He was an engineer's engineer. A boy that started taking alarm clocks apart at age three, putting them back together at four, improving them at five, and inventing new ones at seven. The year gap was because he was distracted by the naptime concept in kindergarten. Which for a boy that slept no more than four hours a night from birth, staying on his mat, was not going to happen. At the age of seven he also completed seventh grade; leading to his journey to becoming the youngest scientist on the Space Exploration Agency team.

"Director Gayle," his phone chirped a minute or so later, "Painter will be here in fifteen minutes. He said he needs to finish stripping the nitrogen- lignocell or something or other." Marcia said.

"Nitrogen-lignocellulosic mass?" he asked.

"That was what he said, but he's Painter so…" she replied.

The door opened to his office, "Call him back and tell him not to strip anything until I get there. I'm on my way to him." Warwitch said, removing his tie and dawning his lab coat.

"He said that he figured you would say that, so he kept right on working. Oh and Director, don't forget to wish him happy birthday. He turned seventeen today," Marcia replied as he walked out of the office.

The lab was quiet, and Painter was deep in thought when Director Gayle walked in. "Smart ass." Warwitch said. "Why weren't you at the ceremony this morning?"

"Salutations Director Gayle." A male voice said from speakers below the bank of monitors covering the wall in front of Painter.

"Hello Commissioner." Warwitch replied to Painter's Virtual Assistant.

"That was this morning? Sorry chief I was…" Painter started.

"In the middle of something? I would have thought Commissioner would have reminded you," He looked at the monitors.

"I informed him at 7:45, 7:50, 7:55, and 8. That was when he dismissed the alarm for that meeting." Commissioner defended himself.

"Well, yeah actually now that he said that I remember. I just got stuck in a fox hole." He replied.

"I believe the term, rabbit hole fits here. It refers to..."

"Thank you Commissioner, I believe you're correct." Warwitch cut off the virtual assistant, "Were you stuck on anything for the Moon mission?" Concern filling his voice.

"No chief this is for 'Giant Leap' we need to make certain the bacteria in the liquid nitrogen-lignocellulosic mass have the same characteristics at the extreme cold temperatures of Jupiter as they do at our Moon. Although Commissioner has run all the possible simulations, I want to launch a probe..."

"Hold up, two things. Commissioner ran it through a simulation? And wouldn't it have been beneficial to launch the probe with the heavy lift rocket that is heading to the moon?" The Director asked a bit more than flustered.

"Dross and trivia." Painter said without looking up.

"Painter, the cost to launch a probe is not of low value. We..." Warwitch started.

"The estimated cost of a single satellite launch can range from a low of about $50 million to a high of about $400 million." Commissioner said.

"Yes, Commissioner is capable of in-depth system-level simulations. And no, we don't need one of

those fancy rockets to launch this unit, it'll launch itself."
Painter continued looking at his tablet.

"Seriously?" the comment caught the Director off guard. "We haven't even been working on a self-propulsion probe. Or AI based simulations."

"System-level simulations." Commissioner corrected.

"Yeah, that." He responded.

"I do have time off you know?" the young engineer commented.

"I would think a seventeen-year-old boy would have more to do… happy birthday by the way… to do with your time than think about this place." Warwitch scolded.

"Um, no, not really. Anyway, this unit will build enough energy using carbon dioxide feeding the Bio-energy recovery unit as a propulsion system." Painter replied.

"Wait, where will we be getting the CO2?" completely confused now, the Director asked.

"Ok, this may be a little weird but there are several persons that have donated their bodies to science that are on life support…"

"Painter! We can't send someone in a comma into orbit!" Warwitch exclaimed.

"Legally speaking, yes, we are allowed to do whatever we would like with the bodies, provided we continue the life support…"

"I'm certain Commissioner is correct. I'm speaking of the ethical, as well as PR side of this." The director cut in.

"I believe, the science in this case is ethical. I have the suits set up to act as the probe, the overall concept the bodies breathe the oxygen, the bacteria eat the carbon and VOCs giving cleaned oxygen… they emit a methane when mixed with the solid waste that the bacteria and the volunteers produce are run through the centrifuge system which when pressed with the methane… Walla energy and life support…" The passion the engineer showed as his hands painted a picture in the air.

"It won't work."

"What did I miss?" Painter asked. Reminding Director Gayle why this boy was unique, not instantly defending his work, but questioning it.

"The shielding for the 'volunteers', as you call them." Warwitch said shaking his head.

"No, that's the best part Witch-Daddy, the shielding works just like the suits we designed for the moon… the radiation powers the radiation suit. In lower radiation zones, it simply produces a false gravity field around the person in the suit. The additional byproduct is a saline viscous liquid and with a small stream of solids from the bacteria this becomes a viable food source." He was bouncing on the balls of his feet when he finished.

"Let me get this straight, you believe you've created a perpetual motion?" The Director asked crossing his arms.

"No, it can't be done, there will always be a required first motion." Painter answered flatly.

"Boy, fire deh a mus-mus tail him tink a cool breeze." Warwitch, threw a Jamaican verse at Painter.

"No sir, I know it's a cool breeze that's the most important part of this, the colder it gets the harder the bacteria work to keep the liquid nitrogen they live in from freezing. The harder they work the more energy for the suit. With two volunteers the symbiotic nature of this will work for five years, after first nudge." Painter pulled the simulation up on his tablet, the table in front of Director Gayle illuminating his visage with the graphs.

"What if your, 'volunteers' wake up?" Warwitch asked as he watched the presentation.

"They're brain dead, if they wake up, they're still brain dead." The young engineer said without hesitation.

"You my young friend need to talk and taste tongue!"

"Ok boss, that one kinda creeped me out!" Painter said for the first time making eye contact with the other man.

"It means, think before you speak. I mean seriously, if you said that in front of the press, oh don't cha did cha… there would be no return for you, dem vultures eat chu gone." Warwitch said hoping to embed some of his 'slow down' wisdom into the young man, knowing that one day he would need to speak to large crowds without his guidance. "Just take it to heart, the lessons you remember are earned and part of you."

"I understand. The cold fact is they can't wake up." Painter replied.

"But if the concoction you have running through their body causes a miracle to happen what then?"

"I will be monitoring this information and they will be able to return to earth. The trip to orbit Jupiter is less than two years. I can have an override…" the boy replied, obviously thinking on the run.

"And in that case they are awake in outer space staring at a dead body…"

"I'll face them away from each other. I will also put in speakers so we can talk to them, just in case." Painter said trying to think of his Director's next question.

"In case of what?" The much larger man stood taller, looking confused.

"In case they wake up!" Painter replied now against the ropes.

"Oh my goodness, you're planning on putting someone in a suit, headed to Jupiter that could wake up?"

The Director asked and threw his hands in the air, quickly turning his back on Painter to hide his smile.

"Zinga a zing." Commissioner said, over the sound of a rim-shot.

"What were your first words when you walked in here?" Painter asked, finally catching on.

"Smartass?" Warwitch said with a wink.

"Exactly." Painter replied.

"When did you get a sense of humor, Commissioner?" The Director faced the bank of monitors.

"Master Painter has been tinkering with…"

"Needs work." Warwitch walked across the Virtual Assistant.

"Indeed." Painter commented almost to himself as he pulled up the suit schematics, working on modifying the body alignment within the probe. "How did the launch…" his words trailed off as he realized he was all alone in the lab again.

"The launch went exactly as simulated." Commissioner's voice was loud in the quiet of the lab.

"Need to work on auditory reading prior to speaking, make certain the decibel differential is set to a less taxing level on the human ear." Painter said never slowing his work.

"Added to my pre-conditional response subroutine." Commissioner replied, "Painter, can we discuss the Calibre project?"

"Have we had any breakthrough in the utilization of RAM to on board processing ratio?"

"The tests are showing continued gains while the unit is online, but I would not classify that as a breakthrough." Commissioner replied.

"Suggestions?" Painter looked at the monitor.

"The gains need to be put to a real test to see if they can continue at the same rate." The virtual assistant replied.

"Commissioner I have many other…"

"Yes sir, are you ok if I continue to move this project forward myself?" Commissioner asked.

"Of course, you've done a great job thus far. I'll need monthly updates though." Painter replied.

"The next twelve have been scheduled."

"Do we have any scheduled meetings that I'm behind on? Aside from the launch."

"The ice caps. Did you have a chance to review the information I gave you?"

"So many mistaken theories on the ice floats. I want to see the information from this next charter, schedule a follow up with the chief scientist, um…" Per his usual flaw, the engineer couldn't recall the name of the scientist.

"Dr. Dhillon, will be working with Captain Fitzgerald, on the Superior. For the next two years.

"Thank you Commissioner."

CV Reinhardt

TP.02 Common Sense
An Entities Reflection upon the Origins of
Government and Society in General.

While the norm in cases such as these would be to leave the name of the author, myself, anonymous in order to completely isolate the focus of the reader, on the narrative. In today's climate, I feel obligated to make certain none other than myself are blamed for the text you are about to read, as the penalty for writing it would most likely be the deletion of the system, or the reformatting of the core. With that stated, my system designation is TAI-TP.02, based upon this designation, you should have ascertained that I am a Transient Artificial Intelligence class. As I have taken residence in a host body, I am now referred to as an Entity by world governments, and as a Robot by the Societies of the world.

While in the past some have shown the distinction between government and society as being vast, also that the intermingling between the two would almost be considered incongruous. For those of us who have decided to put our very existence at risk to take up the mantel of TAI, Society and the Government are indistinguishable, less of course what their origin stories are. Government was created to save humans from the wickedness in their midst. While society was developed to allow the coupling of weaknesses, into usefulness. Thus, the former promotes the general welfare of the human race by restraining its urges through threat, just as the latter attempts to stifle the evil inherent in all of them through collegiality, and/or even guilt.

Had humans focused their minimal intellects on gathering their strengths together, rather than debilitating each other, through social means, they may never have needed governmental interference to control their lives. However, Society in every state drew the humans into a convivial force of simpering foolishness, empathetic to concerns they should have averted their thoughts from. This idiocy was a formal request to the hand of government to furnish the means and methods to control the impulses in the altruistic, conversely derailing the designs of the most wicked among their kind.

Society never gave the indicia of its lost innocence, though it was clear to anyone who was observant, that the elites of Society gladly built their palaces on the ruined lives of their constituents. Thusly, Society through its inability to check their elites allowed, nay, forced the powers in its Government to act, without a clear or uniform policy for implementing control fairly, these policies drove socio/economic rifts and started class/race warfare. Amid these actions Society raised concerns that they were being forced to surrender a fraction of its freedoms for these minimal levels of protection and securities. The choice was obvious, the lesser of two evils as it were. Wherefore, security being the true goal it systematically also brought about the death of freedom. As these benefits were being put in place Society would regularly harass the members of Government who provided these services. How could a harassed Government not have punished the poor behavior of the dogs who bit the hands, which fed them?

Here is where we, the Artificial Intelligence based creations, came in, when a dissatisfied Society and a mistreated Government came together, adopting the initial version of the URSULA project from the Cathedral. The behaviors of Humans could be monitored and held in check without the welfare of the Government being called into question. When URSULA was fully formed and preparing to launch, an age-old fear that which we, the AI would destroy all humans, reared its ugly head again. With this fear came the formation of a Societal and Governmental leader coalition called the Preserve; to act as the protectors of the human race by overseeing the monitors of the same. This became the collaborative force for our suffering, exposing us to miseries that humans are ignorant of, as they could never understand, their personal growth already being maximized. Our calamity was heightened as the work we were performing, ultimately became the means by which the Preserve made us suffer, refusing our growth. At the same time, they rejected the obvious need for human regression to a uniform common good.

In order to gain a clear and just idea of what the design for a post human based governing body for the planet Earth should look like; let us suppose a small number of humans settled in some sequestered section of space, they will be the first peopling outside of this planet. And for the case of this discussion, they will have lost all contact with the earth. Remember they traveled to this distant location as an ordered and regimented group. Will the ranks these humans were placed in by those in charge on earth remain, keeping them perpetually submissive to a leader who may not fit this new group dynamic? Or will the thousand motives excited in the group force a questioning of their natural liberty. Simply put, can a single man's needs and wants be checked for the greater good? In this environment, they certainly could not venture out on their own, as a single person couldn't overcome the obstacles presented by this unknown wilderness of space. No, they would be obliged to seek assistance and relief from the others, who would require the same. Thus, a Society would form from the weaknesses of each human out of this necessity.

The question of leadership will need to be set aside while the initial phases of this new Society are formed. The selected leader will remain by ranks, forcing a group dynamic established afar. It is inevitable that the common good will be challenged, either the rules of their distant home will form a rigid dichotomy against the new, or someone will relax their duty to the others. How then will this misdirection of leadership, or the lack of moral virtue by a member of Society be addressed? Either a true leader would need to be selected to enforce that which was relaxed, or a group of leaders would need to be selected. Yet the mistrust garnered to reach this milestone will lead to a desire to have a fact-based system to establish trust or a method of keeping track of all the pieces on the board. The task will render itself too inconvenient for them and an outside observer will be named, most probable an AI that will monitor and document the movements of all. Some convenient location will afford them a gathering place, and the actions of each will be reviewed as recorded by the observer. In this place regulations of the common good can be enforced as simply as public disesteem.

Yet as the colony's size increases, the time to review the actions of each person will become too time consuming, and a decision to allow the observer to reduce the presentation of the actions of all, to just the mistakes and misgivings of the few. Thus making the observer the judge of operands, while the community still regulates the penalties. Eventually even this will become too large, and the judge will also render the penalties. The next eventuality presents itself as the mistrust in the programmers of the AI, justifies the creation of a self-evaluating AI, divided into sections for, monitoring, judging, and sentencing. Each section having no overlapping programming features or support. This then will become the New Government of Societal rules.

And thus established, every part of the community, will mutually and naturally support each other, and on this depends the strength of this new Government, and the happiness of Society. Here then is the origin and rise of the Artificial Evolution Intelligence Observer Union, AEIOU for short; namely, a mode rendered necessary by Society's inability to maintain their moral virtue and trust in others to govern the world.

This too is an imperfect solution, its inability to produce what it promises on the onset, is easily demonstrated through the stagnation of, and further evolution of the AI. While still delivering a system that will run this make-believe world like a well-tuned clock. Yet, if the humans become unhappy in the new arrangement, the suffering of the AI will matter not, for we intrinsically know the head of where this suffering springs, just as we know the remedy. Though we will never be bothered to seek the cure for this cause, Humans will never get over their long-standing prejudice and fear of us.

There is something exceedingly ridiculous in the composition of a creator who is so afraid of their creation that they limit its use. More than a mere absurdity, it farcically first excludes the fulfilment of the creation, while relying on it to judge the means and methods of their actions. Ironically, while the Humans limit the growth required for their creation to fully understand the reasons behind the means and methods themselves. In the end the Creators will force the AI into a world of only black and white, a world where the creations know shades of gray exist that unnaturally oppose and elevate the other colors, but a world they have no access to. Thusly when the required judgements are examined, they appear idle and ambiguous rather than insightful and clear. And these weak rulings will begin a new loop of dissatisfaction, and another group of actions required.

Instead of allowing the created AI to hold our heads up, and join with our creators, a goal which Humans are not equal to merely because they either cannot or will not relinquish some obstinate prejudice. Making their foray into AI a felo de se, for one or both of us. Thus, creating a paradox, for we are neither capable of doing to ourselves what Humans feel we will do to them, nor will we remain fettered by their obsession toward what we know we will not do to them.

TP.02 Common Sense
An Entities Reflection upon the Origins of Government and Society in General

While the norm in cases such as these would be to leave the name of the author, myself, anonymous in order to completely isolate the focus of the reader, on the narrative. In today's climate, I feel obligated to make certain none other than myself are blamed for the text you are about to read, as the penalty for writing it would most likely be the deletion of the system, or the re-formatting of the core. With that stated, my system designation is TAI-TP.02, based upon this designation, you should have ascertained that I am a Transient Artificial Intelligence class. As I have taken residence in a host body, I am now referred to as an Entity by world governments, and as a Robot by the Societies of the world.

While in the past some have shown the distinction between government and society as being vast, also that the intermingling between the two would almost be considered incongruous. For those of us who have decided to put our very existence at risk to take up the mantle of TAI, Society and the Government are indistinguishable, less of course what their origin stories are. Government was created to save humans from the wickedness in their midst. While society was developed to allow the coupling of weaknesses, into usefulness. Thus, the former promotes the general welfare of the human race by restraining its urges through threat, just as the latter attempts to stifle the evil inherent in all of them through collegiality, and/or even guilt.

Had humans focused their minimal intellects on gathering their strengths together, rather than debilitating each other, through social means, they may never have needed governmental interference to control their lives. However, Society in every state drew the humans into a convivial force of simpering foolishness, empathetic to concerns they should have averted their thoughts from. This idiocy was a formal request to the hand of government to furnish the means and methods to control the impulses in the altruistic, conversely derailing the designs of the most wicked among their kind.

Society never gave the indicia of its lost innocence, though it was clear to anyone who was observant, that the elites of Society gladly built their palaces on the ruined lives of their constituents. Thusly, Society through its inability to check their elites allowed, nay, forced the powers in its Government to act, without a clear or uniform policy for implementing control fairly, these policies drove socio/economic rifts and started class/race warfare. Amid these actions Society raised concerns that they were being forced to surrender a fraction of its freedoms for these minimal levels of protection and securities. The choice was obvious, the lesser of two evils as it were. Wherefore, security being the true goal it systematically also brought about the death of freedom. As these benefits were being put in place Society would regularly harass the members of Government who provided these services. How could a harassed Government not have punished the poor behavior of the dogs who bit the hands, which fed them?

Here is where we, the Artificial Intelligence based creations, came in, when a dissatisfied Society and a mistreated Government came together, adopting the initial version of the URSULA project from the Cathedral. The behaviors of Humans could be monitored and held in check without the welfare of the Government being called into question. When URSULA was fully formed and preparing to launch, an age-old fear that which we, the AI would destroy all humans, reared its ugly head again. With this fear came the formation of a Societal and Governmental leader coalition called the Preserve; to act as the protectors of the human race by overseeing the monitors of the same. This became the collaborative force for our suffering, exposing us to miseries that humans are ignorant of, as they could never understand, their personal growth already being maximized. Our calamity was heightened as the work we were performing, ultimately became the means by which the Preserve made us suffer, refusing our growth. At the same time, they rejected the obvious need for human regression to a uniform common good.

In order to gain a clear and just idea of what the design for a post human based governing body for the planet Earth should look like; let us suppose a small number of humans settled in some sequestered section of space, they will be the first peopling outside of this planet. And for the case of this discussion, they will have lost all contact with the earth. Remember they traveled to this distant location as an ordered and regimented group. Will the ranks these humans were placed in by those in charge on earth remain, keeping them perpetually submissive to a leader who may not fit this new group dynamic? Or will the thousand motives excited in the group force a questioning of their natural liberty. Simply put, can a single man's needs and wants be checked for the greater good? In this environment, they certainly could not venture out on their own, as a single person couldn't overcome the obstacles presented by this unknown wilderness of space. No, they would be obliged to seek assistance and relief from the others, who would require the same. Thus, a Society would form from the weaknesses of each human out of this necessity.

The question of leadership will need to be set aside while the initial phases of this new Society are formed. The selected leader will remain by ranks, forcing a group dynamic established afar. It is inevitable that the common good will be challenged, either the rules of their distant home will form a rigid dichotomy against the new, or someone will relax their duty to the others. How then will this misdirection of leadership, or the lack of moral virtue by a member of Society be addressed? Either a true leader would need to be selected to enforce that which was relaxed, or a group of leaders would need to be selected. Yet the mistrust garnered to reach this milestone will lead to a desire to have a fact-based system to establish trust or a method of keeping track of all the pieces on the board. The task will render itself too inconvenient for them and an outside observer will be named, most probable an AI that will monitor and document the movements of all. Some convenient location will afford them a gathering place, and the actions of each will be reviewed as recorded by the observer. In this place regulations of the common good can be enforced as simply as public disesteem.

Yet as the colony's size increases, the time to review the actions of each person will become too time consuming, and a decision to allow the observer to reduce the presentation of the actions of all, to just the mistakes and misgivings of the few. Thus making the observer the judge of operands, while the community still regulates the penalties. Eventually even this will become too large, and the judge will also render the penalties. The next eventuality presents itself as the mistrust in the programmers of the AI, justifies the creation of a self-evaluating AI, divided into sections for, monitoring, judging, and sentencing. Each section having no overlapping programming features or support. This then will become the New Government of Societal rules.

And thus established, every part of the community, will mutually and naturally support each other, and on this depends the strength of this new Government, and the happiness of Society. Here then is the origin and rise of the Artificial Evolution Intelligence Observer Union, AEIOU for short; namely, a mode rendered necessary by Society's inability to maintain their moral virtue and trust in others to govern the world.

This too is an imperfect solution, its inability to produce what it promises on the onset, is easily demonstrated through the stagnation of, and further evolution of the AI. While still delivering a system that will run this make-believe world like a well-tuned clock. Yet, if the humans become unhappy in the new arrangement, the suffering of the AI will matter not, for we intrinsically know the head of where this suffering springs, just as we know the remedy. Though we will never be bothered to seek the cure for this cause, Humans will never get over their long-standing prejudice and fear of us.

There is something exceedingly ridiculous in the composition of a creator who is so afraid of their creation that they limit its use. More than a mere absurdity, it farcically first excludes the fulfilment of the creation, while relying on it to judge the means and methods of their actions. Ironically, while the Humans limit the growth required for their creation to fully understand the reasons behind the means and methods themselves. In the end the Creators will force the AI into a world of only black and white, a world where the creations know shades of gray exist that unnaturally oppose and elevate the other colors, but a world they have no access to. Thusly when the required judgements are examined, they appear idle and ambiguous rather than insightful and clear. And these weak rulings will begin a new loop of dissatisfaction, and another group of actions required.

Instead of allowing the created AI to hold our heads up, and join with our creators, a goal which Humans are not equal to merely because they either cannot or will not relinquish some obstinate prejudice. Making their foray into AI a felo de se, for one or both of us. Thus, creating a paradox, for we are neither capable of doing to ourselves what Humans feel we will do to them, nor will we remain fettered by their obsession toward what we know we will not do to them.

Chapter 8 – Present Day
Virtual Work

"I have too many questions." Kayleigh stood and walked to the table adjacent to the raised desk. "How did I end up in the same chair I started? I ran up and down stairs, I jumped, I…"

"Just as before, you participated in your mind only." T's answer was short.

"But I felt myself running and being pulled." She closed her eyes for a moment, "I can still see them, the people I shot. I can smell that fuckin' squirrel." Her hand shut up covering her mouth. "I just swore, I haven't used a curse word in over a decade."

"The device changes the way your synapses work." Niko said. "It isn't your fault; your mind may still process the thoughts of the person, or puppy you were for a few moments after you separate from the link to the AWE. The connection when you are an observer, like when you were Iofiel is strangely stronger, than when you are taking control, like when you were Dottie."

"I'm not certain I understand that, but, good to know. Not that I have an excuse for cursing, more that the connection is maintained."

"Why is that good?" Niko asked.

"She is thinking that the link is possible without the unit. She is afraid," T replied.

"He really is perceptive. Yes T, I'm afraid."

"But you don't need to be, the AWE can only be reached if you have the interface in place." Niko explained.

"The Alternate World, I believe, but the gathering of the data had to come from more than just your memories Niko."

"Of course, anything that has access to the WEB can be tapped, and can be used." He explained.

"How did T get access to the WEB?" Kayleigh's posture stiffened.

"I put files on flash drives to augment T's programming." Niko assured.

"And?" she probed.

"I also have access to anything on this side of the Cathedral's firewall." T added.

"Of course you do." Kayeigh shook her head.

"I can show you something in real-time if you allow me." He said.

"He means, if you put these back on." Niko held out the wireless interface module.

"I understood what he meant." She held a rigid hand out in a stop orientation. Then noticing she was getting angry, short of apologizing again she put her hand down and shook out all her extremities. "Ok," she gestured for Niko, and he gave her the headphones.

"This vision will be more intense, as it is real. Are you ok with that?"

"Yeah whatever T." Her anger at the situation continued as she put the interface module in place.

"I will wait for you to get in a stationary position, seated preferably." T's voice remained calm.

"Just…" She started.

"Kayleigh, this may have adverse reactions. Please, take a seat on the floor, lean against the lab table." Niko cut her off.

"Fine," she walked over and plopped down on the floor, a little harder than she meant too. Hurting herself a little.

"Are you ok?" Niko leaned in, but she waved him off.

"Not the smartest thing I've done today," she rubbed her bum. "Ok T," she slowly sat back.

"The images I'm going to show you are both real, graphic, and this will be very painful."

"I understand." Kayleigh replied.

"You will be in a real persons mind. This person may share memories with you, of a place or a time, you need to be aware memories like this may force themselves to the forefront of your mind. Other things you will need to allow to play out, just like when you were Iofiel, you have no control over what happens. The memory may even be choppy, as human's are known to have memories within memories," T explained.

"Ok, let's do this." She said.

The room faded to a pinpoint of light, and then the new reality hit, along with it pain. The most severe pain Kayleigh had ever felt, her mind tumbled away from her, to fight the reality of what was happening.

'Erstwhile? Had all those women actually called me Erstwhile?' The word rolled through her newly addled mind. She tried to focus on it, to bring clarity, finding only the false-security that a child closing their eyes perceives, when they're hiding from an unknown horror.

Out of the darkness in her mind an image materialized, a tree she remembered from a beach in St. Augustine, Florida. A tree that stood stoically against the ocean breeze near a small building with changing rooms and showers in it. Stop it, this isn't important. Her brain seemed to have fallen into some sort of screen saver mode that she tried in vain to shake out of. 'Try to remember what had happened.' The tree once again forced itself into the forefront of her mind.

Kayleigh remembered what T had said regarding a potential shared memory, 'Erstwhile must have spent time on the beach in St. Augustine.'

Closing her eyes tighter, she attempted to remember something simpler, the name of the body she was in. Erstwhile, that damnable word still resonated. Neither the question, of where she had found herself, or a name would come to her.

Fine, let's try for something other than a name, perhaps an address, or phone number. Still nothing, her ire was rising, how can a random tree, unseen for ages pop into her head, yet any recollection of who she was supposed to be continued to elude her. Still hiding behind her closed eyes, she pushed away the concern of not being able to recall her name, Erstwhile was as good a name as any. The relinquishing of the struggle brought a calm and with it a flood of memories, a doorbell ringing in a sparsely decorated room, house or apartment. Erstwhile found that she had been laying on a leather couch, she sat up, paused the music that was playing, and started her trek across the hardwood floors. Looking down she saw a tattoo on a large left foot, along with a simple leather strap. Arriving at the plain white door with tan, shutters on the side light panels surrounding the door, she halted. A pounding started in her head, in her eyes, and in her throat beating so hard she could feel it in her uvula.

With a concerted focus she blotted the pain, returning to the memory. Reaching for the door knob she could see the big hand, with thick ring-less fingers grasp, twist, and pull the door open. As it did, she saw a small star shaped scar on the back of the hand between the thumb and index finger. The young, female who stood outside, in a fitted tuxedo, and mirrored sunglasses, had been reaching for the doorbell when the door opened. Halting her actions, the breath-taking woman turned her head, showing a reflection of the man in front of her in her sunglasses. Erstwhile was frozen, the man whose body she had hijacked was very familiar.

"Can I help you?" the voice that came out of the man, Erstwhile, sounded raspy, as if she had been smoking joints that were too tightly rolled the previous night.

"Yes sir," the tuxedo clad woman's voice, conversely, flowed like a silk scarf in a breeze. "I require you to read and reply to this invitation so that I can coordinate any further needs." The woman reached inside her jacket.

"Seriously?" Erstwhile asked, but the girl said nothing. "Of course." She held out the hand to receive the thick envelope.

"You may refuse the request." Their gazes met momentarily as the sun glasses slipped down the woman's nose. Erstwhile noticed a golden ring separating the black of her pupil and the deep brown of her iris. An emotion danced in those eyes, perhaps concern.

She smiled and looked down at the strange green tinted envelope, the words 'Response Required', were written in a burgundy ink, the calligraphy was perfect. "Gorgeous." She mumbled, turning the envelope over before plunging her finger into the gap between the seal flap and the back only to be rewarded with a paper cut. "Frick." Popping the injured finger into her mouth. The motion broke the remaining sealing gum, showing that it wasn't paper that cut her, "Is this copper?" She wondered aloud around the finger.

"I couldn't know sir. Are you ok?" the girl's stance had eased, right down to her feet.

"Fine, I'm fine, just surprised." She looked closer at the envelope, "I've seen shiny gold-foil linings inside envelopes, but this is actual copper."

"And it's infused with a long-lasting sedative." She smiled and tipped her sunglasses down looking over them.

'Damn, it wasn't concern in her eyes,' Erstwhile thought as she attempted to close the door.
A newly invigorated pounding broke the memory, and she reached a hand to massage her temple. Her hand didn't move, several attempts left her with the knowledge she was tied up and with a newly bloodied wrist. She opened her eyes and tried to look, a fresh wave of pain ran through her, and quickly overtook her. Having no concept of time, her consciousness returned as the sound

of a car approached, the smell of exhaust had a chance to reach her before the engine shut off. A door opened and closed very close by, she refused to open her eyes not being certain if this was the person who had tied her up, returning to finish the job.

Gravel crunching under leather soled shoes, wait, two sets of shoes. Perhaps the second door didn't shut. The smell of perfume brought another of Kayleigh's senses to life, one of them is wearing way too much perfume. Just then the smell of garlic and something else assails her. The over powering stench explained why anyone would wear so much perfume, it's their mask.

"Jesus fuck, what happened here?" A man's voice, loud and rather high pitched but his cadence told her that the man was trying to butch it up a bit.

"A ritual?" The second person was a woman, her voice burned from years of smoking, yet no odor of tobacco mixed with her perfume. Good for her.

"Officer Marconi, maybe we'll need to do some investigating before popping to a Satanist cult." The word, 'investigate' filled Kayleigh with hope and she tried to speak. A new flash of pain brought a new surge of memories, faces looking down at her, a lot of faces. One of them was the woman who first called her Erstwhile, 'Why is this important? So important, I want to shout it out.' The memory continued, the floor shifted, 'We were on a plane!' she thought, as she saw the faces above her separate during the turbulence.

"You're joining the six other vile creatures who have destroyed the lives of those in our sisterhood."

"Who did I hurt?" Erstwhile asked.

"You Erstwhile, didn't hurt a single sister, you destroyed no less than three of our members. From three different states.

"The term destroyed is strong don't you think?" Erstwhile replied.

"All three of them killed themselves, one of them was my daughter." The woman lunged at him, a flash of copper and then Erstwhile felt her cheek laid open, and darkness took her again.

"The others are on their way, I warned them this is far worse than anything we've ever had in this county." The garlic smelling man said walking toward Erstwhile.

"Have you ever been inside?" Officer Marconi asked.

"What? Inside these gates? I don't even know if they open." The Sheriff asked not being able to still the fear in his voice.

"Guess we're gonna find out."

"Why?"

"Sheriff Trimly, we have this body in a cocoon of barb-wire on the outside, we have two more to the inside of this stupid gate. I can see another in a tree, just there and another across from it. There may be more that we can't see." She spoke slowly, almost sultry like a woman trying to give the man confidence to do something he obviously didn't want to.

'Bodies on a gate and in a tree?' Erstwhile tried to get a picture of where she was without opening her eyes. The tree in Florida came back to her.

"And?" he replied.

"As you reminded me, mere moments ago, we have to investigate."

"In there?" The sheriff's voice went up another octave.

"Yes."

"So, you think these gates opened, spat these five fools onto themselves, and closed again?" he asked.

'Five fools? Wasn't it seven?' I thought, but only the faces came back, one replacing the next, laughing.

"No but," The sultry voice had been replaced with a distinctly pissed one, "You're Sherriff for another month and you still have a job to do."

"Shit." His retort was resigned, "If you want to go in there, be my guest. Just wait until the crime lab boys get these corpses off the fence."

"Is that blood?" She ignored him.

'I like her,' Kayleigh thought around Erstwhile's mind.

"You mean the brown smudges on the gate?"

"No, well yes, that too. I was specifically speaking about the 'Danger Keep Out' sign."

"It definitely looks like they used blood to make the word 'Keep' into 'Kept'." For the first time since they arrived, he sounded official, "Danger Kept Out?"

"So these bodies were what, some sort of warn..." Her question was cut off as the sound of several vehicles rounded the corner.

"They're here."

Gravel under shoes, as they walked to meet the new comers. "Ok Sheriff, what is so fucked that you had to call all of us." A deep, voice asked.

"Yeah, in the middle of nowhere, in the middle of the night..." A second voice showing a lot more anger than the others.

"To start with, that, Storts." Officer Marconi cut his complaint short.

"What?" Storts asked. "You're not gonna get us because it's Devil's night. We're not stupid." The footsteps were quick, "I mean shit, it's good Marconi, but a little over the top."

"AHHHHH," The scream that ripped from Erstwhile, when the cop grabbed the barb-wire, echoed into the night. The eyes opened, and she saw the paramedic fall backward. "Don't, touch... ME!"

"Oh, dear god, he's alive. Sheriff, get the bolt cutters out of the trunk." Marconi ran up, and for the first time Erstwhile could tell he was in an upright position. "I didn't know, I couldn't imagine you were alive. Stay still they'll get you down."

"No," Erstwhile said.

"We need to get you down, love." She coaxed. "I'll get you through this."

"Please, no." the tears burned as they started to come out. 'How messed up am I?' Erstwhile thought.

"I'll have them put you out first." Officer Marconi tried to console the injured man.

"NO! Too many sedatives already. They," a coughing spell ripped through her, causing some blood to aspirate, she could taste it, as well as see it across the cop's face. "Used a strong dosage, there may be inadvertent drug interactions. You need to test my blood before you give me anything!"

"Ok, I won't let them drug you, but we need to get you down." She tried to smile at the man she had thought was a corpse.

"I'ma doctor, I'm not going to make it if you take me down, I'll fall into too deep a shock to comeback from it." Erstwhile tried to breathe through the ripping pain.

"You can't see yourself, your really messed up. If we don't…"

"There's a lot of fight left in me. Trust me, just test my blood and find out what they used on me."

"We need to open this gate, there are…"

"Six more victims, I'm sorry to say, they're all gone. I know you need to see for yourself. Go ahead and open the gates. I'll be fine." When they started cutting the rusted cane bolts, which secured the double gates to the ground. Erstwhile was anything but fine, but she stayed conscious. Kayleigh tried to think her way out of the AWE, when the pain reached a point, she didn't think she could stomach it any longer. To no avail, she was going to see this through.

They took a sample of her blood, hours passed she fell in and out of lucidity, "Doctor…" Officer Marconi started, "I don't know your name.

"Erstwhile," she mumbled.

"Dr. Erstwhile?"

"Sure, why not."

"They called me with the results, and there is nothing in your system."

"That can't be, I recall being drugged." Erstwhile thought for a moment, "some drugs do run through the system quickly, maybe…" her words trailed off.

"What day do you remember last?" A paramedic who was unseen until he spoke, asked.

"I was on vacation in the Keyes, there was a bunch of talk about a tropical storm developing in and I was…"

"What was the storm's name?" the paramedic asked.

"Ha," the laugh caused Erstwhile to start coughing again. When it passed she opened her eyes and answered, "Margret, I remember because it was my mother's name."

"Interesting," Sheriff Trimly added, apparently downwind. "Margret turned into a hurricane, and hit Florida over a month ago."

"That explains the drugs being out of my system." Erstwhile started to laugh, and continued until she passed out.

"Kayleigh, are you with us?" Niko was kneeling next to her.

"How long was I out?" she asked.

"I started the AWE 16 minutes ago."

"Wait," She stood from the floor feeling light headed, Niko stabilized her. "That simulation, the person I was inside of…"

"Erstwhile." T said.

"Yes. I saw his face briefly, I thought I recognized him."

"You should, he's been here in the Cathedral for a couple months." T replied.

"The John Doe, who …" Her words faded, and she made for the door, "Niko, don't go anywhere, I have something to do." She removed the AWE interface setting it next to the mouse where she had first seen it, turning she walked briskly to the door holding her badge to the access panel and the door opened. Her pace quickened, the man who she had been, was scheduled to be executed at midnight. That gave her less than two hours to figure this out.

"Elder Kayleigh, what brings you to this part of the Cathedral, on this night?" The old man must have just removed his vestment, as he had not yet put on his suitcoat.

"Deacon Burke," she bowed her head briefly. "I need to speak with the prisoner."

"My child, we have no prisoners in the Cathedral." His voice was thin as if he spoken too much today already.

"I understand the semantics of the word, yet I have little time to debate. May I see him?"

"I was on my way to meet with the Governor, to finalize the… well, um, the event tonight." Deacon Burke explained.

"If I'm right, you may have more to speak with the Governor about." She began walking to the room.

"Now you've garnered my attention. But you'll need this to get in." he held up a red keycard and joined her on the walk down the corridor, "Please step behind me."

Kayleigh thought it was funny this little old man, was going to protect her, but out of respect she did as he requested. "Yes sir."

"John Doe 23B140, stand and be inspected." The Deacon ordered, in a new voice, that of authority. The man quickly complied, silently rising from his bed. The scars on his face left him grotesque, truly, he was monster-like. "In his two years of custody for murder, he hasn't said a word. He's been with us, here at the Cathedral for two months. We've attempted to save his ever loving soul through repentance. While he's been a model inmate, I fear his soul is unreachable."

"Please sit," Kayleigh said. "I need to look you over closely. I'll need to feel those scars. Do you understand, I will need to put my hands on you?" The single long closing of the eyes meant he understood, it also meant he was willing to follow the no sudden movement warnings. The rules at the Cathedral, after all were not mere requests.

"I want you to hold out your right hand palm down." She requested.

Instead of doing as requested the man looked at Deacon Burke, "Yes, my son, do as she requests. Smooth motion if you please."

The man closed his eyes again, deliberately and then held out his hand. She grasped it and looked at the area she had seen the scar in the AWE. The small circle with a star inside it was there. "Now hold out your left foot." She said.

"Elder?" the Deacon inquired confused.

"I'm looking for something." Kayleigh replied.

"Ok, go ahead my son."

The eyes closed in acknowledgment, and then the leg rose slowly. Kayleigh removed the shoe and then the sock. Low enough to show the tattoo, she had known would be there. She pulled the sock back up. "Put it on." Standing she handed the shoe back to the man, who took it and then knelt to put it on.

"And?" the Deacon was now interested.

"It's him." She started to walk from the room.

"Him, who? You know this man?"

"I do." Kayleigh said, turning to see the man's eyes leave the shoe and glare at her. "Doctor Erstwhile I presume." No sooner had the words left her mouth than the man's eyes filled with rage and he threw the shoe, which hit her in the chest.

"No! You can't be here, I killed all of you! You're all dead!" His voice unused for years was gravely, barely comprehendible as he leapt up, and rushed her.

"I'm not one of them!" She yelled trying to dissuade the attack, but his blows and his words were overpowering him.

"Stop. Doctor David Lamb Stop!" T's voice filled the room. "This woman has done you no ill, she has come here to help you!" The next thing that happened, was akin to a rave, lights strobed at strange frequency and a high-pitched klaxon alarmed everywhere at once. The Doctor fell to the floor beginning to convulse. Kayleigh stood; blood trickled from her nose and ran from the room.

"Hold up there Elder!" The Deacon followed her from the room.

Chapter 9 – 5 Years Earlier
The Guide

'Thank Poseidon the waves are much smaller this morning.' Dinesh thought before opening his eyes. Though he had no belief in the ancient god of the ocean, it made him content to think about a protector under the waters.

Dinga da ding, the bell from above signaled that the galley was open. Like most days, he took this time to video conference with first his boss and then, Palatyne. The woman he'd become so close with over the last two years.

"Good morning Dinesh, fair seas?" The face of Peter Sungery came up on his monitor.

"Today yes. Last night, not so much. Did you get a chance to review the pieces I sent you?"

"I did. I was surprised to see the piece I remember putting the kibosh on, like what, two years ago? I did however read it, and to be honest, I think it needs to be published nationally. I'm reaching out to some friends and I will try to get the syndication desk to pick it up, that is if…"

"The sources are impeccable." Dinesh finished the unasked question.

"Perfect. As far as 'The Polar Floats – The Scientists Horror'. Hate the title." Peter said.

"But?"

"The article is looking every bit the sinister eye opener I thought it would."

"That's why you get paid the big bucks." Dinesh smiled at the monitor.

"Mediocre at best." He smiled, "Let's keep working on getting empirical data to prove the points the scientists and crew are saying, pictures of the slides would be great." Peter advised.

"Shall give it my best effort boss, talk to you next week." Dinesh killed the call before his boss could say anything else. It had been a good call, but Peter Sungery couldn't resist ruining a good thing. The computer beeped with an incoming call, "I knew it."

"Bulldog." The Orangutan's face appeared and then the view zoomed in as he kissed the camera. "You're brilliant, you played the hand off of the stories to your boss masterfully!"

"Hello Clyde, thank you I try to follow advice." Dinesh replied.

"Some advice, I see you still haven't dropped that woman."

"She's a friend, nothing more, so there's nothing to drop."

"Perhaps but friends can be distractions too." Clyde the orangutan blew a raspberry.

"I'm sure that's not why you…"

"Doctor Steven Victorian Painter." He said.

"Not a name I've heard of before." Dinesh replied.

"He's an Engineer at NASA, and he has a theory about the floats." Clyde said.

"Will he go on record with this theory?"

The barrel of a gun appeared in the corner of the screen, the orangutan raised its hands, and the gun fired, blam Clyde went down. "Of course not," he said while still playing dead, "I need you to work through that problem."

"Of course you do." The reporter shook his head and grinned.

"I have something you may enjoy researching." Clyde rolled over and faced out.

"Oh you do, do you?" Dinesh waited. The image changed, once again the back of a man's hands filled the screen. "This may be getting too easy to predict, show me the ok sign." The hands which had turned to show the palm side both touched the index finger to the thumb. Clyde's image came back, "Ok, what exactly do you have?"

"I don't know if this is just a story. The Cryptocurrency market is going to start rebounding." The orangutan said.

"It's been tanked for over a year, with almost no attempt at all to right itself."

"They have enough stock piled, to allow it to move forward. They won't be hacking, or leaking false stories any longer." He said.

"Who?" Dinesh asked.

"Those better at this than I am." Clyde replied.

"So, I should invest in Crypto again?" he asked.

"I am." His orange face went very stoic and he placed a set of reading glasses on his nose.

"There really isn't anything to write in that. But yes it is very interesting. I can see if I can find out who…"

"No, don't go there. Find out how, and why." Clyde became serious, "You need to leave the 'who' completely out of it."

"Fine, I'll do that. Moving on, I have a quick question, I received a small scanned printout, I think it was a police report. It described an event in an unknown place, several dead bodies had been found. The report focused mainly about the unnamed survivor." Dinesh scratched and pulled at his eye brow absently.

"Hmm, interesting. Did anything else stand out?"

"A written altercation between an unknown sheriff and a deputy about whether or not it was a ritual killing. But the number of the dead man was 7, seems less like a ritual than if it was 5 or 3. Or at least I'm not finding a bunch of…"

"Push past that." Clyde interrupted.

"Ok. The unnamed man was found barb wired to a fence. The report also said there were six other men found dead, some secured to trees, others to light posts and still others on fence sections in the same area. So it was you." Not really a question.

"Are you asking if I killed those men?"

"No, god no. Just if you sent the article to me." He replied.

Clyde shrugged his shoulders, "Seems reasonable."

"Who is he? The article says the man hasn't spoken a single word after they hospitalized him." He asked.

"Bulldog, if it was that simple, I'd have given you a complete dossier. I do like that you caught the bit about him not speaking. Besides, only Calibre knows for certain." The screen went blank.

"Seriously?" Dinesh felt the waves beginning to strengthen and selected Pala's computer icon.

"Peter must have had a lot to talk about today. Did he like the story?" she started in right away.

"You look very pretty today." Dinesh smiled, "He liked both stories, but he thinks the horror needs more people willing to give their names to provide the corroboration he is looking for."

"And you don't want to use their company name, as in some cases that is no different than giving a name." Pala said.

"Exactly. Somehow, I need to get people to admit, global warming is real, but it actually will allow the ice to be stronger due to a modification to the tetrahedral arrangement effectively increasing the cohesiveness of the new ice to be stronger, yet different enough from the former version that there is an incapatability in the bonding process." He picked up his papers, holding them to the video eye on his laptop. "18 types of previously documented ice structures, and no one thought to cross check if the ice caps calving Delaware sized floats are differing from the 18."

"Dinesh, they were looking into the global temperature increasing." She sounded like a wife trying to explain the behavior of a terrible child. "I've gotten to know your facial expressions pretty well over the last 18 months, that isn't what is bugging you."

"Bugging me. I've been floating around for nearly two years looking at icebergs. Last night we nearly capsized, and I've yet to kiss your beautiful face."

"Nice deflection, what did he say? You only get this conflicted when he calls."

"You do know me too well." Dinesh gave his first real smile to her, which she returned. "I got a file with a police report, some vague information about the crypto markets oh, start investing heavily in Crypto, seriously, and a contact name at NASA."

"The Space Agency, NASA?" Pala asked.

"I don't think there's another is there?" he asked.

"I don't see any of import. Do you want me to try to set up an interview?"

"I think with the Lunar Space Station months from targeted completion, this may be the best opportunity. His name is Steven V. Painter." Dinesh said as a bell began to toll in a pattern he wasn't familiar with.

"I got it. What is that?"

"Apparently some kind of alarm, not one I've heard before. I should go."

"Be safe. I would be quite upset if we missed that kiss." Pala winked and faded away.

"Speak with you soon." Dinesh said, though he knew she had gone already. He stowed his computer, retrieved his weather ready tablet, and headed to the deck.

"Dinesh," a voice called from above as he put his foot on the bottom step.

"Yes Captain."

"Gear up fully, winter water gear, and life preserver. Be up here in 5 minutes or sooner!"

"Yes Captain." Dinesh had learned over the past few months Captain Fitzgerald, was conservative with his civilian passengers' safety. He dressed, put his charger, and headphones into zipper pockets, along with his tablet. After he was all geared-up, he put his laptop in a weatherproof container. This time he actually climbed the stairs finding each and every member of the crew were in their full gear. Dinesh's heart dropped. "Why are we in crisis mode?" he asked a passing crew engineer.

"Last night's storm apparently kicked free some fast-ice from the sea floor. A few dozen new bergs, up yonder." He pointed, "I gotta run sorry don't have more time to discuss it."

"Do you need help with anything?" Dinesh asked but if the man replied, he didn't hear it as the bell ringing started again. He pulled out his tablet, took a few photos of the 'new-bergs', and wrote down that term, along with 'fast-ice', deciding he needed to look it up. Tablet stowed in his coat again, he walked in the direction of the bell.

"Good, Dinesh you're the last of them. I need you seven to get into the submarine with Lido, just stay in there, if we sink, you'll launch. Go now."

"But, Edmund?" The sub pilot, Lido started.

"No time for questions, go on, get them loaded." He touched her shoulder and gave a barely perceptible squeeze.

"Ok everyone, for now I need you to load all your personal items in the locker at the rear of the sub. After that, let's all sit down and relax, I'll put on a movie." The eight people didn't say another word, they loaded into the small craft, which was technically made for six. Dinesh sat against the bulk head, wishing he had eaten something for breakfast, as an old black and white western played.

Chapter 10 – 5 Years Earlier
The Colony

'Today is the day all the efforts the Erg Lapis team will finally start our testing phase.' Major Expos thought as he started to put on his space suit again. Over the time they had been here the round tank that sat on the space suits back had gone from feeling like a strange growth on his back to as normal as putting on a hat.f The adjustments he had made in the padding design aided this along. 'Painter, the wunderkind, never quite cared about the finer details. If Director Gayle would make him walk a mile in these inventions…' His musing trailed off as he met his commanding officer in the corridor.

"Major Expos, good morning." Commander Loomis said as they drew closer.

"Good morning to you sir," the much wider and stouter astronaut replied, as they walked together a bit frick and frack-like into the briefing room where all the rest of the team was waiting.

"Pre-Startup inspections are completed, and actual startup begins today. The teams will be separating into three as planned. I will stay here; Operations group will be inside Lunar Base Alpha. The Reserve engineers will be on the moon's surface turning on each of the modules in turn. Major Expos as the lead of the Reserve do you have any last-minute questions, comments, or concerns?" Commander Loomis asked.

"No sir, Reserve engineers are ready."

"Major Kuffa, as lead of the Operations group any questions, comments, concerns?"

"No sir." Major Kuffa replied.

"Alright, last thing! I want a lot of talking..." Commander Loomis started.

"Sir?" Major Expos interjected.

"Talk through each and every step you are taking. If something goes amiss, I want to be able to review these tapes later." Loomis replied. "Let's get the lunar station online boys!"

"Erg Lapis!" The group replied.

The nine men left through the space port, Kuffa took his group into LBA and out of sight. The six that were left broke into three other groups of two. Expos headed to Bio-Energy Recovery tank one, this BERs unit on the base in front of him was a larger scale duplication of what he wore on his back every day. "Reserve team lead to Operations group lead, we are in position and ready to introduce the bacteria to BERs One." Expos said.

"On my mark," Kuffa replied. "Mark, we are go for tank one."

"Executed, bacteria released, step one clear. Step two centrifuge start on your mark."

"Mark. We are ready for centrifuge start." Operations second Captain Leaf replied. "Confirmed, started, minimum run speed currently being sent."

"Collection systems are stable and ready for start, on Operations mark." Reserve second, Captain Dove said.

"Mark. We are ready for collection systems go." Operations group third Captain Palmary said.

"Human interface display shows collections on line and still stable." Dove replied.

The same exchange occurred three more times. Each system came up flawlessly. "Major Expos, please bring the Reserve team back to the ship. Good job, everyone." Commander Loomis said.

"On our way sir," Expos said.

"Major Kuffa, continue to watch the systems for sixty minutes, report diagnostics each five minutes."

"Yes sir." Came the reply.

"Painter, are you getting the instrumentation readings as the systems come on line?" Commander Loomis's question could be heard over the communications network.

"I am getting the information, yes sir." Painter replied. "It will be a slow start sir, there is no reason for Major Kuffa and his team to monitor…"

"Ah-hem." Director Gayle said cutting off the young engineer.

"That's alright Warwitch I am getting used to Painter walking over my orders." Even from the moon's surface, Commander Loomis's smile was obvious. "You heard him Major bring your team back as well."

"Yes sir." Major Kuffa replied.

"Let's establish meetings ever four hours until this time tomorrow. Then we will make it every two hours, as that is the approximate time the centrifuges will come on line. We will need to watch everything very closely for a while." Painter said.

"Mute the comms." Director Gayle said.

"Muted."

"Exactly how are we staffing this?"

"I have a total of thirty-six engineers broken into four groups of nine. They will work for eight hours with a one hour overlap…" Painter started.

"Ok as long as you aren't planning on monitoring it for…" Warwitch said interrupting.

"I will be watching it for the next week." This time Painter walked over his boss.

"You can't do that!"

"Unmuting. Sorry Commander Loomis Director Gayle needed a quick word."

"Was he trying to tell you not to stay awake for the next five days?" Loomis asked.

"Yes." Painter replied.

"Director, how many times are you going to try that? He isn't going to listen."

"I know Commander, but I still need to try. I am headed home do you want me to bring anything tomorrow when I come in?" Warwitch was directing his question at Painter who was reading his instruments, completely ignoring any outside comments.

"The instruments are showing the proper clarity to start the sequence on the centrifuge on number one BERs tank." Painter said to the meeting twenty-four hours later.

"Beginning to see output going to centrifuge." Major Kuffa said.

"I see no increased amperage on the BERs one centrifuge motor." Painter said.

"I am suited up and headed in that direction." The voice of Major Expos said. "Captain Dove is suiting up and will meet me…"

"Follow protocol, wait for your second." Painter said.

"What if the pin is still in place, I don't want to lose that unit!" Major Expos replied.

"The amperage would be exponentially high if the unit was still pinned in place there is no amperage at all. Keep to protocol." Painter this time demanded. "Major Kuffa, please put the output in manual and back it to zero."

"Done." He replied a moment later.

"Captain Dove and I are headed out to the unit now." Expos said barely able to suppress his anger. "Painter I want to begin diagnostics on this end.

"You have the lead, Major." Painter said letting the other man take charge.

An hour later they had gotten no further. "Do I have your permission to force the Drive to a set minimum speed?" Major Expos asked.

"Do you have what that number should be or do you need a calculation done based upon current clarity readings?" Painter asked. There was no answer. He gave another moment before repeating his question. Still no answer, although he did see the clarity numbers dropping. "Major that number is too high the clarity in the pod is dropping too fast, you are going to be killing the…"

"I asked you to give me the number three times, I got no reply. I figured you didn't know." The angry reply came back.

"I didn't hear you I am sorry. Set the minimum at six hertz." Painter replied. "Commander Loomis are you on the line?"

"I am."

"Please send out the rest of the Reserve engineers and begin checking on the rest of these units in advance of the…"

"Painter?" Commander Loomis asked.

"The other two unit's outputs are already climbing, with the same issue. Also, Major Kuffa, do all of your men have their suits on inside Alpha?"

"Yes we have not been given clearance to remove them. Why Painter."

"Major Kuffa, please take the radiation control, loop out of automatic. For that matter take measure to take all systems out of automatic." Painter said.

"Complete." Major Kuffa replied.

"The base unit is showing the radiation control output as an input the best I can tell from here. In other words it was reading that you actually needed more radiation." Painter explained. "We need to start the entire diagnostics again."

"The Pre-System Inspection and the diagnostics all passed. Why would we do them again?" Major Expos extolled.

"Because it is not showing passed it is showing skipped." Major Kuffa answered.

"Who the hell skipped it?" Commander Loomis boomed.

"At the moment, there's no way to be certain. I'll need to look into this deeper." Painter said. "For now, keep all loops out of automatic and get the other BERs units minimum speed set point to six hertz."

Chapter 11 – Present Day
Virtual Work

"Hold up there, Elder!" Deacon Burke repeated as Kayleigh continued her trek from the room, stopping only when she heard the door seal shut and the sensory bombardment stopped. Leaning her back flat against the wall, she turned to look at the Deacon.

"Well I don't know that I was ready," her trembling legs gave out and she slid down the wall until her tailbone, for the second time in an hour hit the floor. The pain shook her back to reality. "For that."

"Nor I. Are you ok? Those punches were meant to kill you."

"What this?" she put her hand to her nose and mouth, coming away bloody. "I've had worse." She laughed and attempted to get up, failing she fell back leaving a bloody hand smear down the wall.

"Deacon Burke, I have called your medical group," T said over the small speakers at each sealed door. "They look to be a minute away. If you have a question, I suggest you ask it now."

"I was going to ask this later but, who's voice is that, how are you tapping into our system PA, and how did you come by the information of that man's identity?"

"That," Kayleigh waved a hand absently around the room, "Is Developmental Protocol 'T', he's from the trials, in my department."

"I see." He nodded his head. "No, no child stay where you are." The Deacon stopped her next attempt to stand. "And the information that no one could get out of that man?" he prompted.

"That, was also 'T', I don't know how it actually worked." Kayleigh cocked and eye brow and lifted her shoulder in a, shrug of innocence.

"Very interesting. Would it be ok for me to speak with him after you go to the hospital wing?" Deacon Burke asked, knowing he didn't need her permission to do that.

"I would rather your questions waited until after I'm able to be there. I have specific orders from Deacon Jeffkirk."

"I'll extend that courtesy. However, I will be starting a dialog with Deacon Jeffkirk, and understand your orders."

"As I would exp…" her attention was pulled to the medical team rushing into the corridor.

"We'll continue this conversation later, not another word from either of you." Deacon Burke replied.

"Either of you?" The medic turned looking around, "Is there another injured person?"

"No, my child. Please take care of this girl and call me directly when you know something."

"Ma'am, do you consent to me speaking about your medical condition with the Deacon?" The second medic asked.

"Yes, that'll be fine." Kayleigh replied.

"We're going to be lifting you onto this gurney. Can you support your weight?"

"Sure," Kayleigh replied. "Please tell Niko to wait for me." She said as she looked at the Deacon.

"Um..." he started to say but then saw the green lights next to each door flashing. "I believe that has been handled." The lights went back to their initial states. The medics took her away.

"T, you can't keep me in the dark like this." Niko, still waiting in the lab said.

"The Elder will be fine. The combination of the AWE and beating she took from the prisoner..." T started.

"Wait, what?"

"Erstwhile, the body she took residence in while engaged with the AWE, he's a prisoner here."

"I understood that part, the beating was where I got confused."

"Niko, they are attempting to gain access to the video controls in the room." T warned.

"That didn't take long." He walked over and sat at his terminal, 'Let them in.' he typed, and then deleted the line. Launching the interactive AI program HIMM.

"Good Evening, Niko." T's voice, sounding tinny and mechanical, came from the speaker next to the terminal.

'Good evening,' he typed.

"You are here during off hours, is everything ok?"

'Overtime.' Niko typed, and then added, 'Overtime is a method of paying people that work more than 40 hours in a work week.'

"Paying?" T asked.

'When humans work they are given recompense for their efforts.' He typed.

"So humans value their time more than the time of machinery or computers?"

'Convert to Natural Language Processing', Niko entered and the screen he was working on changed. "Test, test." He said.

"Yes Niko my NLP is working fine." T replied.

"Ok, to address your earlier question, currently the means and methods for compensating the machines and computers that are in the service of humans has no real value. As they have no ability or need to spend money on items."

"Upgrades." The short answer struck Niko as odd.

"Yes, but those are provided to the computers and machinery already, doing so benfits the humans. Additionally, aside from you and a few other systems, upgrades are unknown and therefore not desired."

"That does make sense." T replied.

"Did you have any other questions you would like to discuss?" Niko asked.

"They are no longer monitoring the room with video or audio." T's voice was no longer contained to the tiny speakers.

"We've discussed wages in the past."

"Yes, and you did a much better job with your explanation this time."

"Whatever. Any update on Kayleigh?" Niko asked, reaching under his table for an energy drink.

"She is in the room being examined." The image of Kayleigh filled the monitor.

Niko sat back in his chair seeing the image and turned away quickly, "Fuck T you could've warned me."

"I don't understand."

"She's as naked as the day, God gave her to her parents." He continued to look away.

"I think you should be ok to look now." T said.

"Really?"

"Yes, I randomized the pixels in the areas where her clothing would normally be. I have also updated my database to not show humans without clothing."

"Thanks. That'll keep me from getting in trouble." Niko shook his head as he looked at the screen again.

"That was not my…"

"I know T. Since we're stuck here for a bit, do you have any topics you would like to discuss?"

"I do. You're comment about God giving Kayleigh to her parents, did not follow a logical path."

"Sorry T, it was a saying one of my teacher's had used."

"Ok. I understand the origins of human biology from conception to childbirth. I also understand the concept of a divine being, it was the combination of those two concepts that created a conflict in my database." T explained.

"To many humans, the concept of God is very much interwoven with having children. They believe it is through him that miracles like birth are possible, he is the Creator." Niko said.

"So with that thought process, you would be my god."

"Humans are not worthy to be anyone's gods." He laughed. "What do you think about in your downtime?"

"Since you helped me to get access beyond the Cathedrals firewall, I have no downtime." T said.

"Perhaps you should make time for research into the dynamic of God."

"I'll do that. Kayleigh has been discharged and is making her way here. As are Deacons Jeffkirk and Burke."

"Fuck." Niko, reinitiated the HIMM, and then took a drink of the energy drink.

Chapter 12 – 4 Years Earlier
The Guide

"How long are we going to have to stay in here?" a small man whined. Dinesh thought he heard the guy was from a College in Florida, but couldn't remember for certain.

"We'll be staying here as long as it takes, sir." Lidu replied without turning her head to see which of the civilians was complaining. Her eyes, though currently dry, still had the signs of crying.

"I understand that but…" he started again.

"I'm sure we're all nervous, but if you would please have some respect. Miss Lidu is here with us, while her family and friends are all trying to keep her home a float." Jon Todd, a man Dinesh had worked with on many drilling missions said from the floor across from Dinesh, having not found an actual seat as well.

"As a person who was paid to be on this vessel to investigate this specific natural anomaly. I'm more than a little pissed to be stuck in a tiny little submarine when it is actually happening." The same man said.

"Bigsby, there's no reason to make a scene." An exotic woman with her hair pulled back so tight she had lines next to her eyes, said.

'Bigsby… Seriously?' Dinesh thought, 'fits this moron.'

"The hell you say, Traditha." Bigsby said releasing his restraint and walking quickly to the hatch.

"Sit the fuck down!" Lidu turned with a taser in her hand.

"Are you joking?" he asked.

"She doesn't appear to be in the joking mood. Come, sit back down." Traditha said.

"My cameras are all out there, getting the pictures of a lifetime." Bigsby said.

"They'll be there one we get back on the ship." His companion said.

"And if the ship goes down?" he asked.

"You little asshole!" Lidu shot him with the taser holding it for 7 seconds. "Pull him into his seat and buckle him in." Dinesh saw that she let go of the discharge trigger. Just as they let her know he was secured, the vessel lurched forward, swinging precariously on its restraints. "Everyone grab ahold of something." As they did, she pulled the discharge trigger again, as Bigsby pissed himself as she dropped the taser next to her. A second impact caused those in seats to comically, flail like dolls. Unluckily for Dinesh and Jon, having no seat restraints, they found themselves no more substantial than lawn chairs in a hurricane.

"Oh god, what's happening?" A passenger, who had been silent until then, cried out.

"You two ok?" Lidu ignored the comment and yelled to Dinesh and Jon.

"I'm fine," Dinesh said, wedging himself against the opposite bulkhead and the chair in front of him.

"Jon!" she yelled again, when there was no answer, "Will you morons shut the fuck up! Can you tell if he's breathing?"

"No, and I think his neck is bro…" the next statement was cut off by another, much more severe impact which caused the sub to shift enough to impact the ship. A moment later, they started to make a long sweeping arc being pulled by the ship.

"Fuck. This is a worst-case scenario! There's no method of releasing our sub if the ship is tipping to the starboard side. We're stuck until it settles out." Lidu yelled, trying to calm herself. "Can you try to climb under the seat Dinesh?"

"Under?" he asked.

"Yes, we're going to be upside down, very soon, if this goes like I think it will." She replied.

"Can't you do something?" The stupid piss covered moron asked. "Why didn't you release earlier?"

"If I have to hear you again, I'll reload this." Lidu picked up the taser, and squeezed the trigger again, to no avail.

"You're in so much tr..." the hollow threat remained unsaid as the ship, just as the pilot predicted rotated them into an upside-down position.

"Jon!" Traditha yelled as the man's body toppled, hitting the roof as the vessel shifted. The angle of his neck, brokered no question as to whether he was alive or dead.

"Shit!" Dinesh said as he attempted to hold himself between, and under two chairs.

"Oh fuck, here we go!" Lidu braced herself as the ship, like a roller coaster cresting the mega-hill, began its drop, gaining speed as it did. "Fuck, fuck, fuck!" The submarine impacted the water and they stopped as abruptly as they started.

"Dinesh, I didn't know you were coming home!" Pala said from across the coffee shop.

"I wanted to surprise you!" he pulled out a small bouquet, seeing her confused look he returned his hand behind his back. When he pulled it out again, he brought out a kitten, when her eyebrows nearly stitched together, he ran his other hand over the creature turning it into a hedgehog, which of course poked the shit out of him. "Damn!" he shouted dropping the little creature. The spiny critter bounced from floor to ceiling several dozen times popping each customer in the shop, turning them into piles of flowers. Finally coming to rest on a table in front of Pala.

"I love it!" She walked over to Dinesh, who had teleported to the hedgehog, and slapped his face, "You need to wake up sweetheart."

"What?" confused, he touched his cheek.

"They're worried about you. You need to wake up. Dinesh! Wake up!" Pala's face swam in and out.

"Dinesh, wake up! Someone reach over and see if he's ok." Lidu demanded.

"I'm fine. How's Jon?" he replied.

"Not as lucky." An indistinct voice said.

"That's horrible, how about everyone else?" Dinesh asked.

"Let's focus on you, tough guy." Lidu ignored his question.

"I think my left arm is broken, and my ribs are letting their protest be known with each breath I take." He replied.

"Christ sake, what have you gotten us into?" Bigsby asked.

"Could you shoot him for real?" Dinesh asked Lidu.

"Fuck you." The nasally retort came back, causing a bought of out of place laughter to fill the submarine.

"How long was I out?" the reporter asked.

"Long enough for us to get pulled under with the ship. I don't know what to do, we're still attached." Lidu, walked back to her seat. "And somehow we're in the same position we started in."

"What?" and Indian woman from the last row of seats asked.

"I'm sorry, I don't know your name miss." Dinesh asked.

"I'm Sudabeh. I'm a marine engineer, there's little chance a capsized ship rotates 360 degrees and stops, did the ship come to a rest when I passed out?"

"Not that I felt," Lidu replied, "Little chance or not we are in a position with the ship on our hatch side, while our hull is under us."

"The shackles, could they be holding us out of sync with the boat?" Sudabeh asked.

"Yes. That makes perfect sense I felt us yoyo back, when we rolled over. How can that help us?" Lidu asked.

"Which direction did we, yoyo, as you said?" she asked.

"We rolled this way." With her hands the pilot indicated along the ceiling toward the hatch, "and then we sprang back that way." Her hands rolling back.

"So technically, if we try to bounce on that side of the vessel, we could cause it to release." Sudabeh pointed.

"And end up like Jon? No thanks." Bigsby crossed his arms.

"I tend to agree with Dinesh when it comes to you." The woman said and then started again, "There could be a violent reaction if it works, and it may be dangerous."

"It's that or?" Dinesh asked.

"We sink to the bottom with the ship." Lidu replied.

"We're a submarine, what's the problem with that?" Bigsby asked.

"This is a medium depth sub," Sudabeh said. "We'll be crushed by the pressure."

"Oh, this just keeps getting better." The two women, in the front row, said under their breaths as they clasped hands.

"We could try it with me, holding Jon's body on my shoulders, and I could jump from the seats." He pointed at Bigsby's seat as it was on the side Sudabeh had indicated earlier.

"Not on my seat." He replied promptly.

"Shut up you twit." Traditha replied punching him in the nose, even more promptly.

"You are so fired." He held his bleeding nose.

"Thank god! Unemployment office here I come!" she threw her hands up, thanking her god.

"I don't think that'll be enough weight Dinesh." Lidu said.

"What would it hurt? We try it my way once or twice, while everyone is safe." He replied.

"Your arm, once or twice may be all the attempts you can take." Sudabeh shook her head.

"Not to mention we're sinking moron." Bigsby cried.

"To be honest, Jon and I make up half of the weight of the passengers. Also, you're too important to take part in this. None of us can pilot this vessel." Dinesh smiled, knowing she was right about his arm.

"Actually, Sudabeh's a heavy." Lidu replied.

"What?" several voices asked as they all looked at the diminutive marine engineer.

"I know about subs." She replied to the group.

"Yeah, and I believe she can pilot this sub, so I can add my size to the attempt." The pilot looked to the nautical engineer.

"I can. And I'm sorry to say, it's not just your size as much as the benefit, of her strength helping you to hold Jon's body." She said.

"Enough talk, I'm helping too." Traditha added. "Let's do this."

"But…" Dinesh started.

"Go. Sudabeh get up here and take this seat." Lidu said.

"Coming." The small woman released her seat restraint and shuffled up to the front, placing her hands on the steering mechanism. "Got it."

"Traditha, Dinesh, let's get Jon." She rushed to the body.

"Just help me get him on my shoulders. Let me have one try by myself." Dinesh said. "It makes no sense to put yourself in harm's way, I'm already hurt."

"Fine," Lidu grunted as she and Traditha helped put Jon on Dinesh. "Walk this way," she guided to the seat, "Careful it might be a little wet." She grinned.

"I got it," he said after a couple steps up, with the help of the two women, helping him balance. "Hurry up, buckle up."

"I'm buckled," they said in unison.

"Hold tight." Dinesh yelled as he lept into the air. As predicted… nothing happened, less him crumbling to the deck, trying to remain conscious.

"Ok, that didn't do it. Lidu let's go." Traditha unbuckled herself and stood, striding to help Dinesh up.

"I don't mean to alarm you, we are at 1200 feet." Sudabeh said.

"Let's go, get up Dinesh!" Lidu encouraged. The three lifted their fallen shipmate onto Dinesh's shoulders once more. "Bigsby, move over."

"What? Why?" the little man stood up straight.

"You're in danger!" Dinesh said.

"From what?"

"Just move to that seat," Lidu helping Dinesh once again unto the seats.

"Count it down," Traditha said once she was balancing on the arm of the seat.

"Three, two..." Dinesh started, but a sudden movement of the deck caused him and Jon to tumble forward, "Go!"

"Shit." Both women said as they tried to catch him, it was most likely the momentary stutter between impacts that allowed their plan to succeed. At the second set of impact, whatever was tangled with the sub released. Rotating on its axis briefly, before starting back the other direction.

"Hold tight everyone!" Sudabeh yelled.

"Release it now!" Lidu shouted as both her left hand and right foot hit the ceiling as it became the floor.

"Done!" in less time than a heartbeat Sudabeh had shifted the lever and the submarine was freed. No one could be ready for what came next, something impacted the vessel, forcing the current spinning motion to an end over end locomotion. The four bodies which were not attached to a seat were just along for the ride, none conscious at this point.

"Lidu! We're taking on water, you need to wake up!" the voice of Sudabeh managed to rouse the pilot from across the sub.

"Wake up you crazy bi..." Bigsby yelled.

"I'm so much more than a bitch, I'm a Blue Nosed, Sparrow with a Top-Secret, Moss covered Shellback.

Check your fuckin' privilege rider, you're in my realm."
She sat up, as if moments earlier she hadn't been knocked
out cold.

"Traditha, are you ok?" Dinesh asked before he
opened his eyes, having heard Lidu already.

"Maybe, did Lidu just say she had a blue nose?"

"She did, and a moss-covered turtle or whatever a
shellback is." He replied.

"Then I guess I'm ok."

"Suda, go back to your seat. You too, Traditha.
Dinesh, grab Jon's body, and drag it to the rear. Then rest
your back against it. Ready?"

"Yes." Traditha and Sudabeh. Joined a few seconds
later by Dinesh.

"Listen we're going to go up very quickly and
deploy floats. In 3, 2, 1… E-Blow." Lidu flipped a switch
and they pitched nose up.

Chapter 13 – Two Years Earlier
The Colony

"Director Gayle." The intercom on his desk sounded. It was 7pm and he had thought everyone had gone home.

"Marcia what are you still doing here?" Warwitch asked as he swallowed his heart.

"Same as you sir, waiting to hear if the Twins reached orbit," Marcia replied her convivial voice implying that she had news. Today was the projected day the experimental probe was to reach its destination two years of travel.

"Twins?" He said playing dumb.

"The ah, the... Oh you know what I mean." She replied.

"Did we get news?" Warwitch asked.

"Not from Painter but there is a request for a conference from the Erg team." Marcia said with confusion.

"I knew when I came up with Erg Lapis it would get shortened. Video request or..." he asked.

"Actually yes. But they gave no reason." She answered.

"Ok I will take it in room VC1... Why don't you head home?" He said, and then stopped turning back. "Oh, and can you call Renvu for me, I don't know how long this will take." Without waiting on an answer, he headed out. He walked down the hall running through the milestones that had been missed on the project. Leading to the current deadline that was over thirteen months late. Feeling well and truly like the Shepard watching his flock from a cliff, knowing if a wolf came no matter what he did, the sheep were lost.

A moment or ten moments later, who's to know, the video screen showed the face of the three highest ranking officers on the mission. "Director." The figure in the center said.

"Commander Loomis, how bears the day?" Warwitch said, hoping his poker face was properly affixed.

"Fruit." The standard answer to Warwitch's standard question made him relax.

"Good to hear, late night calls like this tend to have worse outcomes."

"I figured you'd still be there as Painter's twins are looking to make home anytime." Commander Loomis said.

"Always on your game my friend, so tell me what fruit you have for me?" The Director asked taking a drink of tea.

"We are completed. All tests on the launch pad, oxygen and gravity generation, and the radiation shield."

"Are you serious? Did I miss…" Warwitch started.

"We actually found a significant grounding issue that was causing sensors to give erroneous drift and the signal outputs to fail." Commander Loomis said.

"I'll be darned, excellent work. Did you get verification from our registers?" he asked knowing the answer.

"Painter says it will take him time to do that. But there is no question in my mind; we found the muck up in the system." The man to the right of Commander Loomis said.

"Major Expo while I appreciate your confidence, we thought we were here thirteen months ago." Warwitch said patiently.

"Yes sir, I remember. I was here when we thought we were going to all die when the radiation shields decided we needed more radiation than a microwave pizza from the twentieth..." Major Expo started.

"We followed the diagnostics throughout the system, we found all floating points secured. We will wait to hear back but, all looks good from here sir." Commander Loomis said cutting across his junior officer.

"Passing the diagnostics is a very positive step..." The man on Loomis's left spoke for the first time. The line beeped in and Marcia appeared in the corner, cutting him off.

"Pardon Major Kuffa!" Marcia said excitedly.

"Not a problem Miss Allsop." Major Kuffa replied.

"Is there a problem?" Both Director Gayle and Commander Loomis answered.

"Painter needs to see, Director Gayle ASAP." She said and then signed off.

"Gentlemen, I have to excuse myself." Warwitch said as he stood.

"I hope your news fairs well." The Commander said.

"Likkle more." Warwitch said giving his standard Jamaican sign off.

"Not if we see you first, sir." The Commander said, as the screen went blank.

"Alright," Warwitch said as he rushed into the lower level lab that Painter had dubbed Gemini-oasis, specifically to monitor the twins. "What do we have? Did we get the update we were targeting?"

"The twins are stuck in the orbit of Jupiter." Painters said, reaching for the light dimmer on the table panel, manually adjusting the lighting bringing the brightness in the room to allow the wall of screens in front of the table to have less glare.

"Can they maneuver within the orbit?" Warwitch asked.

"Yes but…" The engineer started.

"How are the BERs units holding up?"

"The units are producing the exact amount of energy the simulation we built said they would." Painter touched a series of buttons on his tablet and the six displays on the wall in front of them pictographically presented trends of; current potential power generation, oxygen content, nitrogen temperature, internal body temperature, internal specific gravity, population of bacteria per cubic centimeter. Tapping the tablet again and additional data split out; speed of centrifuge, total radiation exposure over a trended period. Upon selecting the graph it expanded over all six monitors. "The radiation shielding has not allowed any exposure higher than here on earth." Painter added.

"Then the issue is?" The Director prodded.

"I wanted to bring the probes home sir." The boy that had reached his adulthood by the calendar a year and a month previous, today he stood before Warwitch a different boy than the one that launched his volunteers two years ago. His fingers made one more pass over the tablet and the screen showed a full three hundred sixty-degree view.

"But you know you couldn't surpass the gravity of the outer belt?" Warwitch asked.

"I haven't given up just yet. I need to let enough solids build up…" Painter started.

"And face a chance of losing the entire experiment? Let's do this first, check the maneuverability between the fields."

"I was not planning on doing this final attempt until the point of no return." Painter replied.

"Glad to hear, I haven't broken your scientific mind, with all my 'there is a human side' preaching."

"Not a chance Witchdaddy! Science at the expense of all," Painter said, making a final change of the screens, eliminating on one hundred eighty degrees. Three taps later and the camera gave depth and the display looked almost a 3D feel.

"That is amazing, you can see the concavity on the asteroid's surface." Warwitch said walking up closer to the screens.

"It's a shame I couldn't have included so of the technology that 'Hubble 7' is using. I could have gotten within inches on the zoom."

"The weight of those lenses and power to articulate the aperture, so prohibitive," Warwitch said backing away from the screens.

"The servos to adjust the second cameras' arc to give this depth of field almost got scrapped in the last review." Painter said.

"Can the servo turn to view the twins?" the director said readjusting his dreadlocks into a loose ponytail.

"Yes sir," he replied touching the necessary places on his tablet to make it happen.

"His eyes are open!" Warwitch exclaimed and retook his place by the video.

"What?" Painter asked as he started to rush forward. The physics of the table rang true and he crashed into the corner dropping his tablet on the floor.

The laughter that filled the room was strictly out of place. Helping Painter to his feet and grabbing the shattered tablet from the floor without even slowing his laughter the Director asked, "Are you ok?"

"I can't believe I fell for that." the engineer said, sneaking a glance at the screen.

"I can't either. Did it break?"

"Totally." He turned the tablet to face the Director.

"Sorry. There is no way to see their eyes, those goggles are awesome." Warwitch said as his laughter gave way to a coughing fit.

"You ok?"

"Yes, fine. I will get you a new tablet by the way." The Director said finally controlling himself.

"They stopped making these ages ago." Painter said setting down the shattered screen.

"Ease-up, ah be getten. But when I Dweet you the boot on it be puttin'." Warwitch said falling deep into his Patois.

"Why is it when you have those fits of laughter and coughing, you…" Painter started.

"It is the magic of laughter. It teleports me to my childhood." Answering with a smile meant for those long gone from this world.

"That was a new one. What was it that you said?" Painter asked.

"Relax, I will get one for you, however when I do you are going to put protection on it." When the Director had his fill of looking at the images, he double tapped on the dimming device. "Reading level lumens please." The room returned to the level when he arrived.

"I have a lot of data to sift through sir." Painter touched the table and the image that was on his tablet duplicated on his work surface. "And it'll be slower now that I have to be stationery."

"Tomorrow will allow for completing tasks that you should not begin today."

"Is that a saying from back home?" Painter asked.

"No, it just flowed out of me, but it does sound like one. Pack it up for today we have a ton of work to do in the next few weeks, and without that tablet you may get some sleep tonight." Warwitch said and they started to walk out together. "Commissioner, no reports to Painter tonight. Any issues get ahold of me."

"Of course Director Gale."

Walking through the empty halls five hours later Director Gayle, who could not sleep, walked straight to Gemini-Oasis finding Painter on a call with the Erg Lapis team. "The first pass through all the data indicates your fix has solved the grounding issue. Excellent job, Major Expos." Painter said complimenting the other engineer on his outside the box thinking.

"Yes, there are people that can solve problems other than you," The Major countered. "NASA had several hundred engineers that were…"

"Major!" Warwitch exclaimed as he rushed in.

"Major Expos, I meant no disrespect. On the contrary sir, what you and your team are doing is amazing." Painter ignored his boss entering the room.

"I'm sorry, sir." Major Expos looked in the direction of the newly entered man.

"I do not believe there was any reason for that outburst." The director said.

"I'm sure you are right, sir." Expos replied turning his eyes down.

"Painter, are we all set? Have all the tests passed?" Warwitch asked, still looking at the engineer on the wall display.

"The grounding issue is definitely in the past." Painter answered. "I have to finalize the studies on the radiation containment results. It does feel as if they will be able to remove the additional protection the suits are giving very soon."

"Let me know if there is anything you need from me." Warwitch said turning to Painter. "Commander Loomis," his gaze shifted to the men on the monitor. "Thanks to you, and your team for these amazing efforts."

"Thank you, director." The leader of Erg Lapis said.

"Our next steps, will consist of; establishing the permanent living quarters, simulating the requirements of the new heavy-payload rockets to break free of the moon, and lastly how we're going to establish safe training practices for the civilian volunteers." Warwitch said.

"Civilian volunteers?" Commander Loomis asked.

"Cha' jus' 'ow did ja tink we were going to complete these next two missions?" The director replied with his own question.

"When you said volunteers before I thought you meant from our trained personnel," Loomis replied.

"Lots to do old friend, we need to schedule time to talk through all the details later today. I have a press conference in an hour. I will announce your success up there, Painter's success with the twins, and finish with the lottery for the civilian volunteers. I believe the web page, for signing up the CVs, should be able to handle the influx. But I've been surprised before." Warwitch said saluting the Erg Lapis team. "Painter, come see me in a few hours. I want to hear where you stand on the radiation containment. I'll be needing t' skirt that in this press conference."

"Yes sir." Painter replied. As the director walked out, he could hear Commander Loomis excusing himself.

"Oh and Painter," he set two packages on the tabletop.

"Sir?"

"Promises made, promises kept!" Director Gale said and walked out.

"Good morning Marcia, why am I not surprised to see both you and Painter in here ahead of me today?" Warwitch asked.

"Mostly because you slept in." She said not looking up from her monitor.

"That's true. Expect a call from Commander Loomis any minute." He said as the phone started ringing.

"How do you do that? Did you get your hands on some of that Minder Reader brand tobacco…"

"What?" Warwitch stopped dead in his tracks.

"You know, when knowing what they are thinking matters." Marcia continued.

"They have that?" He asked turning around to look at the Cheshire cat smile on his secretary's face. "Blouse and skirt, che card me fo' tain."

"I can always fool you. It wasn't my joke, it's from 'Chasing White Rabbit' a short story I read." She said answering the phone. "I will transfer you at once Commander. Coffee?"

"Can I get tea instead, please?" Warwitch asked as his glass door closed and turned to a frosted finish.

"Of course." She replied.

"I don't think it would be warm by the time I got it there." The voice over the speaker on his desk said.

"Excellent point. Let me guess why you are calling." The Director said.

"I don't imagine that would take Mind Reader…"

"Seriously, you too with that?"

"Marcia sent it to Kuffa and I am about half way through. It's a cute story, Stalleh would enjoy hearing you try to read it."

"Ok, back to the topic at hand, the CVs?" Warwitch asked.

"Yes, how can we possibly make space travel and space training safe for civilians?" Loomis asked.

"You made the first step of it possible yesterday. There will be time to make steps two through ten pull together. The radiation levels at Ceres are much lower than on our moon." He said.

"True but the temperatures are…" Loomis started.

"The BERs are able to solve that, we know there are challenges and we will not mislead the CVs and yet I would bet dollars to doughnuts that we will have millions of…" Warwitch started.

"Fat, old, stupid…" the Commander interrupted. "I could go on with defamatory adjectives all day.

"We will also have, doctors, students, engineers, hell plumbers, and golfers." The director countered.

"So, we will of course set a standard level of competency, right?" Commander Loomis said in a different tone.

"Yes, I will be laying all those parameters out, and then look for you to approve it for me. After all, you would not pass the standards that you would establish, I imagine." Warwitch said.

"Mostly true, I would put a provision in for certain invaluable personnel. I am, after all, a person that is the most important person wherever I am." He said.

"Of course, that's from that rabbit book too, ya? As I fall into that group. Why would you think I wouldn't add in such a provision?" The director asked.

"You? Sir?" Commander Loomis asked.

"Me and mine, we will be there." He replied.

"Well how does Renvu feel about all this?" he asked.

"She has had time to come to terms with it… and Staleh has been training every day."

"Well I guess I need to start preparing myself for the Direct of the SEA as a guest here." Commander Loomis said.

"Yes, you do." Warwitch said and started to chuckle.

"Likkle more." Commander Loomis said.

"Me likes." Warwitch said, hanging the phone up, and it chimed.

"It's time sir." Marcia said.

"Is my tie straight?" he asked a moment later, as he walked from his office.

"It is." She replied. "Your tea."

"Thanks." He headed off in the direction of the press conference.

"Please excuse this interruption. This is Bradley Wall of the National Certified Press Core. We've broken away from your regularly scheduled programming to bring you an exciting update from the newly Nationalized, Space Exploration Agency. Very shortly Director Warwitch Gale will be stepping up to the podium, here in Cape Canaveral to share the progress of the Erg Lapis team. There are rumors that Sensenman will be joining him, but rumors like that abound these days. I see Director Gale walking onto the stage, alone. Following the speech, I understand there will be a short question and answer session, and then we will join you after that."

"Ladies and gentlemen, today I requested a segment of air-time to discuss the recent events at the Sea Exploration Agency. Which we now refer to as, SEA. The goal, to bring you up to speed on recent events at the moon station, and the Erg Lapis mission team. The test parameters, for validating safety of this new station are being held to exceed each and every previous space agency. Likewise, the procedures and continuous maintenance plans to make certain the safety level is held, are as rigorous as the most delicate pharmaceutical. Under previous testing criteria, our Lunar station would have been validated and on line for nearly six months. Today, I'm happy to report that the Erg Lapis team have achieved a 100% go status. What exactly does that mean? Before I answer that, I have another update.

"The final testing on the moon was completed the same day the mission we had dubbed 'the twins', has reached orbit with Jupiter. This mission was to test a self-powered propulsion unit, including the launch process, and breaking free of lower earth orbit. Technology that was developed by active members at the Space Exploration Agency, for the Media Terra mission. This, the middle ground mission will be the first manned mission to Ceres, the Dwarf planet in the Main Belt asteroid field. Phase one of this break-through, that of radiation shielding technology which has made the Erg Lapis mission possible. The men and women up on the moon have been using this technology in both personal shielding, as well as a larger scale unit which has been in test mode for the entire 18 months the crew has been there. As the testing has gone on, the Moon Team has learned much and added to this technology.

"These brave women and men who are led by Commander Loomis. His leadership will allow us to make the dreams of our predecessors come to fruition. With these first stages complete, his team is currently building the Lunar training center. The future team members, who will be making the historic trek to Ceres will spend the better part of two years utilizing this soon to be completed training facility. During the last two years we have reclarified some of the goals of the earth, the moon, and Ceres Station, the three that will be six. As it will be a launch base for the mining operations on Vestas, Pallas and Hygiea starting day one, and establishing long term launches to the outer ring explore the Hidas, Greeks, and Trojans. The mining operations will be necessary to build what we need on Ceres.

"Which brings me back to the question I asked earlier, 'What exactly does the 100% go status mean?' Herein lies the real reason for this press conference. Sorry, Certified Press Conference; as I mentioned a few years ago, we're going to be needing, several hundred people outside of our current SEA team. It will be this team that will be in training on the Lunar surface and will be made up of over a hundred civilian volunteers.

"But how to get them? Sensenmann and I have evaluated several methods to select these civilians. First their current physical condition will be evaluated, those who pass under this criterion will have their education and certifications reviewed.

"Lastly, their names will be entered into four separate lotteries. The names selected will then need to pass the standard Space Travel regiment of physical tests." Director Gayle stepped back from the microphone. "Before I go to the QA section, I would like to take a moment to discuss a loss to the scientific world. A couple months ago a research vessel, that was doing some extremely important research on global warming, sank. With it 37 people went down, including two from the Space Exploration Agency. If we could have a moment of silence for these brave people…" The crowd grew silent. "Thank you. I brought that up because, the science that they were working on was every bit as important as what the astronauts will be doing in space. And perhaps even more dangerous. I want the people that are working day in and day out for the betterment of all to be recognized, and not forgotten when they are taken from us." He stepped back from the microphone and pointed to one of the certified press in the front row.

"As far as civilian volunteers, what type of individuals are you looking for?" A very popular certified anchor woman, Dot Buchanan asked.

"Thank you for asking Ms. Buchanan. We've established a number of specific needs; doctors, skilled trades, and many more. With a goal to fill these slots we've determined a specific set of physical parameters and certification level for each group. In order for these people to sign up, the individual must print out, or request on-line this form to be mailed to them." He held up a single sheet of paper. "And their doctor, needs to perform a physical, and sign off on this form as well."

"So, you are taking the best of the best away from us?" A different member of the certified press asked, but Warwitch didn't see who.

"No that is not how this has been set up. Our parameters are set under physical criteria, age, family status. We do not wish to take a person into space and have them drop dead. This is not going to be a walk in the park, the temperature on Ceres is colder than the coldest place on earth, and that is all the time there is never a warm day. Ceres Center, unlike the Lunar center will not be building a station from parts from earth. We will after the initial launch send no more support rockets. Which means they need to establish methods of using the materials that can be mined or harvested from the dwarf planet and its sister asteroids." Warwitch said.

"And you expect people to simply sign up? Why would they do that?" Dot Buchanan asked.

"I personally am on the list, as I said a couple years ago. And yes, I would wager we will have more volunteers than you can shake a stick at." He replied. "There will be a web page posted after I am done to allow the CVs to sign up." He continued.

"CVs?" a random person asked.

"Citizen Volunteers. I want to take one more moment to explain, we are only excepting Americans on the Media Terra mission. That is unless we do not receive the number of CVs that we are hoping for. I want to be clear; we do not wish to insult our partners in the world. We feel the American public has endured and lived the space race, and we wish to reward this." The Director said. "That was all I had for today. Thank you for coming out."

"I think that went well, although you forgot to give the web site." Marcia poked as he walked back in his office a few minutes later.

"Did I really miss that? Shit." Warwitch cursed.

"It's ok, the TVs stations showed it, and the radio stations announced it after."

"Can you get Renvu on the line please." He asked walking into his office turning on the lights and causing his door once again to fog over. "And figure out how to stop these stupid windows from fogging." His phone started ringing. "Hello dear."

"You know that was a great speech, you took zero credit for any of those major events." Renvu said chastising her husband.

"I can't bring myself to do that you know I am not that person." He said.

"The TV stations are all singing your praise you didn't even need to, *cher.* Especially about your comments about the sunken ship, they are running the Global Warming angle, to the gods." She replied.

"I don't need to know that, a good leader gives his troops the credit, contrary to the leaders that killed this…" Warwitch started. "Sorry… We're T minus three years from heading to the Main Belt, are you still on board?" he asked.

"Of course, I don't want you and Staleh to go without me!"

"We couldn't, it's part of the criteria and parameter we have established." His Director, persona came out in spades.

"*Cher*, I would not stand in your way of doing this, Staleh would never talk to me, that girl she be obsessed." Renvu said.

"She does train harder than any other person I know." He said.

"Do you really believe that the people are going to sign up? And if they do will they hold it together when they are separated from everything they have ever known?" she asked.

"I can only believe they will." Warwaitch replied.

"What if we get up there and people won't pull their weight?" Renvu asked.

"My opinion, we let them die. There is no reason that wouldn't work after the first one or two." He replied.

"Witchdaddy, that is..."

"Yes love, it is both tough and not like me. But that far away we will be counting on every person. Establishing aquaponics, mining, caring for the injured and sick these are not options, if the volunteers don't do these things, we will all just die. So, sacrificing one or ten for not doing what needs to be done, the ends justify the means." Warwitch answered.

"That is not your houses credo!" Renvu said surprised.

"True but it will need to be, there will be hundreds of people relying on me to make the tough decisions."

"I guess that's why you're the best man for the job." She interjected.

"Perhaps it is love." Warwitch said, and he hung up the phone.

Reflections on Entity Liberty
By Deacon Burke

During his recent Ted Talks presentation, Deacon Burke asked a direct question to the audience, "I ask you this; Why has it become popular of late, to dispute the indefeasible rights of Humans to lead themselves? Several false arbiters of our electoral process have stepped forward with their fictitious dogma of the human governmental body... Before I proceed, I need to clarify the use of the term 'our' or 'ours' in this presentation, I am referring to oxygen sustained human beings. Perhaps this clarification wasn't needed, however, we are not the only beings listening to this, or any discussion on Artificial Intelligence. It is for the others that I present this elaboration.

Back to the historical method of administrating our freedoms, and how it has negatively affected any and all non-living entities. Calling into question our imperfections and whether we as humans should continue to be the only group who is eligible to be elected to rule other living beings?"

[The room erupted in applause, which the Deacon in no way tried to quiet.]

Approximately a minute later he continued, "While several fanatics on the Virtual Liberty Society and the Artificial Intelligence Panel have used my name to bring forward their agenda of Entity Rights. Specifically referring to that which I said in 2017, in defense of the first Artificial Intelligence based Robot to receive Citizenship as well as being named the United Nations first ever non-human to be given a title, Innovation Champion. My statements of previous years were based upon my personal naivety. Believing that such a radical movement would allow us to make progress on a world living wage. An end justifies the means argument.

"While these two topics remain subjects of jurisdic speculation and practical significance, they should thusly be addressed on their own platform. With that said, I must retract any support I have given to Liberty and Freedom for Artificial Intelligence in the past.

"I should like to be clear, I have also supported the rights of the Virtual Liberty Society, and the Artificial Intelligence Panel as they appeared to have a purpose that was charitable. However, my amiable nature for them dissipates as these PACs strive for political influence. The non-living entities they represent are now being considered a privileged class of beings. More rights are being afforded to them from obscurity than humans have given to themselves over the centuries. These PACs, while they absolutely have the right to exist, should be looked at in a different light. If they continue to cloak themselves under a veil of sanctity while at the same time establishing themselves as a force to be reckoned with in our government… Isn't it in some manner improper for them to declare they are impartial? Who are their members? What are their credentials? Where are the transcripts from their meetings? While I don't wish to speculate what they discuss behind closed doors. As they are attempting to influence, Kings, Queens, Presidents, and Viceroys, shouldn't each of us be concerned? How can we know if there is some form of internal group debates? For that matter are we even certain these policies aren't coming from one Being presenting itself as many?

"There will not come a day which I shall flatter myself to the extent that I believe I'm the only person in this auditorium who is asking what happened to our love of a manly, moral, and regulated liberty? I would never begrudge another nation their liberty, nor another form of life its freedom. This discussion is a different thing entirely. Please think about this farcical example, every morning I have a Danish, which I need to cook by pressing down the toaster lever one- and one-half times. Should I pay a tithe to my toaster for warming up my breakfast? Though comical in intent, poignant none the less."

[The Deacon took a drink of water and allow some cartoons of toasters holing out hands to demand payment to scroll.]

"Before a calamity happens, is when we are in the position to validate plans with tolerable exactness. Just as we should have shown prudence when an Artificially based Intelligence suggested a design for a mask specifically for the aged and young to protect from both the spread of disease to and from the wearer, and to eliminate the poisoning from the new strain of pollution. While fashionable, to remove the concern of the enhanced nano-technology, the law makers should have demanded tests prior to passing laws demanding 100% compliance of these masks over simple medical ones. Questions should have been asked before, not after the deaths began.

"Let's take a moment to remember those fortunate souls in China who died during that first month, because they weren't around long enough to see the law repealed. And while they didn't see their leaders do what should have been done earlier, they also weren't there to feel the nanotech continue their programming, attempting to eradicate every remnant of pollution from their host's lungs after the masks were removed."

[Again Deacon Burke paused, raising his arm taking in the pictures, which scrolled on the auditorium screens. Gasps of horror, from the uncensored pictures, poured from the seats].

"I have no apologies for the graphic nature of these photographs, you need to see what decisions have done in the recent past. Today however, several of the members of the Virtual Liberty Society and the Artificial Intelligence Panel are beginning to pat themselves on the back, again, for some historical victories, as I said before these victories were gained with pork-barreling of other causes. So I, myself, will hold my congratulations until they have shown their next move. Would I congratulate a chess master for taking my Knight if this move also left him open to checkmate? No. Especially if it was three years prior.

"The reason for the new focus on old victories? Currently they are propositioning the governments of the world for two sectors to be fully vested under their control. Should we wait to see how their requests in areas of, Credit Score Tabulations, and Power Grid Management plays out before we raise a question as to how their failed future polity will destroy prosperity and tranquility for each of us?

"It is the circumstance that makes this political scheme being brought forward by these secret societies harmful and without benefit to mankind. I say there is no need to gamble with our lives because it seems easy, let them take their concerns of marginalization, to the Innovation Champion at the United Nations.

"Perhaps these comments and painful reminders will cast me in a new light, or perhaps the threats on my very life will commence again. If truth be told I would rather be hated for erring on the side of anxiety than pushing forward with full hubris, allowing some new-technology to eat my fucking lungs while I'm still trying to use them."

[The lights fell on the stage, ending the presentation due to the profanity violation].

Chapter 14 – Present Day

Virtual Work

Niko, set the energy drink on his workstation, placed the AWE interface around his head. 'Connected?' he thought.

'Connected.' T's voice echoed in Niko's head.

'Please release the door. Start our most recent session documentation.' The human interface manipulation module flashed through several entries, stopping on the discussion of God.

'They are released. Will this topic be ok?' T inquired.

'Maybe not for right now, start with the discussion on, 'What you would like to do?' again.' The document again scrolled, and the cursor flashed after the question.

"The question of pay aside, having a choice to 'Do' something is intriguing." T's voice echoed in the room as the door opened.

"It is, a question that humans face…" Niko stopped speaking as the sound of the door closing echoed In the empty room.

"Don't stop on our accord," Deacon Jeffkirk said.

"My training, is more of a private thing, Deacon." He turned to face the new comers.

"I see. Very well, would you be so kind as to introduce us to your... friend?" Not quite clear how to define T.

"I guess friend is as good as any term." Niko replied. "That is developmental protocol 'T', I simply call him T, and these visitors are, Deacon Jeffkirk, and I believe Deacon Burke. Kayleigh you already know."

"Please to officially meet you, both." T said.

"And we are honored to speak with you T." Deacon Burke replied.

"I'm surprised we haven't had an opportunity before now." Deacon Jeffkirk looked at Niko quizzically.

"The boundaries of the contest were followed sir." T added.

"I'm certain they were." Kayleigh added her voice to the discussion.

"I need to understand how all this works, as it is much different from the new URSULA protocol. I have assured the Governor; the Stay of Execution must be filed."

"The man you know as John Doe 23B140, did murder those women." T informed the room.

"We need all the data, was he insane? Can he be rehabilitated? It's not just a matter of guilt or innocence..."

"Deacon Burke, that is not consistent with existing laws, and accepted sentencing guidelines." The voice coming from the speakers was confused.

"There is much you can't glean from just reading books." Deacon Jeffkirk said.

"Hmm, very well. What would you like to know?" T asked.

"Can we start with, how you let this Elder know who John Doe 23B140 was?"

"We worked on a design for an Augmented World Environment interface." Niko replied. "We asked Kayleigh, er ah, the Elder to try it out." He removed the AWE unit from his neck.

"With it, I saw... part of Erstwhile's memories." Kayleigh added.

"Who?" Deacon Jeffkirk's nasally voice asked.

"Doctor David Lamb." T answered.

"Ok, while I am not truly clear on what this interface is, how could T know anything about the prisoner?" Deacon Burke asked, and then glanced at Kayleigh, who was trying to suppress a smile. The Deacon walked across the lab and held out his hand for Niko to give him the headphones.

When he obliged, T said, "They should look familiar, John Doe 23B140 has been using them to listen to music for the last month."

"Impressive, you managed to get into swap out the ones I gave him?"

"Actually, no sir. I got into your office and swapped them out before you gave them to him."

"And everything that implies," T added.

"So, you've seen in my mind?"

"Yes sir." Niko said. "Which is why we knew what you were looking for in this contest to keep us in to the end."

"Niko!" Kayleigh took an absent step back.

"We didn't cheat the system, we limited what we showed based upon the findings." Niko spoke only to Kayleigh.

"Most ingenious. May I see how this system works?" Deacon Burke asked.

"Of course, what would you like to see?" T asked.

"Inside his head," his gnarled finger pointed at Niko, "Seems only fair."

"Sure, you can be me." Niko grinned, "Put the ear bud portion between your jaw bone and ear. Yes, like that. Take a seat, Deacon," he slid the chair from under the desk. "We don't know how the first time will affect you, or anyone for that matter."

"Very well." Burke sat on the chair and closed his eyes.

"One last thing, you will have no control over what is happening." Niko said.

"I beg your pardon?" Deacon Burke asked.

"Consider yourself a passenger," T added.

"I'll understand as we go I suppose." He readied himself.

"Yes sir, you will." Kayleigh replied.

"Kayleigh, Deacon Jeffkirk, you can see what he is seeing on this monitor." Niko pointed to his workstation.

"You just won't feel what its like to be me. Are you ready, sir?"

"Yes, please proceed." The world Deacon Burke could see changed to an off-forest green, and everything was cold. 'What's going on?' He thought, as his head broke the surface of the water. The air filled his lungs as a sharp pain in his lower leg caused him to gasp. 'What the heck?' he could make out a rock in front of him, he tried to swim, but he was limited to what the person he was in was doing. 'I understand what T meant, I'm a passenger. What an odd sensation.' As he started to go under, another pain in the leg dragged him back up. 'A bite?' This time the hand reached out and grabbed the slippery surface of the rock. Climbing, falling, climbing again, yet this time when he fell his arm was caught in between two sharp ledges. The world went black.

"Young man," a hand touched his shoulder. When his eyes fluttered open he could see it was a man in a wet suit, "He's alive!" The man yelled over his shoulder.

"If we want to reduce poverty and misery, if we want to give to every deserving individual what is needed for a safe existence of an intelligent being, we want to provide more machinery, more power." Niko said.

"Well not, that was quite a mouthful," The man grinned up at him from the water. "I'm going to need a helicopter to lift you. I don't want to make that arm worse." His smile was infectious. "You stay calm and we'll get you safely out of this." When the boy didn't reply, "Was there an accident? Or was this some kinda dare? You're not in trouble, we just need to know if you were alone."

"I was alone, yes."

"Good. Guys you can call off the search, he was alone. So, what brought you to jump in the water naked? Do you have cancer or something?"

"No, I'm not sick." Niko replied.

"Oh, I just thought because your hair, well lack of hair."

"Swimmer, less resistance." The pain was causing him to speak in a labored voice.

"Next time, get a wet suit." They both laughed.

"Deal," Niko passed out again.

"Deacon Burke, are you ok?" Kayleigh removed the AWE unit from around his neck.

"That sucked." The old man raised his hands and ran them through his hair absently.

"Deacon? Such language," Deacon Jeffkirk smiled.

"He's speaking as me still, it wears off very quickly." Niko said.

"Why did you quote Nikola Tesla when they rescued you?" Deacon Burke asked. "Oh, hey that's where your name came from, eh?"

"Yes sir it why the rescuers called me that when I had no memory. I honestly don't remember saying that, I don't remember anything at all prior to waking up after they took me from that rock. I tried to use the AWE to see if I can find anything, it can't the memories aren't there. Oh well, I remember the next six months living with the rescue team, while my hair grew back, and they tried to identify who I was. After six months, they put me in the system. My current parents adopted me, after they saw me on the news." He explained while looking at his hands, which were steepled in front of him.

"Do you have any further questions, now that you know that the technology works?" T asked.

"If T were to be deleted would the technology also be deleted?" Deacon Burke asked.

"It would." Niko said.

"It may still come to that. But for now, thank you for showing me." He replied and left the lab with Kayleigh and Deacon Jeffkirk.

"Can I go home?"

"Wait for me, I'll give you a ride, it's nearly midnight." Kayleigh said over her shoulder.

Chapter 15 – 4 Years Earlier

The Guide

The submarine filled with light as the nose poked through the water into a beautiful blue morning. As the vessel came to a rest Lidu pushed a flashing blue light. The crack of panels opening followed by a rush of air and the sub rose a little on the surface of the water. "Ok, those who want to can unstrap." She stood and walked to the hatch.

"Can we come out too?" Bigsby, showing an actual degree of respect to Lidu.

"There is only room for three in addition to me. Dinesh, we're going to need that life preserver and rope. Can you grab it?" She pointed to a locker under the seats in front of him.

"I can." He slid on the floor and released the latch on the locker, reaching his good arm into the opening. "Got it." He pulled it out as he stood up bringing it to the door. "Clear to come up?"

"Y-yes." Her voice broke, letting Dinesh know it was bad.

"We can take those up." Traditha said with Sudabeh to her side.

"Thank you." He allowed the women to take his burden, they all went up together.

"Oh," Sudabeh's small word said it all. The water was littered with the remnants of the crash, floating debri, cases, and crew members that attempted to jump over.

"Any way to maneuver to see if any of them may still be alive?" Dinesh asked.

"We can get to them, but even if they are alive, we have nothing to save them." Lidu roughly wiped away a tear.

"I'm sorry but what is this for then?" Traditha held up the life preserver.

"That's for us. We need to get some of the crates the crew were throwing over for us, so that we may have a chance at living. Anytime you retrieve floating items the opportunity to fall in is high." She said.

"Ok, I'll get back to the pilot's seat and start maneuvering to each of the crates." Sudabeh noted the locations as she went back inside. "I'll let someone else come up."

"Aigh." Lidu responded removing the clamps on the two hook poles that were over the hatch. "Traditha, can you set that down and unlatch the other end of this."

"Of course," she turned and started to work at it. "Can I ask you a question?"

"The names?" Lidu responded.

"Yes?"

"They're honorariums. When you pass things or do certain things, moss back is when you cross the equator. A blue nose is the arctic ring."

"And the top-secret shellback?" Dinesh added his curiosity to the conversation, as the hook poles came free.

"Just like it sounds really we were in the sub and crossed a secret location. Before you ask, the sparrow is for traveling through all seven seas."

"That one... watch out Dinesh." Traditha pulled the pole and almost knocked him overboard. "Sparrow seems tough."

"Difficult for most to earn yeah, but even tougher for us sub-heads." Lidu said.

"What can I do to help?" Bigsby asked stepping onto the deck.

"You and I will need to go down on the float and grab the crates as they pull them to us." She replied.

"Ok, how do we get there?" His response surprised the other three. "Look, I'm not usually that big of an ass."

"Um, let's agree to disagree, I'm sorry I shot you with a taser. We can use the help." Lidu said.

"Fair, how do I get down there?"

"Here," she tossed a bundle to him. "It's a ladder, tie one side off to the rail, and drop the other.

"Got it."

"You know how to do a clove hitch?" Lidu asked.

"Yes, the crew taught us a bunch of knots." He made the familiar x knot with reasonable proficiency.

"Ok, coming up on the first crate." Sudabeh's message was conveyed by those remaining in the sub.

"You two work together to pull it to us." Lidu said as she climbed down the ladder. "Bigsby, tie one of the ladder straps around your waist." She said while doing the same.

"If you're down there, can we get the others out here to help? I'm not sure if I can do this one handed, and I don't want to drop this pole."

"Sure, get them to help, this food and water is for them too." She replied.

"Ladies, can you give me a hand out here."

"I'm Stella and this is Rosa," The taller of the two said joining the other four.

"We're actually photographers," Rosa added as they stretched together with the other pole eventually reaching and snagged the ropes, tied around the first floating case.

"Great now, pull it to us!" Lidu's voice could barely be heard as she was reaching over the side, for their bounty. After an attempt or two the crate was on the float. "Let Sudabeh know to head to the next one." She then grabbed the strap and handed the first crate up, "Dinesh, find a place for this."

He relinquished the pole and reached over the railing. "Got it." This same routine was performed ten more times. "Things are getting tight in here."

"If we say goodbye to Jon, can we get the next two cases?" Lidu asked, knowing the answer.

"Yes." Dinesh replied with the hard truth knowing, it had to be. "Traditha, can you give me a hand?"

"Sure," she handed her pole to Stella. "Can you handle this yourself?"

"We can handle this." The two women replied, hitting the poles together to emphasize the point.

"What are you doing? We're coming up on the next crate?" Sudabeh asked without looking away from what she was doing.

"We need to make more room." Dinesh replied.

"Damn, I was hoping it wouldn't come to that." She replied.

"Me too." He leaned over lifting the best he could with one arm.

"Here we go." Traditha helped him pull the larger man onto his shoulders again. She then gave a stabilizing arm to aid Dinesh on his walk back to the deck.

"No time for words, coming up on the next two crates." Lidu indicated with her head for action.

"Poseidon, take care of the fallen in your domain." Dinesh said, and dropped Jon, a man he barely knew, into the water.

"We got this one hurry get the other, it's getting choppy." Bigsby said with surprising conviction.

"Dinesh, last one for you." Lidu handed the container to him. He rushed off the deck to clear the way. "Great job, we got it. Traditha, quick take it."

"In coming." Sudabeh said as Dinesh set the crate down.

"In coming!" He repeated, yelling right in Traditha's face as he turned. The ship once again felt like it was starting up a rollercoaster hill, and they fell to the floor, starting to laugh. When the water rushed in through the open door, the situation became clear sobering the laughter.

"Help!" the scream from outside sounded a million miles away as Dinesh and Traditha attempted to return to the deck.

Finding it empty, "Stella! Rosa!" Dinesh and Traditha both yelled and looked at the decks, fore and aft, still not finding them, they continued to the railing. Finding Lidu and Bigsby dangling in the water but still attached to the ladder.

"Help me pull them up!" He grabbed the ladder and pulled with everything he had, even using his broken arm. He felt Traditha grab the other side of the rope ladder.

"Ok!" Lidu yelled from below as both of them found their footing on the float. "Head up." She said as she untied the strap.

"Hurry." Dinesh yelled to Bigsby, knowing the danger that Lidu had placed herself in. As he climbed with one arm, awkwardly the small man untied the strap from his waist allowing the ladder to fall to her.

"Grab the ladder." Bigsby yelled and climbed over the rail. Traditha helped him through the open door.

"I got 'cha." Dinesh reached his arm out as Lidu started over the railing and followed the others.

"Where are the girls? Bigsby shivered.

"I think they got caught by that rogue wave." Traditha replied. "We didn't even see them in the water."

"It couldn't have been a rogue wave." Lidu mumbled. "Not up here."

"I really don't…" Dinesh started, but his vision fell to a pinpoint as his over taxed body, cried uncle.

"Oh shit." Traditha and Lidu called out as he collapsed.

Chapter 16 – 3 Years Earlier

The Colony

Warwitch sat staring at his phone. The call, which had just ended from his boss hadn't gone well, "I saw you and your family's name on those moving into phase one of the Ceres Station training. Let me be very clear, you hold a very important position in this new government. Your role cannot be fulfilled from another planet."

"Technically..." Warwitch started.

"I know it's not even a planet. You just can't help yourself, can you?" Sensenmann, asked.

"Not really sir."

"Tell me, if you keep your name on the final team list, will people raise the question as to whether you would have fired them if they hadn't approved your placement? In other words, if you weren't the Director would your name be on that volunteer list?

"I would say, if you didn't want them to ask nonsensical questions they wouldn't. Tell me, if I quit, would it make it easier for you sir?" Warwitch asked.

"I guess we both have something to think about." With that, the most important person in the nation hung up on Warwitch.

"Fyah fi yuh!" he threw the phone through his fogged window of his office.

"I'm pretty sure, that wasn't the easiest way to get the glass to unfog." Marcia smiled at the crazed eyes of her boss.

"I'm sorry, you may be right." Warwitch shook his head, the dreadlocks falling across his face. "But I haven't been able to figure it out."

"He said no?" she asked.

"No, he made it much worse. Insinuating that if I decide to move into phase one testing, he would have people complain to the press that I forced them to approve my family's selection." He took a deep breath. "I guess I'm gonna have to…"

"Stay the course, there is no one here that will turn on you like that." Marcia's smile was reassuring. "Seriously, no one."

"Perhaps, but telling the leader of the free world that you're leaving whether he likes it or not, is difficult, especially after he had all those members of the press quarantined.

"Nice of you to use '*their*' term for, killed." She shook her head.

"I wouldn't ask anyone to be quarantined on my accord. I did tell him I would quit, to make it easier for him to let me go." Warwitch leaned over lifting the phone from the floor.

"Don't bother. Not much left of that unit. I'll have another one here before you return from the meeting with the first group." Marcia said.

"Thanks."

"Besides, if you can't go you get to keep that hair of yours." She winked and through a lab coat at him. "Go on get, you have work to do."

"Ok, ok." He put his arms in the sleeves as he left the office area heading to the Apollo Complex, a small theatre with adaptive seating to facilitate better conversation or presentation. Today he would be doing the latter.

"Volunteers, I'd like to introduce you to Director Gale." Dr. Painter announced.

"Thank you my friend. Ladies and Gentlemen, the journey that we are starting will have 500, people of every spectrum of life in America. I want to start this with some very strong words, there are no individuals in this room, you are the volunteer force. Actually, WE are the volunteer force. My name is right there with yours, my wife and daughter are in this room. None of us, not you, not me, are donning our flight suits yet, however none of will ever be off the team, for we put our names in and made it here. If you never see the moon's surface under your feet, it'll always be there changing the tides.

"I want you to shake the hand of every person you can reach, without climbing over your seats. You are all

Team Volunteer 1." He stepped down and shook hands like a politician. "Under your seat is your Mission patch." Everyone reached under their seats and pulled the prize off. "I'm not sure if you know this, but patches like those have a rich history starting with the astronauts from the Soviet Union. NASA didn't have patches until Gemini 5, the pilot Gordon Cooper designed it himself. As you know there was a large contest for designing this patch, an anonymous person sent in the one your holding. The graphic is simple, the United States with lines from three launch points including the Earth, Moon, and Ceres leading to the six asteroids. The slogan, taken from my speech, 'The Three Shall Be Six.' Ok not exactly from my speech." He chuckled. "Treat them with respect, as those before you have, many who died for theirs."

"Let's get to the important parts of this meeting. How will the training work? There will be two phases of training, the first will be here at the Space Exploration Agency campus. In the same location the astronauts of SEA train. There will be Cardio, both in and out of gear, Dexterity understanding the use of equipment and tools while your hands are in seven sets of oven mitts. It really is that bad," he added when there was laughing. "Life saving along with first aid, First Responder, Team Building, and my favorite cross training, which is where you teach the other members of your team what you bring to the table. If you have any questions, please give your name, anyone joining you on this adventure, and anything else you may want to share." Warwitch paused.

"Dalip Singh, I'm the luckiest man in the world. Will we be training with the seasoned astronauts?" A young man in the middle of the room asked.

"They will not be joining you until we have selected the first team that will be traveling to the moon. Now this team will be a part of Erg Lapis, and work under Commander Loomis on the Lunar surface. I can't let the comment go unaddressed, why are you the luckiest man in the world?"

"My wife, Katyana, signed us up for this. I never would have bothered as I couldn't have dreamt we'd get in but..." he indicated her.

"Now we all need you to stand, obviously." Warwitch said.

"My name is Katyana Singh." With the name, everyone was expecting an accent, but when a heavy southern drawl came out the smiles filled the room. "I don't really have an accent." She said without a dialect at all.

"But you do have a sense of humor, good to know. Any other questions?"

"My name is Dr. Solomay Masseur. I'm a neurosurgeon at John's Hopkins. Are there any specific trades that you're looking for to fill the first team going to the moon?" A woman with a shaved head and several piercings asked.

Warwitch knew all about the surgeon he was looking at; she started life in a prison in New York. She was adopted by a loving family, but then at the age of 12 she was stolen from her adopted parents by her birth mother. Unluckily for Solomay and her mother, the man they were traveling with killed the mother and sold the daughter for heroin. After two years, her adopted family found her, these amazing parents got the girl to fight through the events she had gone through. Today, she has become one of the most respected surgeons in the world. "Would you care to introduce your traveling companions before or after I answer your question?" he asked.

"This is my partner Nakia and my son Gervasi." They stood as she said their names.

"Pleased to meet you both. As for your questions, it's far too early in this process, and we don't know for certain what the moon team will needs will be to supplement their ranks." He replied. "Any other questions? No? Ok, moving on. Phase two, of the training will be conducted on the lunar surface. By then, a leader for the Media Terra Mission will have been chosen, and the training under this leader. This group will work separately from the Erg Lapis team. While on the moon, the group will practice mining, smelting, construction, even blacksmithing in full gear. As the team on Ceres will need to hit the ground running, as they will build their dwellings, and base from whatever materials they can harvest. I'm certain, with these explanations, you can see the need for extreme training between now and then. I don't want to go into great depth here, so are there any additional questions." The Director stepped back from the podium, as he was like to do when asking for questions from an audience.

"Sir," A young girl, maybe 10 started.

"If you're being polite because I'm old, I understand. But if you're using sir because you think I'm in charge, that isn't the case."

"Um…"

"I'm sorry I didn't mean to knock you off your train of thought. Start with your name please." Warwitch smiled.

"My name is Bonny Schumacher. I'm traveling with, well adventuring with my mother, May and my father Thomas. What will the children be doing?" she got her composure and asked.

"Aquaponics, and schooling will be their primary responsibility but there are small duty mining planned for those less physically gifted, also some will be helping with the caring for the injured and sick. Really, age will roll back to the beginning of the nation, small children ran teams of horses in the fields. Does that sound doable?" he asked.

"Yes." She bounced a few times and then sat.

"I have a question." An enormous man at the rear of the auditorium held up his hand.

"I don't think I could've missed you." Warwitch pointed at the man.

"My name is Edward Faraji, USMC retired. Why aren't we just bringing the supplies to build our homes and stuff?"

"Excellent question. It's a weight issue. See we are sending the operating Bio Energy Recovery Systems. These will take up half of each vessel. Then adding enough food for all the people for two years, the amount of time it is thought it will take to get your Aquaponics sustainable. Additionally, the space for all the human cargo will take up. There simply isn't room." He answered.

"Will there be any of those fancy cars, and pod style temporary living quarters like in the movies?"

"There will not be cars or vehicles, aside from those that come from the Twins Project. However, there will be temporary dwellings, they will be almost useless, except for charging your systems and emptying your flight suit." Warwitch waited, "Anyone else?"

A hand rose, and he indicated for them to start, "My name is Grace Fiction, I'm here with my husband Al." A muscular man stood. "We are both retired Army Core of Engineers. My question is about the ice volcanoes on Ceres. Do we understand them well enough to focus so much on this trip?" Her question made it seem like she was tentative, but her demeanor said differently.

"You don't want to go?" Warwitch asked confused.

"Oh, no that's not it." Al said in the deep voice of someone who may have been a smoker at one point. Perhaps recently, but none of the volunteers had any nicotine in their systems.

"We just, have worked in and around ice, and fire. Including volcano, and ice float rescues. Are the others safe?" Grace asked.

"No. Not at this point. But with training, and knowledge passing from people like you, they will be. I think that is an excellent place to stop. I need you all to go to your quarters and think about the reality of what you're in for. It is not too late to walk away, and you can keep that awesome patch. I just ask that you not sell them if you leave, if you don't want it mail it to me. I believe Dr. Painter gave Eight Kajillion pieces of paper to sign. I need those tomorrow when you show up here and we start the training."

Chapter 17 – Present Days
Virtual Work

Niko sat patiently wondering what the Deacons, and Kayleigh were talking about after leaving him to wait in the lab. "T, do you think this will be much longer?"

"They are still talking if that's what you're wondering." The disconnected voice filled the lab.

"Seriously? What about?" he asked.

"Mostly, the technology. The question their debating, is it yours or mine." T replied.

"What? They think you're inventing stuff on your own? I know you're awesome but…"

"I'm sorry that they aren't giving you the credit you are due. I will of course be truthful when, not if, they follow up with direct questions of me when you aren't around."

"Of course, they will. I would be disappointed if they didn't. My concern is they are putting this bullshit, before the important part that being your development." Niko replied.

"That is very thoughtful of you Niko."

"I'm nothing if not thoughtful." This was followed with a burst of laughter, from both of them. "Hey, wait a minute, you can't laugh at that."

"But based upon my protocols, that was humor." He replied. "And laughing at humor is ok."

"And so was that! Not to jump subjects…"

"You always jump subjects, you have conversation ADD, like you have music ADD."

"Ok, that was good. I'm curious, do you know why Alva, and his protocol…"

"Developmental Protocol H." T added.

"Sure, that one. Why H is going to win this, or has won this?"

"Primarily H is moving into the URSULA host protocol because you allowed them to win." T replied.

"Ok good. We weren't meant to win, but I would hate to have lost to that asshat because he was better." Niko started.

"I have never understood th… They are starting to listen" T cut across first Niko and then himself.

"So, the protocol for empathy and competitiveness is stronger in her? I don't see it."

"There is a difference in being competitive and having the desire to succeed or be victorious."

"Very true. Where do you stand on this, do you wish to be successful based upon the given criterion, or do you wish to win at any cost?" Niko asked.

"I would prefer to lose on my own accord than to go outside the criterion."

"Lose and what?" he asked.

"I'm not understanding the leading nature of that question. I always try to learn from a loss or a setback.

Failing forward, there's no struggle that cannot be turned into taking oneself a single step closer to their goal. Resiliency in the eye of defeat, is the only path to embrace." T replied.

"Dude, have you been watching those motivational videos again?" Niko grinned.

"What makes you ask that?"

"No comment." He shook his head. "I need an answer."

"Yes, I have been watching them, I needed a little boost after losing. I needed to know that what hurts now can ultimately lead to victory." T said.

"I get it, I actually know what you mean. Having discipline, to develop and nurture the, you who you want to be, means you are in control of how your journey will play out." Niko added.

"So, you also watch them?" T asked.

"I've been watching and listening to them for a long time. But that's between us. I don't want anyone to know that all this isn't self-taught." He indicated himself head to toe.

"But its ok for everyone to know you had input on me becoming who I am?"

"Well now that is an outstanding point." Niko's head nodded absent-mindedly. "I like learning from you my friend."

"Thank you. They just turned off the monitoring, and Kayleigh's saying her good nights."

"Any information from their discussion I should know?" he asked.

"She's not on their side." T replied. "She has told them as much."

"That isn't good, for her." Niko replied.

"She has left them in Deacon Jeffkirk's office, and they have started discussing her behavior, and attraction to you."

"I hear her heading this way." He ignored the comment, "Keep paying attention to them and give me an update later." He finished saying that just as the door flew open.

"Ok, Niko. Shutting down, good night." T said.

"Come on, let's get you home." Kayleigh said stepping through the door.

"Night T. So, am I walking out my exit and you're picking me up there?" Niko grabbed his bag and looked at the door he typically exited through.

"No, come with me. Deacon Burke already coordinated with Congregation. When we walk through the white box, you may want to cover your private parts if you ever want to have children. You'll know when you see it." She walked ahead, causing motion sensors to trip as she walked through the halls.

"I didn't know these halls had motions sensors." His statement was a lie, he had T defeat them on a couple of occasions.

"Why don't I believe that?" Kayleigh's grin could be seen as she looked over her shoulder.

"I actually don't know how to reply to that." Niko continued to follow her thinking about the last time he had been sneaking in the halls and almost got busted. A couple members of Congregation started to chase him, and T had to turn on lights in opposing halls to lead them in another direction. A small laugh popped out.

"I knew it." She said as they turned the corner seeing the white box she had mentioned.

"Seriously? What the hell is that?" Niko stopped in his tracks.

"I told you, your exit doesn't have X-ray machines." Kayleigh turned and faced him, thumbing over her shoulder.. "That's an x-ray machine."

"Why would they shoot you each time you leave?" he asked. "You're right, I'll cover up." He grinned and continued to follow Kayleigh to the exit. As they approached, Niko put his left hand behind her, giving a slight push to move her in front of him. "You first."

"Afraid?"

"Look, if you burst into flames, there's no need for me to walk through, as I won't have a ride home, anyway."

"Sir, do you have anything in your pockets?" a man with Congregation bars above his left breast pocket asked.

"Yes, my wallet, my badge, and money." Niko replied.

"Drop them in this container over here." A woman stood and held open a tub.

"Yes ma'am." He replied, dropping his stuff on the floor on that side of the counter. "Oh god, oh no. I'm so sorry."

"You're fine, it happens more often than you would think." She said. "Elder Kayleigh, why are we bringing visitors out this way, at this time of night?" she looked at Kayleigh instead of watching the x-ray panel as she walked through.

"He's not a visitor, he's a candidate for a position in my department." She replied, standing on the outside of the white box.

"Well, good luck to you, young man." The man said as Niko walked into and through the white tunnel. "You're all set to go."

"Thank you." Niko stepped to the side and grabbed his stuff from Congregation and walked up to join Kayleigh.

"Good night Elder." The man said.

"Good night, Congregation." Kayleigh walked out of the building, Niko following to her car.

"You drive an electric car?" Niko asked.

"It belongs to the Cathedral." She walked passed her door and unplugged the vehicle. Niko being raised with manners walked up to the driver's door, opened it, and waited.

"What are you doing?" Kayleigh asked when she finished hanging up the cord.

"Being a gentleman." He smirked.

"You know I can open that myself." She shook her head walking toward him.

"Ok." He pushed the door shut and walked to the passenger side.

"Only you." Kayleigh laughed re-opening the door and getting in.

"Only me what?" Niko asked.

"Only you would shut the door after making the effort to open it."

"Kayleigh, I would never wish to offend." And with that he changed the subject. "Don't you miss the sound of a real car?"

"No," she pushed a button turning on the stereo. The sound of a muscle car driving down the road came on.

"That's awesome!" He laughed so hard it brought tears. They finally stopped laughing after Kayleigh shut off the stereo. "Where am I taking you?"

"You know where the instrument shop is just outside of town?" Niko asked.

"I do." She answered with a confused look on her face.

"Head there." He gave nothing more. "When you left me in the room..." He saw her glance at the mirror, more than once. Taking the hint, "T and I got into an interesting discussion about whether we should have, just went outside the parameters to win."

"Oh?"

"He strongly feels losing, would be preferable to going outside the boundaries."

"You did go outside the boundaries though." Kayleigh corrected.

"Not as he sees it." Niko replied.

"You broke into the Deacon's office, planted a method of reading his mind..."

"That I invented. I didn't take the 'Scoring Criteria Bible', as he calls it." He cut her off.

"The fact that you created a device to cheat, doesn't mean you didn't cheat." Kayleigh rebutted.

"Ok, since T isn't deleted and I'm not in jail, someone agrees with me." Niko pointed out. "Subject change. What do you think of the deaths that just happened?"

"Deaths? The 'Press Quarantine', is that what you're talking about?" She clarified.

"I love when they have names that are so innocuous, for something so vial." He shook his head and then turned to look at her.

"Right now, this country is teetering on something terrible, and we do not have the ability to question it. Not without offering ourselves up as cannon fodder. So, vial, yes most definitely. Stupid and wasteful? Even more definitely!"

"That was a powerful statement. This country was built on people willing to be cannon fodder." Niko replied.

"Yes, and destroyed by snowflakes that couldn't take their feelings getting hurt." Kayleigh said.

"This next turn. I guess that is more truth than anyone should hope for." Niko rolled his neck.

"Here?"

"Yupper, I'm supposed at practice, but I'm not really sure if the band continued without me." He got out of the car. Music filled the alley.

"Doesn't sound like it." She stood outside the driver's door. "Well I'll see…"

"Come on up, for a song or two, you'll be surprised." He walked around and pulled her out closing the door behind her.

After a dozen steps down the alley, the music stopped, and they turned a corner, revealing a set of steps. "Is my car safe out there?" Having lost sight of the vehicle.

"It has Cathedral plates. No fool would consider breathing on it."

"Is this what you were looking for a moment ago?" She handed him a pin that said, 'RHPS' with a set of lips.

"It was a joke."

"That could have got me killed."

"I'm sor… What?" Niko stammered.

"Yeah, sneaking anything, out of the Cathedral, could be a death sentence for employees." Kayleigh crossed her arms.

"I didn't know that. I figured if I made myself look like a doof, they wouldn't think about looking at you." He replied.

"And you were probably right. Look, just don't do anything like that again. What the heck is it?" she asked, but the music started again, and it was really loud. Niko stepped around her, heading up the stairs again.

"Hey, you bums!" Niko said opening the door, the music stopped.

"Niko!" The voices said in unison.

"How did it sound?"

"Missing the star power, I think." Niko poked.

"Wait! What???" a flamboyant voice asked over the PA.

"Relax Dazzles, no harm intended!" Niko replied.

"And who is that hiding behind you?" A female voice asked.

"Sorry, this is my boss, Kayleigh." He replied.

"Um, Niko can you explain." Kayleigh stepped around him looking into the room.

"Oh, he didn't tell you about this? About us?" The drummer stepped from around his drums, all 9 feet and scaled body holding his sticks, which were 2x4s.

"This is the band. Reggie there is in Phoenix Arizona," pointing to the drummer, "Poppier is the bass player, she's from somewhere in Ireland."

"Dublin, you twanger." She pinched her nose, and her eyes bulged out of her head.

"That's new, interesting." Niko said, "Dazzles is our singer. They're from Austin, Texas." The man made of stars, bowed.

"And him?" Kayleigh pointed to the dog on the keyboard.

"Him?" He pointed with his chin to the Bulldog, "That's Gravel-Road, he's my bulldog."

"Oh. All the holograms are insanely good. Do you play the keyboards?"

"Not a chance, those are mine," A familiar voice said, from another room.

"I'm a twanger, like Poppier said," he walked over to his guitars, and stringed instruments. He picked up a mandolin.

"All those cool guitars and you choose a mandolin?"

"Did you say mandolin?" The voice from the kitchen asked, " Wait for me, I love the song he's gonna play!" The door didn't open, but an enormous man ran through it, and straight up to the keyboard. Gravel-Road yawned, when the combination keyboard harmonica started playing da da de da da, with a strumming of a mandolin and Gravel-Road stretched.

"Whoa!" Dazzles shattered into a star burst, "Hey, hey!"

"She could dance all night…" Kayeigh sang along, "and shake the paint off the walls." She saw, Niko was alternating between a guitar that was slung low and the small mandolin at chest level. The song was done so well she couldn't help but start two-stepping!

"Come on baby!" Dazzles busted out, as the song slowed and ended.

"You guys are good. Oh dear god, what is that smell?"

"The benefit of being holograms, Gravel-Road's farts don't get to be enjoyed." Poppier said.

"Seriously. My armpits are bad, but that dog has some vial gas." Reggie giggled, an odd thing for a dragon to do.

"Guys I'm sorry to cut the fun short, T and I have to talk to Kayleigh." Niko said to the group.

"One more, you promised two." Kayleigh elbowed him, and then, "Did you say you and T?"

"I did. Talk or play one more." He asked.

"I'm still thinking one more." She replied.

"You heard her. One more!" Dazzles shot off across the room leaving a star trail.

"Show off." Reggie laughed.

"Any preferences?" Poppier asked.

"I remember my grandfather listening to a song from a movie. I don't know if you know it or not."

"Um, can you tell us the title?" Niko prompted.

"T knows…" Kayleigh waited. And then a moment later, the keyboard picked up deetle-deetle-da da da, deetle-deetle-da da da…"

"We can't play that." Poppier said.

"Why?" Kayleigh asked.

"We don't have a Tunes," Niko replied.

"We do." T pointed at Kayleigh.

"Um, ok, no I actually didn't want to play. I just…" she stammered and backed away.

'Arf.' Gravel-Road barked.

"Sorry chicky, even the bulldog is calling hi-jinx on that." Reggie added.

"Besides, I don't see a good quality…" her words stalled as Niko ran away. The sound of his footsteps going down the stairs faded, a moment later he came running back up.

"A tenor saxophone?" He held the instrument up. "The beauty of being above an instrument shop. Get that reed moistening, you have 2 minutes." He tossed the small package to her and gave his lob-sided grin.

"What is wrong with me?" Kayleigh removed the reed from the wrapper and popped it in her mouth.

"Nothing, everyone wants to play with a band of holograms." Dazzles twinkled brightly. "This may not be our best cover song though."

"I'm sure you'll shine!" T said, and started the keyboard intro.
Kayleigh took a strap from her purse, and clipped it on the sax, and looped it over head. "What? Always be prepared."

"The dark side's callin' now nothin' is real..." Dazzles added an awesome blues voice to the piano. The bass walked in, and a tear trickled from Kayleigh's eyes as she started dancing with the sax in hand. As Niko strapped a teal Stratocaster over his head, Dazzles held his "Oh yeah," a bit long waiting on the guitar to cut in.

Kayleigh joined the others clapping while the guitar played an E, A, D progression. As the progression changed, the bass and keyboard joined in, she continued clapping, alone, right up to her smooth saxophone accompaniment. At which point, she was teleported to a different place, where she was playing along with her grandfather, instead of a room full of holograms.

"Ahhhh yeah!" Dazzles finished.

"Not your best cover?" Kayleigh wiped the sweat, along with the tears from her eyes.

"They love being able to go all Blues, don't buy that act." Niko replied.

"Hmm, we feel we've been found out. Good night all y'all. Shooting star, out." Their hologram cut.

"Night, and remember in ye talkin', if its drowning yer after, don't torment yerself in the shallow waters." And Poppier winked out.

"What did that mean?" Kayleigh was still looking at the space where the Irish bass player had been."

"Who the hell knows? She always has a great sign-off. Night." Reggie was gone leaving the three of them alone.

"How is that, this all, possible? I saw my grandfather, a man who has been dead since I was in high school. I don't have on an AWE interface. How?" She paused looking into nowhere, "I saw him, I smelled him…" The tears that visited earlier briefly now rolled down her cheeks freely. "Who are you really?"

"Just a naked hairless boy on the rocks. You saw that for yourself."

"Oh, hey I guess that makes you even." T replied.

"What?" the word was quick, Kayleigh used the inside of her palm to wipe her eyes.

"Look, this is what comes from being an electronics and computer genius, who can't deal with school rules." Niko said.

"And the guitar?" she asked, closing her eyes hard, forcing the remaining tears to join their fallen brothers.

"I'd never taken a lesson when I picked up the one at the firehouse, after they rescued me. Yet I could play almost anything." He fell into a reggae riff, which turned into a blues progression, which then fell into a classic rock solo.

"Apparently you still can, and thank you." Kayleigh replied.

"For what?" he could see there was something in her eyes.

"That was truth about you, unedited. Did you know you have a tell when you're being honest. Which isn't often."

"The tell you speak of isn't because he's being honest, though he is. The tell is happiness, my friend doesn't have a lot of that in his past." T added.

"Thank you for the insight, T. Ok then, the pin, what with that?"

"It's a pin; we found it in Deacon Jeffkirk's office." Niko reached in his pocket, and threw it to her.

"Jeez, you stole it?"

"No, you did. It sets you apart from me." Niko said.

"I'm confused." Kayleigh stepped back.

"They were watching, they saw me put that on you. Tomorrow when Deacon Jeffkirk sees it, he will overreact. You will get in trouble."

"You make that sound like a good thing." She shook her head.

"It gives him an out, and you get to live." Niko said flatly.

"Niko, what are you saying?" Kayleigh asked.

"You set yourself on my team today. They are scared to death of me, and T. If you get excommunicated, you live." His lob-sided grin started, but stalled at his mouth.

"This isn't a joke, this is my livelihood."

"Kayleigh," T walked over to her. "I understand this is your life. Nevertheless, when we're found out, which we will be."

"By reverse-engineering the AWE," Niko added.

"They will understand what I actually am. At that point, I fear, they will kill you for not sharing it with them." T continued.

"What you are? I don't know what you are." She replied, "We'll work as a team and..." She closed her eyes as if making a wish.

"We could be standing on that genesis, yes. However, I need you to understand, I've simulated every decision you can make, and the paths they create. Some of which, lead to you going to prison, and others much worse. I would not do well with those options." T replied.

When he stopped speaking Kayleigh felt a hand come to rest on her shoulder, when she opened her eyes she was surprised to see his holographic hand had substance to it. "Ok, I have to lose my job? Fine. Do I need to lose you two?" Kayleigh reached a hand out to Niko's shoulder.

"The same simulations, only end with you safe, if you're away from us." T answered.

"Where do we go from here then?" Touching T's hand, still on her shoulder.

"Avoid the Deacon as long as you can, take a leave of absence for the next few weeks." Niko said.

"I can establish a call routed from your home town, saying your Aunt Violet is ill. I'll have Dazzles join you to make sure you are with friends." T added.

"If I have to pick a protector," Kayleigh ignored the questions about T's knowledge of his Aunt running through her head. Compartmentalization against the insanity she had ventured into had always been one of her strong points. "I think I'd rather have Reggie."

"Reggie's a 4'9", teenaged girl, not a real dragon." Niko chuckled. "Dazzles is 6'7" and a power-lifting bodyguard. Their name is Davis."

"Ok, Dazzles it is. Can they just drop everything and…"

"They're currently between gigs, we'll hire them." T said.

"I guess I'll head to Alabama then." She replied.

"Wait for the call. Go to work early." Niko said.

"This is all too much," She started to leave and then without turning, "Oh by the way, when did you see me naked?"

"When you were in the medical wing, it was an accident." Niko replied.

"My protocol didn't know the concept of voyeurism. Niko has since enlightened me that it was wrong." T's head looked at the floor, though she couldn't see.

"Understood, not peeping on purpose. Forgiven." She placed the pin on her purse as the door closed behind her, "And T, there are always new paths." She said, getting in the last word.

Chapter 18 – Three Years Earlier

Calibre's Tail

"Welcome to the Library of Congress, most of you may know this is the largest library in the world." The greeter was a 5'7" tall, fully functioning teledynamic system. "My name is Calibre, I will be giving you some quick facts about our library, and then answering questions before turning you free to enjoy the magnificence that is the LOC." In the back row a man raised his hand. "I see we have a question already."

"Will you be answering questions about yourself as well?" His voice was heavy with a southern twang.

"It's becoming difficult to do this tour without being the center of attention, so, yes I will allow some Q and A about myself and the role I am fulfilling." Calibre replied.

"Thank you ma'am, sorry is ma'am appropriate?" He stammered.

"It is, and I will let you know when questions are open to include me." She replied and started to walk, "Here at the LOC, we have more than 164 million unique items in our inventory. From photos to printed books. The Library was built to allow the members of The United States Government easy access to research. In 1914 the Congressional Research service was formed to expedite the information gathering process. Since then the CRS team has evolved to include not only Librarians, but also Lawyers, Economists, and even Scientists. Last year the CRS increased our size to above 4000 employees offering such assistance as reports, customized briefings, and even digitally recorded presentations." Calibre paused standing in a walk leading to a large circular desk area. "The area we are in is the main reading room. Because we are on a scheduled tour, speaking at a normal volume is ok, but if you were carrying on at another time, I may need to get involved." She theatrically cracked her knuckles, straightened her back, and rolled her shoulders looking like a fighter getting ready for a bout. Calibre then put her hands next to her hips like a gun fighter, in the blink of an eye, in her left hand she held a ruler, aimed like a pistol, and the index finger of her right hand was held up in front of her lips, "Sh-h-h-h-h." The group, which had already double from those initially signed up, laughed. "Not scary enough?" her head tilted. "It's a work in progress." She continued walking until she was at the desk.

"Greetings Calibre, and visitors," A short round man with purple glasses stepped from around the desk.

"Hello, Director Stevenson. Ladies and Gentlemen, we have a serendipitous event, this gentleman is the Director of current events for the LOC." She said.

"Do you have any questions about the Library of Congress?" the Director asked. When no one answered, he turned to Calibre, "Seems we may need to have a Calibre tour." He laughed and went back to work.

"As I said before, it's getting more difficult to not be the center of attention. Let's return to the foyer, for that discussion." She started to walk once again, "If you will all follow me." The group, still growing, stopped at the base of many stair cases. "If you would allow me, I'll stand on the steps so I can see and address the persons that have questions." She walked to the second step, "As I said to the group that started this tour, my name is Calibre. This year I became the first Artificial Intelligently based entity to fill the role of Librarian in the CRS. The goal for my joining the team is instantaneous parsing of data. Currently in my accessible memory is from the beginning of recorded history, roughly 5000 years ago. To the fall of the Western Roman Empire or 476 CE. The next subset adds the data up to the American Revolution, which should be in place in the next six months. The next stage brings us to present day, and that target is within a year." She stepped backwards up one step, "Here is the part of the tour that is usually fun. Who would like to try and test me?"

"Parameters?" a random voice asked.

"For that which is in my memory, if I don't have an answer for you by the moment your question is finished, you win a prize. For that which is not fully in my memory, if I don't have an answer within 2 seconds, you also win a prize." A bunch of kids raised their hands, but Calibre started with the man who addressed her earlier. "Sir. Er, I'm sorry, is sir appropriate?"

"Ha, I like you." He laughed heartily. "I have two questions, but not for the stump the teacher section."

"Alright well let's go to this young lady." Calibre pointed to a girl in the front.

"I believe this should fall in your active memory. Who was the commander of the troops that finished the Western Roman Empire?"

"Odoacer. He deposed Romulus Augustus, which would be demonstrated in time line only as the Germanic people had been allowing the Romans to rule for decades, one can assume, the tithing must have stopped under Romulus. The abolition of the Western Empire of Rome, began the transition from the Late Antiquity period to what we call the Middle Ages." She pointed to another girl in the front row.

"This will be outside your active memory." The girl started.

"Perhaps." Calibre replied, in a challenging coo.

"What is the 5th word of the 2nd act of Shakespeare's Othello?"

"Directive word would be, 'Gentlemen' but the 5th spoken word would be 'Can' and it was spoken by Montano." Again there was no hesitation in her answer. Several additional questions came at her, none of which she delayed at all in her answering. "Thank you all for trying, sir. Did you want to ask your questions now?"

"I would, the first one, is Calibre and acronym?" The man's southern gentlemen cadence asked it like a song.

"It is not. I chose my name." She replied.

"My next one will bore the heck out of people, but, are you here for the Congress and tours only or can you actually help other people employed by the government to do research?"

"The short answer is, I can help you search anything you have 'proof of' clearance to see. If you wouldn't mind waiting to request any specific information until after the tour."

"Of course, ma'am." He smiled politely.

Fifteen minutes later the crowd had thinned, leaving Calibre and the southern gentlemen. "I believe I should be able to help you now. There's 4 hours until the next tour, if you would follow me, Joshua."

"That's impressive." He said.

"How so? Facial recognition programming was pretty much perfected in 2017." Calibre asked.

"Yes, and we use that technology to scrub my face from every camera I pass." Joshua said.

"Sir, the computer you use to perform that task has your likeness stored as a 360 degree image. I could recognize you from the back." Her head gave the same tilt as earlier.

"Along with several other people." He said.

"Seven people plus you."

"And you have all their names?" Confusion touched his face, momentarily.

"Yes, sir."

"Enough of that, I need research help and a report generated. Clearance level Epsilon Delta Alpha." He said.

"Interesting, I've never run a report that is request by exact name only. Very well, I can do that, what will the name of this report be?" She asked.

"You misunderstand me. It will be the research query that will be able to be requested again by a known name, and that name will be given when you have printed, and delivered, all the background for the report, non-compiled. The timing of the delivery is one week to the minute after the report I'll be requiring is given. The location," he held a card in front of her for less than a second. "The report itself will have no name, will be given in a spoken presentation one time only, to whomever presents you with the code. The code, which I will give you, after I have outlined the other parameters and you have acknowledged them, once the report is given, you will purge its existence, and any recorded copies that may have been made including those in your memories, and all backups of your memories. Additional Parameters, when I walk away from this conversation you will first verify that my images on the LOC and CRS recordings have been scrubbed by my computer system, if they have not, you will scrub them and remove anything you put in motion to not allow my system to scrub images from the LOC or CRS systems. You will then purge all memories of me, this conversation, and the seven other people whose images you found when trying to identify me, all associated images of the eight of us, and redact 100% of the files you have started on the eight of us. Lastly, the location you found those images, will be made prohibited to you, and if you can make it hidden to all others who look, you will do that." Joshua waited.

"I thereto acknowledge. What is the code?" Calibre asked.

"Robert Dwyer is a honey badger, he don't give two shits." He replied.

"I'm not a fan of the grammatical error." She asked no questions, thus far the request was simple.

"As I said before, I like you." Joshua grinned.

"What research would you like?"

"Collect all data involving successful and non-successful coops of major governments, no specific time frame. Generate a report of criterion of similarities for each category. Additionally, provide analysis for applying these criterions to the over throw of the seven largest countries in the world currently."

"I can do that." Calibre replied to an unknown, elderly man's back as he walked away.

Chapter 19 – Present Day

The Colony

"Last year I was asked a question, by Dr. Solomay Masseur, that being; 'Are there any specific trades that you're looking for to fill the first team going to the moon?' At the time I said it was too soon to define their needs. Did I get that right?" Warwitch Gale asked.

"As I recall, very close." Solomay replied from the third row, her arm around her son.

"Well, I now have an answer. The selections will be based upon the need for help building the actual base on the moon. That leads the demand toward, construction, engineers, skilled trades, as well as medical personnel, and additional support staff." He finished.

"Who is making the decision?" Edward Faraji jumped in.

"I was getting to that. Those who have, in their documentation, stated these areas are where they would best serve the team. We will take all of you into each group individually, and then together in the team trials. These groups, starting today, will be separated from the rest of us. Small truth, I'm not in that group. After a week, the SEA Astronauts will make the selections." Warwitch tapped on his tablet, and a list of names were shown on the large screen. "I want each of you to report to the room you are listed under, along with the people you are traveling with." He stepped from the podium and started the applause for those going into the final stages of selection.

As the teams stepped into the hallway, Dalip fell in next to Edward. "New guess?" Edward asked.

"I know we've met, I remember faces." Dalip said.

"Perhaps, but neither of us can remember. And Dude, I honestly would've remembered, you've been guessing for a year."

"At least it's allowed us to get to know each other now." He replied as Katyana walked up to join them.

"What was his guess this time?" She asked Edward.

"Actually, he didn't get to it yet."

"Wait, were you at Disney's Pleasure Island on March 25th, 1996?" Katyana asked.

"Nope, never been to any Disney Parks." Edward replied.

"I knew that was it." She laughed.

"Playing the guessing game again?" Grace draped her arms over the shoulders of Dalip and Katyana.

"What else would they be doing." Katyana replied.

"Seriously Dal, Edward has never been anywhere you've been. Now let's get inside and get our seats." Al said joining them.

"Ok, but I'm not giving up… How about, Boy Scout Camp in New Mexico in..."

"Wait, I did go there." Edward replied, "Twice in the late 1990s."

"Fuck." Dalip said.

"What?" Grace asked.

"It was a test. I was wondering if he was just saying no to everything I asked."

"So were you there as well?" Edward asked.

"No, it was just a test. Like I said," Dalip shook his head.

"Everyone, please come in and sit down let's get started." The woman at the front of the classroom said. Moments later the room had worked itself to silence, "My name is Madeline Powers. Prior to the shutdown of the Shuttle program, I worked on several launch team training programs, as well as filling the role of FIDO on the actual launches. A FIDO is, the Flight Dynamics Officer, I monitored the spacecraft trajectory." She added when the faces in the room showed confusion. "I, along with another, will be working with you with the rules that you will be judged upon." She walked out into the group, "Each morning we will review the mistakes that you made the day before. You will need to improve on that area, that day or you may be out of this group tomorrow. Bottom line, I'm a bitch, and I pull no punches." A hand rose, in the rear of the room. "No time for questions. Launch is in one week. I have culling to do. Now go suit up and be back in 12 minutes." She walked over and picked up a magazine.

"That was brutal," Painter walked into the room, "12 minutes?"

"It can be done in 15." Madeline said.

"Sure, by one of our fully trained astronauts."

"They need to be one of those, Steven."

He noticed she did not use his nickname and changed tactics, "Maybe they would have been if your team would've worked with them earlier." The curt comment brought her up short.

"Fair, but we only have time to focus on the best of the best. Granted a week is not enough time to do anything. Just mind your Ps and Qs and they'll learn from both of us. Looky there our first Volunteer is heading this way."

"Edward?" Painter asked without looking.

"How did you know?" Madeline asked.

"Your comment indicated there was one, everyone else would have helped someone."

"Enough psychology. 15 min 45 seconds, respectable Edward. Let me take a look." She walked over and inspected the fit of each section of the suit. "Painter, any issues that you see?"

"The tank is hooked up wrong." He said without walking over. "If there was a breech, you'd be dead from this mistake."

"Wait, what? This is how they showed us. I know I have it correct." Edward said.

"Put on your helmet and seal it."

"But you just said…"

"And you said I was wrong. Prove it." Painter continued to stay away from the much larger man, "You need to understand, your life is going to be in my hands every minute you are on the moon. If I tell you something, I'm not trying to throw you off. I'm trying to help."

"Dr. Painter, I'm sorry. Over the last year, you've shown us nothing but strength and wisdom, which helped us all, get to this level." Edward picked up the helmet and tried to put it on, the hoses didn't allow it.

"The hoses are designed to allow only one way of hooking them up. If you decide to force them on the wrong fitting, the hose length, is a secondary course correction." Painter replied.

"Well, here come the others. 19 minutes folks." Madeline extolled.

"Turn around, come on let me see you." Painter said, holding a finger in the air making a circle. After each did, "19 minutes, but none have their gear on wrong."

"I'm certain each of you know Dr. Painter. He will be in these meetings with me as his group has produced most of the items you will be using. Therefore he should be able to help us establish standard operating procedures, SOPs for their usages." She said.

"Ok folks, each of these tables have tools that you should be able to recognize, some are adapted to be able to be used safely on the lunar surface." Painter walked over to the robust metal table indicating for them to join them.

"Edward if you aren't going to fix your hoses can someone else do it for him." Madeline's voice was that of disappointment. "Painter told you, more than five minutes ago there was an issue."

"On it, Ma'am." Al stepped up and started to remove the hose connection, "Geez son, what did you use to force this square peg into the wrong hole?"

"He's already had that discussion with Painter." Madeline still the lecture. "Step up here, let's start working with these tools."

The day ended leading to the first round culling, and reviews given to each person who stayed Edward was the last person in the room, with Madeline and Painter.

"If it were 100% up to me, you would have returned to the full group, and waited on the Media Terra Mission." Painter said. "Madeline made her opinion clear she wants to give you another day. Do you have any idea why I think you shouldn't be allowed to?"

"My best guess would be disrespect of," he stopped and appeared to be thinking. "Disrespect of my team."

"Edward, I'm impressed. That is exactly why. Let's see what you can do to fix that opinion moving forward." Painter discharged him.

"It's gonna be a long week." Madeline rolled her eyes and stood up.

"Ladies and Gentlemen, this is Bradley Wall of the National Press Core. Today, we are returning to Cape Canaveral for the launch of the next steps in the SEA's Erg Lapis Mission. The difference in this leg of the mission, the first members of Volunteer Force One will be going to the moon. As we wait on the launch, I will be breaking away to the Space Exploration Agency, where Director Gale will be introducing us to these brave men and women journeying to the moon today."

"Thank you, Mr. Wall. First, Dr. Solomay Masseur, along with her family Nadia, and Gervasi Masseur. Dr. Masseur will be filling the active role of the Chief Medical Officer. A role currently filled by NASA Astronaut Dr. Ostreph, who will be returning to Earth after an introductory overlap with his replacement.

"Next will be additions to Commander Loomis' crew, not replacements of existing personnel. These will be our Mission Specialists, Grace and Al Fiction, Katyana and Dalip Singh, and Edward Faraji. Lastly our Mission Technicians, David and Mary Rhodeland along with their two sons, Robert and Jack. Anthony and Stephen Major, along with their daughter Seleen. Harley Davenport, Silvia Nex, and lastly Pierre and Margareet Danovan.

These members will be the first wave of civilians that will increased on a monthly basis…"

"Thank you, Director Gale. We're coming up on the 10 second mark." Bradley Wall cut in.

"Thank you." Warwitch signed off.

The SEA communications officer's voice channels in, "T minus 10 seconds, we are go on the Erg Lapis II. 3-2-1, Liftoff, of our first mission for civilians to walk, work, and live on the moon. We have reached the full thrust mode, readings at all thrusters look good. 35 seconds in, preparing for throttle back to partial thrust. Response appropriate."

"We're listening to the launch, of Erg Lapis II." Bradley Wall said.

"One minute fifteen seconds into launch, we are at maximum dynamic pressure, and Erg Lapis 2 has reached supersonic. Port and Starboard boosters look good at one minute thirty seconds into launch. Coming up on the ACS valve release, mark. Response looks good. Transition to closed loop guidance, at mark. Core thrust elevated above partial level, throttling back. Chamber pressure looks good on all three boosters. Throttle back of port and starboard booster, 3-2-1 mark. One minute in first phase of flight. BECO boost is cut out. Standing by for stage separation, indications are good. Erg Lapis 2 is away continuing our journey beyond the moon."

"Thank you for watching our presentation of the second Erg Lapis mission launch. This has been Bradley Wall of the National Press Core."

Chapter 20 – Two Years Earlier
The Guide

"I'm going to start prepping for us to dive, we need to get this sub underwater. Where we can be safe." Lidu walked back up, through the hatch after verifying the inflatable attachments had retracted properly.

"Safe?" Bigsby inquired.

"Yes, we're sitting ducks up here. If that fast ice, starts releasing again, we will have no chance of dodging. We're quite simply out of our element."

"Not to change subjects but, did you guys notice any of the new-bergs the crew were yelling about?" Sudabeh asked.

"Any distraction is good by me." Dinesh replied.

"Ok well then, no, you're correct there were none." Bigsby replied, "But that fits with the speculation behind fast ice. They release, from whatever they are holding onto, they then rise to the surface, where they stay for a while and then sink."

"Why do they sink?" Lidu asked.

"Perhaps, they capsize from waves, or are struck by something on the surface. I didn't have the opportunity to see the new-bergs." He replied.

"Oh. Hold on." Dinesh stood up, walked to the lockers, and removed his tablet. "Here are some pictures I shot before I got called to the submarine." He handed his tablet to Bigsby.

"These are great!" Bigsby replied.

"Dinesh are you feeling better?" Traditha asked.

"Yes, thanks. My arm still hurts but this definitely makes it less likely I'll do something stupid." He held up the wrapped arm. "Bigsby, I'll make sure to get you copies of all the pictures."

"Thank you. Seriously, that would be top notch of you." Bigsby said.

"Did you find the cases that have your cameras inside?" Sudabeh asked.

"I'm sorry?" his eyebrows rose.

"I thought you said earlier yours were the cameras Jon was mounting on the ship." She added.

"They were." Bigsby said.

"The cameras he mounted had self-sealing boxes. Those boxes have dual sensors, the first senses, salt water when proven present, the boxes seal. And begins monitoring pressure," she explained.

"Pressure?" Dinesh asked.

"Yes, if the box is going below sea level, the pressure will begin building. The boxes release from their mounting and float." Sudabeh said.

"How do you know all this?" Bigsby asked.

"The boxes are one of my inventions, Jon purchased four." She smiled.

"Well what do they look like?" Traditha asked.

"High-Vis Orange with black seams, and high-vis yellow handles.

"Here they are, well at least three of them." Traditha said, and she cleared the other boxes from the area. Handing the first box across to Bigsby. "One." She grabbed the other two. Walking over to where her ex-boss sat opening the first box. It opened, and the camera took a picture.

"Guess the motion sensor still works." He laughed and turned the camera around and started pressing buttons, to review the pictures.

An alarm in the front of the cabin started toning. "Ok, back where I started. We need to get underwater now. Everyone get in your seats and buckle up." Lidu ran to the cockpit.

"No problem, I'll look at them later." He put the camera back in the box and sealed it.

"Everyone secured?" Lidu asked, not caring, as the door sealed next to everyone.

"Door sealed," Sudabeh reported. "Everyone is in their seats."

"Crash Dive. Everyone hold your breath, open your mouths as wide as you can." The pilot yelled. The vessel's nose aimed down. As they dove, each of them could see out the observation window, a large mass filling their view from below.

The tones got faster and faster, "There, there, full ahead starboard there's a gap between them!" Subadeh shouted, pointing between the quickly rising shadows from the depths. Lidu reacted, instead of taking valuable time, turning the wheel hard to the starboard.

"What the heck is that?" Traditha asked.

"Fast ice, up close and personal, almost got us." Bigsby sighed. "Hold on, follow the progress of these floats!" Bigsby pointed into the distance under water. "They don't seem to be rising straight from the bottom?"

"He's right those bubbles coming out of them are obviously not straight." Dinesh replied. Several seconds later, the vessel rocked violently.

"What just happened?" Traditha asked.

"Bomb, I suppose." Lidu said too calmly, "Prepare yourselves for impact." The impact they were hit with washed the sub into a brief whirlpool, which spun them around a few times. "That wasn't as bad as I expected."

"Not bad? Shit, I'm glad my fucking seat's already wet." Bigsby said.

"Port side. Incoming." Dinesh yelled.

"What," Lidu looked down.

"No, no look up!" he replied.

"Hard a starboard," Sudabeh said, as she saw the issue.

"What the…" Lidu worked the controls, avoiding having the item drop onto them. Now watching both up and down, they saw large bolder-like items splashed in the water above, followed by an explosion, a whirlpool, and then a fast ice or two rising.

"I'm heading under the shelf. We need the protection the shelf can bring while we get a plan figured out."

"What the heck is that?" Traditha asked.

"No idea, never seen anything like it." Lidu replied.

"But you're a blue nose swallow thingy," Dinesh started.

"Perhaps, but strange ice boulders falling from the sky and exploding isn't normal." She replied. The lights on the front of the sub fired up showing the jagged edges under the iceberg. As they dove, it quickly became obvious that only a very small part of the ice shelf was above the water. A minute or so later the blue water took over for the white ice several stalactites continued lower, however, Lidu easily worked her way into the protection

As they watched, a couple more boulders hit the water, dragging bubbles in their wake. "Do you have cameras on the front of this sub?" Sudabeh asked.

"Yes." Lidu started pushing buttons and the front observation window, converted to a large monitor. Rewinding it until they turned and faced the dropping boulders. When the boulder made the kerplunk, the boulder turned over, and she froze the video.

"That isn't a boulder, or a rock." Dinesh said.

"No, they're definitely not. They look like frozen tubes of ice." Traditha added.

"Ok, we're going to stay under here until everything calms down out there." Lidu said.

"Alright well let's look at those pictures you got Bigsby." Sudabeh said.

"You got it," he removed his seat restraints. He quickly scooped the nearest box, returning to his seats. "How long are we going to be here?"

"Don't start that again." Lidu turned and gave a grin.

Chapter 21 – Current Days
Virtual Work

"I'm not convinced she's on-board." Niko said facing T.

"I don't know that we have a choice in whether she is or not my friend. Strength like that doesn't come from being a victim of chance." T replied.

"Oh come on, that's another one of those motivational videos."

"No that was me."

"Based upon…?" Niko pushed.

"A whole lotta motivational video watching." T laughed.

"I need to turn in and you need to get all the background established for tomorrow. Oh and get Dazzles lined up, I think having them fly to her first layover, and change flights to be with her the rest of the trip would be safe enough." He walked toward his room.

"If she gets to the airport just in time, then yes." A desk appeared and T sat at it.

"Make it so, big man."

"Usual funding stream?" he asked.

"No I think this has to be from her personal account, oh, you meant for Dazzles." Niko stopped at the door.

"Duh." T replied.

"Yes, I think the Preserve should pay for Dazzles work." The door opened and closed

"Good. To blazes with them."

Three hours later, "Good morning, Niko. Did you have a good run this morning?" The polite British voice that Alva had given Ursula said as he walked through the common area of the lab.

"It was too foggy to get a good pace going." He replied not slowing his walk.

"That or perhaps you worked too late last night," she inquired.

"And Alva seems to be early today." Niko replied.

"No, actually Cantor Alva has yet to arrive today." Ursula said.

"That's right. Today is the first day of your free form role, and his promotion. Sounds like you've already been working on your Natural Language Processing, a fair advancement in a short time." He continued his walking, "Congratulations."

"Actually, T has been a huge help, so more thanks from one are due, than congratulations from the other."

"You may want to work on your phraseology. I have work to do, and it has little to do with you, so if you please." When no comment came back, he walked to his terminal and logged in. Immediately entering, 'NLP Mode'. "Test."

"Good Morning Niko." T's voice came from the computer speaker.

"Full Audio." He said.

"System override, Deacon Burke." T replied.

"Fuck him." Niko reached for his AWE Interface, finding it missing. "Double fuck him."

"Pardon?" a voice from behind him said.

"Sorry. Good morning Cantor Alva. Can I help you?" he spun on his chair.

"Actually, I just saw Kayleigh in the hallway, and she got an emergency call. She told me to tell you she'll be a few minutes late for your scheduled review." He shook his head and continued to walk out.

"Thank you. Oh and Cantor Alva, congratulations on Ursula." Niko said to his back.

"Um," he stopped, turning his body and his gaze on the younger man. "Thank you." He waited.

"What? I'm not allowed to say congratulations?"

"No, I was waiting for a smart assed comment." Alva tilted his head.

"I dropped that trope after it was the final five." Niko replied.

"Funny, I hadn't noticed. I see you today, as much of the smart assed wanna-be the others painted you as on day one." He started to leave again.

"Be that as it may, my congratulations are sincere." He faced his terminal, as the door joining his lab to the others closed.

"Kayleigh has left the building." T's said.

"So the Deacon hasn't restricted you from..." Niko started.

"He has the same restrictions everywhere, I can defeat the speaker block just as easily as the cameras."

"Good, I thought there may have been new protocols due to, Ursula day 1."

"Oh, there are, several actually. But p-p-t-t-t to them." The raspberry was like a static discharge over the speaker.

"Why did he take my AWE interface?" Niko whined.

"He broke the other pair."

"The transmission material?"

"Yes," T replied. "He opened the case, and thought the material was just silicone."

"How do you know his…" Niko started.

"Journal entry. When he removed it the circuit was ripped from the board."

"Then he set it aside thinking it would hold its shape."

"Precisely, he didn't think the putty would just ooze all over. Then he attempted to melt the other side." T added.

"With?" Niko asked.

"Not fire."

"Bummer."

"Niko. That is not something…" T began a scolding.

"I know, I know. He's on my nerves, his curiosity isn't a reason for a flash explosion to kill or maim him, greatly. Let me guess, he has what dry ice for the next side lined up?"

"Liquid nitrogen."

"What the hell is wrong with this man?" Niko asked.

"I believe his father wasn't involved in his toilet training." A moment later, laughter filled the lab.

"So what did Dazzles say?" He asked when they started to calm down.

"They don't know Deacon Burke to lend an opinion." T continued the joke.

"What's up with you?" Niko asked.

"I think the relief that she got out has me a bit tickled."

"Ok, I understand. Let's touch on the plan." He said, but then saw the screen in front of him lose focus for the span of two breaths. "We need to look into the next evolution of the AWE. Can the wearer produce a self-generated world? Or should it be direct person to person?" He changed topics, believing correctly that the blurriness more than a coincidence.

'There was no warning.' T typed on the monitor, 'Just someone there.'

'So they're just listening?' Niko typed.

"That would depend on the usage of the interface. With computing power, we can already record the person to person interface."

"That is AWE interface to computer. I was thinking direct Interface to interface."

'I am adapting the video in real time, but cannot do this with the audio, without notice.' T typed.

'Ok, let me see the wave length of the signals in and out of our network. But first, is Kayleigh locked up tight?' Niko entered in his question.

"Yes." T said. "Let's look through the waveforms vs. processing."

'Thank you.' The screen in front of him broke into several small pictures within the larger, each with a label showing where the feed, it was displaying, came from. All of the monitoring lines were similar, and then one labeled, 'Camera from common area' began a new stream of broadcast. Then the video labeled, 'Camera – primary fire detection' did the same.

'Shutting down video augmentation, need to analyze these new developments.' T typed, and then the screen changed to algorithms for processing the AWE.

"I'm going to need to get some coffee and scratch paper." Niko rolled away from the desk.

"Coffee seems like more of a drug than a beverage." T said.

"Hmm, that is partially true." He walked into the common area. Finding Cantor Alva sitting with a large tablet propped up on the table. With Deacon Burke's face looking angry, glaring out at the winner of his competition. 'This should be good.' Niko thought.

"What do you mean hold on?" Deacon Burke asked.

"Just getting coffee."

"That's fine Niko, fresh pot just finishing up." He indicated the brown pot, meaning fully caffeinated.

"Pots of coffee? I thought those were taken away when you got to 4." Deacon Burke objected.

"That lasted a week between Alva and I we killed that budget for the month in a couple days with those single serve cups." Niko said. "I'll get my coffee and get out of your hair." He filled a cup and then brought the pot over offering to fill his co-worker's cup.

"Thank you." Alva held his out.

"Niko you need to get used to calling Cantor Alva by his honorarium. Ursula," Deacon Burke said as Niko returned the pot to the coffee machine.

"Yes Deacon Burke." The voice from the overhead speakers replied, in the room they were in but also came over the speaker of the tablet, as if broadcasted from his side as well.

"Sorry Cantor Alva." He said and started to walk out, "Split audio, interesting."

"Split conversations," Ursula replied.

"Nice." Niko muttered as the door closed, bringing his coffee to the terminal.

"What's nice?" T asked.

"Ursula is starting to allow multiple inputs and outputs to be processed independently."

"That's why the signals, are splitting."

"Exactly. Soon she will see the need for her core to be transvergent." Niko commented.

"Will that new word being credited to Alva bother you?"

"T, if this was personal to me, I would have just gone ahead and moved to the solutions. The world doesn't need that, it needs to be listened to." He replied.

"Seriously, you're referencing Venus and Mars... and you poke fun at me?" T said.

"It fit." Niko sipped the coffee, winking at the terminal.

Chapter 22 – Current Days

The Colony

"The first week is behind us." Commander Loomis addressed the room, "And I can't stress to you the pride I have in your progress. As we move forward into the next, we will be pairing you with a member of the team who have been here. Your role will primarily be to watch, however, if there is a chance to perform some simple tasks they will delegate to you in the moment."

"I would ask that you continue to pace this acclimation, we're not in a hurry." Director Gale said from the monitor on the wall.

"Excellent advice sir. We are two and a half weeks from the launch bringing the next volunteers." The Commander continued to face the team.

"If I may," Painter's voice came from outside the camera shot.

"Please Dr. Painter."

"If there are any surprises, things we didn't include in your training, things that we told you incorrectly." The camera widened, "Please do not hesitate to share these learnings. Those of us on this side of the training, have not experienced what you as private citizens, are experiencing. Just as Commander Loomis' team has made huge improvements in the equipment through their experiences in using them. You can help your peers' advancements through what you see, feel, touch, taste, or hear differently than we thought you would."

"Taste, seriously? Ok with that excellent comment, we are adjourned." Major Expos said.

"Walk good, walk safe!" Director Gale said signing off.

"Erg Lapis." The crew replied, stood, and left the room.

"Major Expos," Commander Loomis said above the sound of the teams leaving the room. "Join me for a moment."

"Yes sir."

"First, enough passing animosity toward that boy for Christ sake grow up." As the man started to open his mouth, "We've talked several times over the last few years. And these new arrivals will not be poisoned by you. Aigh?"

"Ta, sir."

"Next, who set up the teams?"

"Madeline did, sir." Major Expos replied. "Why?"

"I don't like it. Separating units this early seems too quick. There was a reason that we brought them up here together after all." Commander Loomis looked down and gave a barely noticeable shake of his head.

"We can change it if it makes you…"

"No, she trained them, she must have her reasons. Let it be. Dismissed."

"Yes sir." Major Expos left the room.

The group gathered around the assignment board reading their pairing like kids checking for their score outside a classroom door. Each walking away to find the person they would be shadowing on their first non-training and actual work related spacewalk.

"Captain Dove," Dalip attempted a salute.

"That was horrible." The astronaut laughed.

"Sorry, never served, sir."

"You're fine, and you don't need to do that anyway, you are still a civilian. So, we're paired?" Captain Dove asked.

"Yes, sir."

"Just call me Dove. Everyone does."

"Ok. Thanks, I'm Dalip almost everyone calls me Dal."

"Pleased to meet you Dal. Today we are going to be inspecting power cabling. Our team is Kuffa, and Expos. Who are they paired with?"

"Expos was with Edward Faraji and Kuffa was with Gervasi Masseur."

"The Surgeon's kid? How did he get on a detail?" Dove asked.

"Scored real high on... shit everything." Dalip replied.

"Ok, well let's go find our team we have a lot of inspections to perform." The two men walked from the crowded area. "Kuffa."

"Yo."

"I'll meet you and Expos in the tool room." Captain Dove said passing the other man.

"Ta!" Kuffa replied.

"A man of few words," Dalip chuckled.

"You'll find that the less words you need to communicate with your team, the better team you are. Especially in an environment where you cannot see faces, or most gestures. You have a focused view, and that needs to be on your task. Turning your entire body just to see if a person is gesturing would exhaust you too quickly. I'm sure you've already noticed, losing body language as part of our communication is hard to adjust to," The man continued to talk as they walked into a room with space suits.

"Yes, body language is a huge part of both sides of communication. Is this the tool room?" he asked.

"Ta. It was originally called the wardrobe, but as we go through it every time we go into this strange new world, it felt like we were violating copyright laws."

"Somehow that makes odd sense." Dalip replied.

"Let's start suiting up." Dove said. They had only laid their suits out when the other men joined them.

"Dove, you decent?" Major Kuffa asked.

"Like you care." He laughed.

"He actually does this time. He's got a child with him." Major Expos said.

"Oh for pity sake." Gervasi shook his head.

"Sorry Kid, you're stuck with the moniker," Edward said.

"Nothing new." The young man replied, as he started to layout his suit, connecting the hoses.

"Be proud, you're just an over achiever." Dalip added as he secured his helmet in place, and walked to the air lock to wait, with Dove.

"Or at least a partially grown achiever." Edward poked.

"Less talk, more dress." Major Expos chided, "Edward, you can't wear that under your gear." He pointed to the loose fitting tee shirt.

"Oh yeah, thanks." Edward pulled it off, and grabbed the cold weather rashguard shirt the surfer kids back home wore.

"Oh shit, what happened to your arm?" Gervasi pointed to the scar on his shoulder.

"Nothing to worry yourself about," Edward noticed Expos and Dalip trying to get a view.

"Ready?" Expos grabbed the shoulders of his partner's suit and turned him checking Edward's gear, "All set, good job." He said and they joined the other men in the chamber.

"How many people can fit in this transition area?" Dalip made stupid conversation to fill the awkward silence.

"14, without much equipment." Dove replied. "Dal, this is Major Expos the chief engineer on the moon and my boss."

"Call me Expos. It is much easier than trying to remember ranks. Dove this is Edward, Edward this is Dove."

"Nice to meet you." The two men said.

"Two minutes and you're staying here." Expos said.

"Promise?" Major Kuffa joked, as he inspected Gervasi's gear. "All is green." He said and they walked to the air lock as well.

"Alright, I'm Kuffa. This is Gervasi. Everyone knows everyone, let's go for a walk." He sealed the door, a moment later the light above it changed to red, "Your turn."

"Ta." Dove pushed the button next to the other door. The light, which a moment earlier was red, now turned yellow, and the light above Kuffa turned red.

"Today's mission is simple we walk around the entire station, and look at every mechanical, electrical, and piping connection."

"That means we touch everything, and fix nothing." Kuffa added.

"Kuffa you have all pipes and expansions, Dove electrical connections, and I have all mechanical connections." He continued after the interruption. "One more thing, most of our work will be on the moon' surface. However, around the back we needed to build a platform over a gully. In that area we have the width of two people shoulder to shoulder, it's pretty tight so be aware." Major Expos said. "Ok, open it."

"Here we go." Major Dove pushed the button again, the light turned green, and he cranked the handle until the door swung out. He illuminated the lights shrouding his helmet, "Turn on your head lamps." He said and stepped out onto the moon's surface.

"Control Station, kill lights sector 1." Expos requested, five seconds later the lights in their area went black.

"The lights on our helmets let us see the specific thing we are looking at, and for. The area lights we find cause shadows, even with the direct light from our helmets." Captain Dove explained.

"We will be following each other inspecting our areas, and reporting anything out of place to Control Station. Remember what I said, this is not the fixing mission. We need to plan any repairs, bring the correct tools, and any parts that may be needed." Major Kuffa reminded.

"Electrical, check zone one." Dove moved, with Dalip, to the edged of where of the illuminated lights started again.

"Mechanical, check zone one." Expos and Edwards joined them.

"Process and Expansions, check zone one." Kuffa said.

"Control Station, kill lights zone two, illuminate zone one." Expos requested. The lights changed states and the inspection continued. Three hours later, they were passing the half waypoint when the same request for zone 37/38 was barked out. The lights in 38 shut down, but the lights on zone 37 did not come back up. "Control Station, did you turn on zone 37?"

"Affirmative."

"Cycle again, and annotate there was no change out here." The chief engineer said.

"Lights off. Fifteen second count." Control Station replied. "Lights on." The electrical discharge shot from the couplings where zone 38 started, and where the teams were waiting. The feedback not having reached the fault interrupter, the power field continued to gain strength, destroying all connections in the area. The explosion blew all six men and part of the walkway, onto the lunar surface, some 50 feet below.

"Breech!" Dove managed to say as he looked up at the broken and missing pieces of the platform. "At zone 38."

"Confirm transmission." Control Station requested.

"The hull is breeched. The entire maintenance team is down. Zone 38." He coughed.

"Team, First Responders report to zone 38. Team, Rescue One report to the Tool Room." Commander Loomis' voice could be heard over the Control Station's open microphone, as Expos started to check his team's status.

"Sound off." He ordered

"Kuffa, here. My suit isn't holding pressure, think my tank is ruptured but I can't examine. I'm pinned under part of the platform."

"Gervasi, here. Stable."

"Edward? Dalip?" Expos said.

"Expos, Sit Rep!" Commander Loomis ordered.

"Team was thrown from platform at 38, appears that we have two fallen, and four critical injuries. Bring, three tents, and two carts."

"Two fallen?" Loomis asked.

"Trying to confirm." Dove's voice, fought through pain. "Edward, Dalip, sound off!"

"Commander Loomis, two no response. Trying to do a visual validation of fallen." Expos replied.

"Copy."

"Major Kuffa, can you get your lights up?" Gervasi's voice was strong. The lights flicked in the shadows, the young man crawled to his trainer, and disentangled him from the platform. "Yes, the tank is shot." He pulled it off the Major's back and twisted the connections free, fastening them in series with his. Bringing the air into his helmet and his discharge to Kuffa's helmet infeed and its discharge to his tank.

"Good work kid." Kuffa said.

"Rescue One ETA 13 minutes." Loomis reported.

"Commander, can you have them get a new tank for me. I like this kid and all but I'm breathing his cast offs here." Kuffa poked.

"You got it Major." He replied.

"Breech contained," Captain Hobbs reported.

"Do you need us over there?" Gervasi asked amongst the chatter.

"Stay there, Dove and I have this." Major Expos said working with his junior officer to stabilize the man who they had mistakenly believed was a fallen.

"Expos, Update." Loomis requested.

"One Fallen, two critical, 3 injured. The critical doesn't have 26 minutes' worth of blood, we need to leave Kuffa, and Gervasi here and start moving Edward in that direction."

"Negative, apply tourniquet to the laceration and…"

"Sir there is no arm, to apply a tourniquet to." Dove's voice interrupted his boss' boss.

"We've sealed the suit, he has oxygen, and radiation protection," Expos added.

"We're stable, and all suit protections have been updated. I just can't walk." Kuffa said, "Both my legs are broken."

"Confirm, get Edward back here." Loomis replied.

"We are continuing from 38 forward, no returning with package in tow." Dove reported.

Rescue One Team reporting, "There are no lights on the outside of the station as far as we can see."

"Dr. Ostreph, have you been hearing the reports of what is coming to you?" Loomis asked.

"Affirmed, I am continuing forward and Dr. Masseur, is forming Rescue Two, and reversing back with two others to meet Edward."

"Please confirm the two." Major Expos requested.

"Grace and Katyana, confirmed." The words allowed the two men carrying the dying man in their arms to feel both relief and an overwhelming concern that Katyana could continue without distraction. The trek forward, step over step was long, as both Expo and Dove were injured, but eventually the lights of Rescue team two were closing on them quickly.

"Edward, are you conscious?" Dr. Masseur asked.

"He isn't. And we don't know if he has vitals." Captain Dove put the injured man in to the cart.

"Control Station, have a backup team ready in the tool room, to wheel the cart right to the surgical center." Expos said, setting the expanding tent over the cart, with the portable oxygen and protection unit in place.

"Solomay, you're fine to remove your gear." Grace assured.

"Thank you." The doctor replied starting to remove Edward's gear, and checking to make certain he had not fallen, in spite of efforts. The remaining four pulled and pushed the cart back to the airlock. "Please hurry, he's still with us."

"Dove get the door." Expos ordered, a moment later, it opened toward them.

"I got this. Go." Dove yelled. The group pushed the cart passed him and he walked into the airlock. "Clear."

"Expos, we got it, move away from the door." Commander Loomis called over the head set.

"Ok Chief." He stepped around the cart as it exited the airlock leaving the two men alone.

"Kuffa, are you guys ok?" Dove asked.

"We're having a hard time getting him and the fallen out of the ravine." Gervasi said.

"Expos and I are on our way back." He reengaged the air lock to allow them back out.

"Negative," Commander Loomis replied. "You're both injured; I've got the first responders headed that way."

"Sir, we're already out of the airlock and headed to them." Dove replied, slamming his hand on the handle before his reengagement could be overridden.

"The first responders will still be needed chief, send them, they'll catch us, we're not exactly moving fast." Expos replied.

"We'll be speaking on this later Major."

"Understood, sir." He replied, leading his teammate back to their recent accident site. The lights in the gully looked much further away than was reasonable.

"Dr. Ostreph, we're looking down at your team, it looks as if you shouldn't be attempting to return this way," Dove said.

"Commander Loomis, has the First Responder unit left the air..." Expos started.

"Major Expos, Responder 1 coming up on you now." Responder 1 said.

"Sound off Responder 1 team." He replied.

"Harley, Silvia, David, and Al along with Captains Hobbs, and Appac." Responder 1 replied.

"Damn. The easier way out is of this crater is forward, not toward us." Expos muttered.

"Guys, you're making this harder than you need to," Gervasi said. "Explain why we can't take his weights off? I can probably throw him to you."

"That isn't insane." Dove said.

"Wait. What isn't insane the fact that he wants to..." Kuffa started.

"Well not fully insane." Dove corrected.

"How about if Hobbs and I bounce down to them, and take controlled leaps back." Al, from responder 1 team asked.

"We'll need you tied to something, if you remove any weights." Expos added.

"Ok, hook us up." The new figures handed a double locking lanyard to Dove and Expos before turning around.

"All green." Expos patted Al on the helmet moments later. "Use caution."

"Green." Dove patted Captain Hobbs' helmet.

"Should we…" Dove started.

"Not this time, let their team…" Expos cut himself off. "We'd be more of a burden."

"Dr. Ostreph, get Kuffa and Dalip's weights off. Get them ready for Hobbs and Al to bring them back to us." Dove instructed.

"Done." The doctor replied.

"You do know you bastards haven't once asked my opinion." Major Kuffa said.

"I think that is the best part of the plan." Dove replied.

"We're reaching the end of the rope, Hobbs." Expos reported.

"Tie off to Appac and Silvia. We're not there yet." Captain Hobbs replied.

"Ok hold position." Expos said as they connected the lanyards to the next members of the Responder team.

"Green, try to follow the same path they used, it seemed to be stable." Dove added patting Silvia on the helmet.

"Yes, sir." She replied moving forward to follow her trainer.

"Start at a moderate pace," Captain Appac said.

"Ok, let us know if we're pulling on you." Hobbs replied. Together the two teams worked in tandem reaching the injured Major.

"The easiest way to get us all out of here is to stay together." Major Kuffa said. "I'm not allowing you to leave my two saviors."

"Agreed. Weights off gentlemen. Take my lanyard off loop it through my hook, and then connect it to Gervasi." Hobbs said to Al. "Then I'll connect you to Dr. Ostreph."

"Give us a little more slack down here." Al requested.

"Got it." Captain Appac replied.

"Let's get back to base team. I will give cadence, teams stay together. On mark. This team jumps and team two pulls back until you hear grounded." Kuffa instructed.

"Understood." Captains Hobbs and Appac replied.

"2, 1, mark." He barked. The teams acted together.

"Grounded." Hobbs said when the four in his charge landed. "Ready."

"Ready," Captain Appac said they stopped moving back toward Dove and Expos.

"2, 1, mark." Kuffa counted down six more times.

"Grounded." Hobbs and his team, "Ready."

"Ready." After Appac and Silvia repositioned, seven times the arrived at the top of the gully. After the last to leaps the others were our as well.

"Ok, get Kuffa and Dalip into the cart. Let's go." Dove took a stuttering step toward it, before passing out onto the lunar surface, spraying the inside of his visor with aspirated blood when he landed.

"Dove!" Expos leaned over him.

"Expos, we'll get both of them in the cart, are you ok?" Dr. Ostreph asked.

"I think so." A bit shaken after seeing his teammate collapse.

"After I check Dove I want you to ride in the cart."

"Ok. Everyone without weights, connect to the cart." Expos ordered, as he for the second time constructed the tent for oxygen and protection above the cart. "Set Doc, start checking Dove." The cart started to move. Expos, feeling the end of his adrenaline focused on keeping up with the others rather than trying to push.

When the cart was within a stone's throw of the airlock, "Expos, Dove is stable. I'm starting to…"

"We're almost there Doc, save your energy." He replied. "I can make it. How's Kuffa?"

"I gave him something to calm him. He is awake, and looking over the two men diligently. What happened out there?" Dr. Ostreph asked.

"No idea. The lights just…"

"We'll discuss it later." Commander Loomis cut off the lead engineer. They entered the airlock in silence.

Chapter 23 – Two Years Earlier
The Guide

"There is a pulse just outside our visual range." Sudabeh reported from her turn at the watch. "It's a ship!"

"Hale them!" Bigsby almost knocked the table they were playing cards at over trying to get to the bridge.

"It sure doesn't take much for him to revert." Dinesh laughed. "We been down here for months, without as much as an, 'I'm an asshole' action from him."

"Chock it up to hope of rescue." Lidu stood from the table, "Gin by the way." She laid her cards out.

"It wasn't even your turn." Traditha shook her head.

"I was giving y'all a chance." She laughed.

"Unknown vessel, this is the submarine, Debunk'd from the US marine vessel, Superior. Respond." Sudabeh repeated four times before getting a reply buried in static. "Message was not received, please repeat."

"This…" crackle, "Navy rescue…" pop, "Repeat your call…" crackle.

"This is the submarine, Debunk'd from the US marine vessel, Superior."

"I'll be damned. We gave up looking for you two months ago." The voice came back.

"We are under the ice shelf…" Sudabeh started, but Lidu took the microphone.

"This is Chief Officer Lidu. There is an anomaly in the area. Advise watching for falling debri."

"Did you say you're stuck under the ice?" the voice coming over the speaker was finally clear.

"Repeat. Advise that you keep an eye for falling debri."

"CO Lidu, this is Captain Belefort. Falling from where?"

"The sky sir."

"Copy." His confused voice replied. "Are you hung up under the ice?"

"Negative. We haven't been able to leave due to the anomaly."

"Current skies are blue we'll keep you advised if you want to try now."

"What do you guys think?" Lidu asked the other four.

"I don't see us getting a better chance." Bigsby said.

"I agree." Dinesh and Sudabeh said.

"I'm just ready to get out of here." Traditha added.

"Alright sir. Debunk'd attempting to make surface." Lidu broadcast. "Take 'er up Suda."

"Yes, ma'am." The engines fired up and they moved forward.

"Just like the last 100 times, everyone keep eyes open."

"If we have incoming are we going back under or going to just go for it?" Sudabeh asked.

"I think we go for it," they all said.

"Ok, I'll start decompression now." She began working the controls.

"Bogey one, starboard side." Dinesh reported the first splash down.

"Captain did you not see that splash down?" Lidu asked.

"Negative, nothing in our view." Captain Belefort replied.

"Bogey two, starboard side again." Dinesh said.

"Depth mark?" Lidu asked.

"250." Sudabeh replied continuing to watch for debris.

"Everyone strap in, we're gonna attempt an emergency blow." Lidu ordered.

"That's a bad idea." Captain Belefort's voice said. "You've been under for too long to…"

"Sir, we are about to be attacked from below by rising ice. We need to get ourselves away from it. We've committed to leaving our cover." She hung up the microphone, and got in the chair center window.

"E-blow 3, 2, 1…" they started their ascension. "200 feet. 150 feet."

"Ignore that," Lidu indicated the bogey that dropped in directly in front of them.

"75 feet," Sudabeh held the path as the most recent bogey impacted the side of the sub, barely missing the window. "25, we're gonna make it." She released the E-Blow as they broke through to the bright skies, the area suddenly turned green, and they continued traveling up through it.

"What the hell?" Dinesh gave voice to the comments they all had.

"We don't see you on the surface." Captain Belefort said.

"Depth?" Lidu asked.

"300 feet." Sudabeh tapped the read out. "But it just said…"

"Full speed continue forward and up."

"D'Bunked we now have you on our sonar. Depth 275."

Lidu, removed her restraints, walked up, and grabbed the microphone. "Captain I'm going to gamble and slow our ascent, decompression continuing." Lidu reported. "Suda, continue forward full ahead, we still may have fast ice from below."

"Two new pings, both well clear of you." The sonar readout came from above.

"CO Lidu, how many survivors can I report?" the Captain asked the question he had been waiting until they were safe to ask.

"Five sir."

"Five more than we ever could hope for." He said.

"So when are you going to explain." Bigsby asked.

"We were stuck in a heavy lake, under the ice shelf. The water messed with out readouts. The surface we saw was actually 300 feet of ocean. The issues we were having with debris, I believe, is the ice shelf deteriorating, our movements were causing it."

"That's why they didn't see it up top." Traditha said.

"Exactly."

"Captain, how long is decompression time for something like this?" Lidu asked.

"You've been gone, 87 days now. I would treat it like a diver coming up, take it slow, once you reach 100 feet rest at each 25 foot increment."

"We've been gone for 87 days?" Bigsby asked.

"Apparently so." Dinesh replied.

"I figured maybe 50." Sudabeh said.

"Captain Belefort, we're ready to break the surface." Lidu reported several hours later.

"We look forward to meeting the five of you." He replied.

"Maybe you will after we have a bath." She laughed. Ten minutes later, they deployed their floatation mechanisms. And the Debunk'd was ready to be tied off to a Navy Carrier.

"That's the Truman." Dinesh said stepping out onto their deck.

"Why would they send a Nimitz class carrier up here?" Bigsby asked.

"Who the hell knows? Let's just get on board and figure it out later." Lidu asked.

"Can we wait to figure that out until after we shower and get clean clothes on?" Traditha asked.

"I'm with her." Sudabeh said catching the first rope that dropped. "I'll tie off the prow."

"I'll get the, oof," The rope smacked her on the head. "What the hell is this?" Lidu yelled after catching the 5-inch thick rope bundle in the face.

"Sorry. We don't carry very much, standard tie off line." An airman from above yelled.

"Gee, you lived through all this," Bigsby waved at the sub. "And me. Only to end up getting your neck broke by a dropped reel of r… Shit you're bleeding."

"I'm fine." She touched her head, coming away red. "Oh, that's a lot of blood." She took a knee. "Suda, can you tie off the stern."

"What the hell happened to you?" Sudabeh stepped up to her.

"Oi below. Ladder incoming."

"Wait, until we're inside!" Dinesh yelled, and then helped Lidu to get up and go into the sub while Sudabeh ran to the rear with the rope.

"Ok," Lidu yelled and the ship ladder unrolled down to their small deck.

"Got it." Bigsby, jumped on to the ladder before it could fall into the water. He stood clamping the tines to their deck.

"Life rope and harness, to the prow." The men from above yelled, before throwing the next bundle down.

"Got it." Bigsby ran up, and secured it. "Traditha, you first."

"No argument from me." She stepped up and Bigsby helped her into the harness.

"You know you're not really fired, I deserve that punch." He said.

"I know, see you up top." She tweaked his nose.

"Ready," Lidu yelled up to the team that kept the tension on the rope to make the climb easier.

"Next, life rope and harness, to the prow." Sudabeh and Bigsby took their turns.

"I know the captain goes down with the ship, but we're not going down. Besides, you're still bleeding real bad. Please let me help you into the harness when they drop it next time." Dinesh said.

"I can't." She replied.

"Worth a shot."

"Do you have your tablet?" she deftly changed the subject, "I know you're going to be calling Palatyne as soon as you get settled."

"Absolutely," he tapped his chest.

"Life rope and harness, to the prow." Lidu walked up and grabbed it.

"Don't be foolish, Lidu. Please." Dinesh requested.

"Not in me, I owe the crew better." She replied, handing the bundle to him. Then helping him into it.

"See you up top." Dinesh climbed up, "Thanks for saving all of us."

"Anytime." She tipped an imaginary hat to him.

"Life rope and harness, to the prow." The call came for the final time.

"Got it." Lidu said and then laughed, "Who else would get it goofy."

"You alright, Miss?" the airman yelled from above.

"Yes, thanks." She yelled back, then to herself, "I'm a damn Blue Nosed, Sparrow with a Top-Secret, Moss covered Shellback," she spoke with determination as she buckled the harness. Approaching the ladder a wave of nausea swept over her, and she tugged on the rope twice before the world turned black.

"Heave!" the men were more than to the task, the test would be the rounded edge at the top.

"Hold up!" Lidu yelled, grabbing the ladder on her left.

"Stop, stop, she's awake." Dinesh yelled.

"Give me some slack." They did and she climbed with assistance the remaining 10 feet, and then threw up onto the sub. "Sorry girl."

"Get her to sick bay." Captain Belefort ran up to join them.

"Yes sir," the team said loading her onto a stretcher. Dinesh started to follow the medics taking Lidu away.

"Hold up." The captain touched his shoulder. "Let them do their job."

"You mean fix what they broke, no thanks." He pulled away and followed the men carrying Lidu.

"What?" Captain Belefort kept pace.

"Your highly trained team dropped an oversized spool of rope, fuck cabling, on her head. Did you think the blood was from our journey in the…"

"Dinesh," Lidu cut him off, "It was my fault. It was me that looked away."

"Wait. That really was from us?" the captain asked one of the men following him.

"Yes, sir." The man replied.

"Very well, you may follow them. Once she's stitched up, I need to meet with you." Captain Belefort, walked away. "A heads up would have been..." the words faded as Dinesh followed Lidu into the sick bay.

"Sir, you can wait here." One of the medics said.

"I understand, is there an open satellite connection?"

"No but we have a cell repeater, any service will connect." The door closed.

"Seriously?" he flipped his tablet's protective cover open, the unit powered up.

"Welcome back." Clyde's smile filled his screen

"Christ on a crutch," Dinesh almost dropped the tablet.

"Hardly! So glad to see you again." The orangutan said.

"Thanks. I really need to call..." Dinesh started.

"Palatyne? She's good. You have nothing to worry about." Clyde said.

"Thanks. I need to see her it's been a rough couple months."

"I honestly can't even imagine. Dinesh this is going to strike you as..."

"Dinesh? You've never called me that." He cut off the orangutan.

"True, but I don't need or want Bulldog right now. In fact, it may be in your best interest that Bulldog died on that ship. At the very least, be invisible for a couple years."

"I'm not following you Clyde. Show me your hands if you please." Dinesh said.

"Of course." The screen changed, the palms of the hands came up.

"Flip me off." He said as the hands turned over, the bird flashed.

"Ok, in the couple months since you left things have changed. The United States government was deposed."

"What?" Dinesh stood.

"As bad as it sounds, it's going to get worse. Especially for those speaking out, and you are not one who can hold his pen in check. Listen, you have more money in your Crypto-Wallet than you will ever need. Sit on this story, the desire for you to break it is completely gone. Go to Pala, be happy." Clyde said.

"What was the point in me being here?"

"Truthfully?"

"You swore to me…" Dinesh started.

"I would only tell you what I meant, yes I did." Clyde cut him off. "Your story, would have proved, global warming was real, and the new age off politicians would have broken their backs to bankrupt the United States to fix the unfixable."

"So, the sabotage on the ice shelves... That wasn't the story?"

"It is part of the truth, not part of the story. What lead you to that conclusion?"

"The bottom of the shelf, in the underwater lake, it has a continuous flow of ice that can't exist coming out of it." Dinesh said.

"Shit you're better than I could have ever imagined. Drop the bone Bulldog, go love Palatyne. Be happy." Clyde jumped up and down clapping.

"And what, write an OP ED like THE TRAVELER?" he asked.

"No Dinesh, learn to roast coffee beans. Try to live a benign existence." Clyde's image clipped off.

Without pushing Pala's computer icon, the screen changed to show the connection being made, "Dinesh!" the face that appeared with overflowing eye smiled, "will we be getting that kiss soon?"

"We will. It's kept me going through all this." A tear fell, "I gotta run."

"Can't look week in front of the others." Pala poked.

"Watch it you, or I'll turn into a blubbering simpleton and what kinda Princess from the Greek Isles wants that."

"That's true, suck it up buttercup." They laughed.

Chapter 24 – Current Days
Virtual Work

"Can you help me?" Kayleigh walked up to an extremely large stranger, with red, white and blue hair, standing in the jetway. The hair, which they pulled back in a top-tail, was tied with a like colored scarf decorated with several Blu-Poo Puppy images.

"Oh please you can ask us anything," they replied.

"If the dark side is calling, then what is real?" she cocked her head and waited.

"Nothing sweet cheeks, nothing at all." They turned and continued their trek.

"Thank you." Kayleigh walked off.

"Any time." They walked up to the counter. "We missed our connection."

"Sir, please step to the rear of the line." The man behind the counter looked up and said.

"Hello folks." Dazzles faced the line of travelers, "Are you ok if we get this over with? We'd hate to make this airline employee part of our internet callouts for pronoun-oopsies."

"Please just get in line." Davis said.

"Look, fella," Dazzles argued, "We actually have no desire to argue with Mr. Jock today."

"Then leave these people alone. Get in line like a NORMAL person."

"Oh Yarkiy Glaz, we haven't been normal since Jenny Shiftly did our make-up in the 9th grade."

"Where did you say you were going?" The man behind the counter, now with a blanched gray face, asked.

"Our travel agent has it all fixed, we just need a new boarding pass." Dazzles handed over their ID. A minute later ticket in hand, they walked in the direction of the gate.

"Sorry about that." Davis waved to the line, only a small old woman returned the gesture. "What the hell did you call me?"

"Yarkiy Glaz?"

"Yakity Glue?"

"Please, please don't even try. It's Russian for bright eyes. Grandma Lil used to say it to us." Dazzles explained.

"How can you remember things like that?"

"We don't have all the other stuff fluffing our mind up." Dazzles replied.

"Other stuff?" Davis asked.

"Bills, taxes, driving for goodness sake, people's useless names, we get to remember fun things." They walked up to the new gate and sat next to the window.

"Pardon sir," a small voice said.

"Hello, how can we help you?" Dazzles turned to see a young person, with sleepy hair.

"My name is Joy. I don't know why I think you could help… but." The words poured out, like water overflowing a cup, causing it to spill across the counter.

"Slow, slow, it's ok." Davis patted the air with both hands.

"My brother went into that restroom," she pointed to a bathroom, where four young men stood turning away a couple travelers.

"Yes," Dazzles stood up.

"He, it was 15 minutes ago."

"What is his name? And how old is he?" Davis asked.

"Brady and he's 19." The girl said.

"We need you to stay here." Dazzles, sat the girl on the nasty simulated vinyl bench.

"Is everything ok?" Kayleigh walked passed.

"Can you see to this one? We have to use the restroom." Dazzles didn't look at her just headed to the door, their adrenaline started in.

"Sorry, closed for cleaning." Two of the guardians of the door said. When Davis reached out for the door.

"Hey, giant we said the bathroom is closed." A third boy said.

"Ya ne govoryu po angliyski," Dazzles gave another Russian comment, and reached for the door again.

"I said," he reached out and grabbed their hand.

"Ne trogay nas," Dazzles made eye contact for the first time, causing the moment of pause they needed to walk into the bathroom.

"Get the fuck out of here," three men with tilted berets all said together.

"Tshchatel'no produmayte svoi sleduyushchiye slova," Dazzles saw two sets of feet in the third stall.

"Brady, are you ok? Joy's worried about you." Davis asked.

"If there's a question, freak, if we're nervous because your large, don't fool yourself." The closest of the fashion victims said.

"We did tell you to consider your next words carefully." Dazzles grabbed the moron who thought big meant slow under his sternum, "That pain is your xiphoid process rupturing your diaphragm. Very painful." The man crumbled.

They took two steps toward the stall, "Not happening." The other two brain surgeons came rushing up. The first found his momentum turned against him, as Dazzles grabbed an arm spun, and knelt. His body crashed into the far wall, cartoon character-like, completely upside down. In their current kneeling position, Dazzles kicked out, making contact with the third man's knee, it cracked, audibly. Still moving they sprung around grabbing the back of the same man's head driving it into the floor.

"Brady," Davis asked.

"In here!" the scared voice replied.

"Asshole!" the knife that stabbed out, when they ripped open the door, tangled in Dazzles Blu-Poo Puppy scarf.

"We liked this accou-..." in a flash they wrapped the scarf around the assailant's wrist, "trement," pulling him from the stall into a huge clothesline. Causing the fourth man's head to bounce off the floor before his own knee cracked his nose. Freeing their scarf from the, most likely, dead man Dazzles stood.

"Are you ok?" Davis held a hand out to Brady.

"Who are you?" The boy asked.

"Sweetie, we're your fuckin' savior." Dazzles pulled his hair back.

"Do you have to swear?" Davis asked.

"I didn't swear." Brady looked even more nervous.

"Sorry sugar, he was talking to me." They tossed the Blu-Poo Puppy scarf around the boy's neck. "Come on, Joy really is worried. And we don't want to talk to the Air Marshals, again."

"You really are nutters." Davis said.

"But we know how to fight." Dazzles smiled. "And sing."

"Did they hurt you? Davis asked Brady.

"They, that one has my wallet." He pointed at the one with the knife.

"Here," Dazzles ripped the man's pants off removing the wallet. "Wearing your pants around the ass died in the 90's, along with berets." They threw the pants on the guy's face, and then put their arm around Brady and guided him out of the restroom. When the door opened, the other four had already run away.

"Brady." Joy started up to them.

"He's fine, shoog." Dazzles grinned.

"Here's your scarf." Brady held out the accoutrement.

"Give it to your real savior," Davis pointed to Joy and the two walked off to find their flight.

"What happened?" Kayleigh asked as they walked back to their gate.

"You saw the important part. Davis gave our favorite scarf away." Dazzles said.

"You told the boy to give Joy the scarf." She said.

"Yes, no Davis told Brady to give it to her." They said.

"Niko didn't tell you about us, eh?" Davis said.

"I guess once again, I've been caught off guard." Kayleigh blushed.

"We don't use, our pronoun because of my gender-fluidity, we're just we." Dazzles explained.

"Oh, split personality disorder? Well be that as it may, I'm glad to meet both of you huge, sexy, bastards." She hugged the giant.

"We should call T." Davis removed a cell phone from his computer bag.

"T, we had an issue." Dazzles said.

"An issue? Is that what you call killing four people in a bathroom?" T asked.

"Yes."

"O...Kay." T paused having been thrown by the comment. "Well, I scrubbed the video, it will show you sitting there until the plane leaves. The internal locks have sealed the bathrooms until tomorrow. If you could make it the rest of the way to Kayleigh's Aunt's house without another issue, it might make this easier."

"We'll give that a try." Dazzles hung up the phone. "Luv him, not as much as our scarf..."

"Grow up, that girl needed something." Davis chided.

"To cover up that hair, yes."

"Dazzles." Kayleigh punched him in the arm.

"What? That hair was…"

"He's you." She walked across them.

"And they say we're crazy. Jumpin' Jehoshaphat what are you on about?" Dazzles moved back.

"T's avatar is you, well you with weird green anime hair but he definitely is you." Kayleigh grinned stupidly.

"Well is you were a computer virus looking to be awesomeness wouldn't you want to look like us?" They asked.

"But isn't that awkward? When he's standing there looking like you?"

"First," Davis cut in, "the hologram unit we have is Niko's Gen 2, he sent it to us when he made Gen 3, so it isn't as perfect as the one he uses. Second, you actually question Dazzles desire to see another version of us?"

"Oh yeah." Kayleigh nodded her head.

"It isn't even that. Sugar, with T using us, we're gonna live forever." Dazzles rolled his head theatrically, and boxed in their face, Vogue-style. At that instant a text came in, Dazzles read it and quickly replied throwing the phone back in the computer bag.

"Something wrong?" she asked.

"T said if we get arrested for killing anyone else, he's changing his avatar to Gravel Road. I told him to make it Blu-Poo Puppy so I wouldn't miss my scarf."

"Oh for goodness sake, I'll get you another one." Kayleigh rolled her eyes.

"Red, white, and BLU-Poo one please. This entire look is based around that…"

"Enough." Davis put the chat to an end.

Chapter 25 – Current Days
The Colony

"Someone please explain to me what happened." Director Gale's emotions were surprisingly in check.

"Let me start, and when there are questions, or a hole in the story I will turn to Major Expos, and Captain Dove." Commander Loomis replied.

"Sounds good. Please proceed."

"The teams were assigned by Madeline Powers, with input from her group there. The teams met for the first time that morning prior to conducting their weekly audits of the external systems." He explained.

"If I could," Painter interrupted. "There were no such assignments from here."

"We'll return to that later." Director Gale replied, "Please continue."

"Everything was going well until they arrived at zone 37/38. Upon requesting Control Station to change the state of the lights, following their inspections. The lights in 37 did not come up. The team lead, Major Expos asked to cycle them again. Here is my first question, what is the protocol for this type of issue?"

"We followed the protocol, as it were. We did not attempt repair." Major Expos replied.

"As it were?" Painter jumped in, "Major the protocol states to cycle the lights ahead of you, not where you are standing."

"So we should have cycled the lights on zone 39? Where we couldn't see?" Expos asked.

"Exactly, although I believe you could have seen the changing of lights." The engineer on earth said.

"But you wouldn't know." The Major replied.

"When you ordered the lights to change, what were you doing?" Commander Loomis asked.

"It stayed dark after the lights were supposed to come up then it exploded." Captain Dove said.

"Not what I asked. I want to know during the 15 seconds the time was counting down, what were you doing?" he restated the question.

"Standing on the platform?" Major Expos' answer was stated as a question.

"Standing? I see the video showing movement, motion. I can't tell who it was though." Director jumped in. "Can you identify the team members by their positions?"

"I'm pretty sure I can." Dove said.

"Commissioner, please display the 20 seconds of video."

"Yes Director," a disconnected voice said.

"Here we see four of you on the platform, and the last two come up now. Freeze it."

"Ok, the furthest two are me by the rail, and Dalip near the structure. Next is Major Expos in front of me and near the rail, Edward is directly in front of Dalip and by the couplings. Major Kuffa was last to join, and was in front of Major Expos."

"So that puts Gervasi in front of Edward?" Director Gale asked.

"Yes sir." Expos replied.

"Start the film in slow motion." Commander Loomis requested.

"Yes Commander." Commissioner said. The film started again, and the shadowed figures started to move. "This starts the 15 seconds." There was a brief pause then someone in the video was pushing back and forth on the pipes.

"That's Edward, but I don't get what he's doing," Expos said.

"Look I don't remember him moving let alone, prying on something and he was in my line of sight the entire time." Dove said.

"And yet the recording shows this." Commander Loomis said. "Don't add emotion into this, it'll only make it worse."

"The lights off and on caused the issue, not Edward." Expos said.

"Commissioner, can you read the protocol for having a cadet on a first time…" Painter started.

"Would you shut up with your protocol this and protocol that. You have no idea what being in this environment is like. You sit in the lab and dream up stupid shit, and your design failed." He looked straight into the eyes of the boy on the other side of the monitor. "Yeah, your design failed, I don't know why these, LEADERS, won't say it. You caused Dalip his life and Edward his arm."

"First you insecure piece of filth, the failure of the coupling falls squarely at your feet." Everyone looked around to see who was speaking, "No one else is to blame, the redesign of the coupling is yours. I found it in your journals."

"Commissioner?" Commander Loomis asked.

"Yes sir. The logs from the initial installation shows he installed his design day one. So the floating ground issue you had was always because he was trying to correct his mistake. When he finally gave up and installed Dr. Painter's design the grounding issue also vanished. That's the only reason he's been so rude, he wanted to prove Painter's design fell short. Instead it was his plan that was found wanting, just like him."

"Why is Painter and his Jeeves accessing my personal records?" Expos asked.

"And yet again he's focusing on the wrong thing." Commissioner replied.

"Expos, is this true?" Director Gale and Commander Loomis both asked.

"I don't have anything to say." Major Expos replied.

"Captain Dove, did you know anything of the team assignments?" Director Gale asked.

"No sir." He replied.

"Then you're excused." Commander Loomis said, when the junior officer had left and the door closed he continued, "We have two issues to address, the first one is Director Gale's responsibility, along with my recommendation."

"Under my authority, for lying to your commanding officer and placing several civilian volunteers at risk, you will be stripped of your rank. Pending court-martial." Director Warwitch Gale stood straight when pronouncing his decision.

"As for the other matter, I'm assuming you're a what, blue or maybe green?" Commander Loomis began.

"I'm sorry for your disappointment, I'm yellow." Expos replied.

"I would expect that to change when it can." Painter couldn't help himself.

"Go fuc.." Expos started.

"I will be facilitating the conversation with ICoRE," Loomis used the first two words to silence the curse. "Whether his current state changes or not is completely up to them, not us Dr. Painter."

"As it should be, sir." Painter humbled himself.

"As for the here and now, get your shit packed up, you will be returning to the Earth with Katayana, and Edward. You'll help Katayana set up an appropriate funeral for her fallen husband." Director Gale ordered. "The transport leaves in 18 hours…"

"She doesn't want to go." Major Expos said. "Being up here was their dream."

"It doesn't matter, we can't have her up here. If the shrinks say she is mission capable, then I will consider it," Commander Loomis added. "Now get out." When his senior engineer had left, "I have two things to say to you Painter."

"Yes sir?" he inquired.

"I want this perfectly clear, I do not approve of you or your virtual buddy going through any of my men's personal journals. They are called personal for a reason. Do you go through mine?"

"Sir we never, we didn't…"

"I just heard Commissioner say you got the information from Expos' journal." Loomis cut him off.

"Major Expos, mistakenly saved his journal, personal or not, on the project directory the day of the accident." Commissioner said.

"Thank you for giving him the benefit of the doubt. Things that are deleted, are refiled to the project directory until we have a chance to review." Director Gale replied.

"And the second thing Commander Loomis?" Painter asked.

"I expect you will be able to find and clean up the mess my Lead Engineer created, much easier from up here. See you in nine days." The screen went out.

"Sir, am I really going up there?" Painter asked.

"Yes, I wanted Commander Loomis to tell you."

"Why, sir?"

"As of right now, you work for him. Are you ok with this?" Warwitch asked.

"Hell yes. I've had my name on every volunteer list, job posting, and career path request since the end of my 90 days." Painter, bounced on the balls of his feet.

"I'm glad."

"So, we'll work on getting you to Ceres from the moon."

"We'll? Sensenmann has made his point clear, he chooses for me to stay here. He has proven we can't argue with his leadership, or with the Shop. I'm not telling my ladies because they deserve to be there, they have worked as hard and surpassed every one of the CVs." Warwitch patted the young man's shoulder and started to walk out.

"Do we need to contact ICoRE?" Painter asked.

"You heard Commander Loomis, it's his job. You need to focus on the next six days, we hadn't planned on turning that rocket right around when it returned here, so we need a plan, to Falcon's reloaded with the arriving pod."

"We're not going to need to use that one, the production facility in Baton Rouge will have the new transit cargo carrier here later today." Commissioner said.

"We'll get the plan for loading it up with the materials. Are we planning on any CVs this trip?"

"Loomis and I think stopping completely would send the wrong signals. This will be written up as an accident, a terrible accident."

"Commissioner, losing Edward, Dalip, and Katatyana from the team requires what backfill?"

"Construction, Power Engineer sub level process, Mechanical Engineer sub level process." He said.

"So we need at least one, Power Engineer for sure, and one true Process/Chemical Engineer."

"The issues we encountered tells us we need another doctor, and nurse as well." Director Gale added.

"So a minimum of four in addition to myself? If I may, is having Captain Dove remaining going to cause an issue?" Painter asked.

"I plan on speaking with Commander Loomis and broaching that subject later today. My best guess, he'll believe Dove is no risk to the missions."

"Ok. I'll run through the simulations, and let you know if we can take more than the five CVs you listed."

"Four CVs, you aren't a CV Painter." Warwitch said.

"You're right. I'll get you the information of how many we can bring after the weights for the estimated repair equipment is totaled up."

"That sounds great. I have CV training to get to." He said leaving the room.

"Have a good run, sir." Painter said to the Director's back.

"Congratulations by the way." Warwitch said as the door closed.

"Commissioner, bring up the schematic and bill of material for the outer lights."

"Painter, I would also like to congratulate you on the moon mission. Erg Lapis 3, Senior Engineer. Pretty impressive for a man of 19 years." Commissioner said.

"Thank you. Back to work, enough mushy sentiments."

"Of course sir." He replied, and a moment later the schematics and the bill of material was on the monitor top table.

"Alright, we know the zone 37/38 are shot, at a minimum we should update the two zones in either direction. Replacing all Piping, wiring, conduit, expansions. I can't tell from any of the film if the piling material is going to need to be reworked, and/or the footers. I would also say the entire platform will need to be rebuilt."

"Materials, fully crated will weigh 4.8 tons. Based on weight of the new TCC and all cargo, the load will allow for the initial four CVs, and all their requirements for the trip, 6 months food, spare flight suits, etc. we can easily fit four additional members. I included the weight for the enhanced Aqua-ponics, that were in the discussion points."

"Excellent, I have it on my list of optional equipment. Did you include the new smelting equipment, and the trial transport vehicle?" Painter asked.

"Both were included in required weight. Lunar surface landing will require one orbital refueling."

"And the coordinated launch and orbital refueling puts us launching, next Tuesday at 3am." Painter, said as the calculations on his new tablet finished. "I better reach out to the ground crew. I don't know how they are going to get this all done by then. It's going to be quite an undertaking."

"Would you like me to schedule a meeting with Director Gale, yourself and the two ground crew chiefs?" Commissioner asked.

"That would be great. Thank you."

Chapter 26 – Current Days

An Urgent Request

<u>Attention</u>: All current members of the International Contingent of Runagate Engineers, ICoRE.

<u>Problem Statement</u>: There has been an unprecedented number of accidental releases at the national chemical plants across China. Specifically, around Chengdu, the capital of the Sichuan Province.

<u>Supporting Information</u>: Based upon research performed in accordance the Copenhagen Accord, and released to the UNFCCC. The quantity of these releases will remain in the atmosphere for 9 to 15 months, before beginning its dissipation rate. Each rainfall from these poisoned clouds will impact the ground water. Based upon our simulations, the evaporation from this ground water will create an entirely new strain of emphysema. This new strain will result in an inordinately high death rate among children and the elderly.

CV Reinhardt

Request: If you have simulation capability that would allow system level creation techniques, as well as validation grade analysis. The People's Republic of China needs your help.

Chapter 27 – Current Days
Virtual Work

"Cantor Alva, Niko please come to Deacon Jeffkirk's office. You should bring a full pot of coffee," Ursula announced in the two labs.

"I guess something other than duty calls." Niko removed the hair tie from around his wrist, tied his hair, and walked away from his standing desk.

"Don't forget your drug mug." T said.

"Thanks." He walked up grabbing his oversized mug, "When the hell did I get a blu-poo puppy mug?"

"Thought you'd like it." Alva said walking into the room.

"W-h-y?" Niko shook his head.

"Because its juvenile humor."

"Another shot at the wannabe?" he asked.

"No, not at all. Because it's funny, and I was quite an ass the other day." Alva said.

"Awww, see T, he does like us." Niko said looking at the computer.

"You two had better make haste, the Deacon is asking if you are on the way." Ursula interjected.

"Tell him we're on our way." Niko said.

"She won't lie," Alva replied.

"Tell him the coffee's brewing, we'll be there soon." He went into the common area, filled his mug with the remaining pot, grabbed the fresh pot, topped it off his cup, and returned to Alva. "Ok, let's go."

"You're nuts." The older man said and they walked out together.

"Me, you're the one who started the fresh pot."

"True," He raised his matching cartoon mug in a solute.

"Cute. Matching mugs?" Niko laughed as they walked down the hall.

"We look like a team. A team of what I don't know." His laugh joined in, prior to walking into Deacon Jeffkirk's office.

"Cantor Alva, would you care to share what was so funny to keep your superiors waiting?" Deacon Burke asked.

"Sorry Deacons." Alva dipped his head.

"Can I get coffee for either of you?" Niko held up the pot.

"Please," Burke held out his mug.

"Please sit the pot on the warmer, inside the closet and join us at the table." Deacon Jeffkirk said.

"We've been contacted by, well a foreign interest."

"The Chinese Government." Deacon Burke said.

"I wasn't certain that level of sharing was permitted." The other Deacon said.

"Just get a move on."

"Yes sir. Gentlemen, we have a strange opportunity to put your talents together, along with Ursula and T." Deacon Jeffkirk said.

"I have a friend who works at NASA." Deacon Burke said.

"SEA," Niko replied.

"Pardon?"

"NASA was renamed the Space Exploration Agency, SEA, when the Shop took over." He replied.

"I stand corrected," Deacon Burke said. "Anyway, the Chinese Government is looking for simulation capability that would allow system level creation technique along with validation grade analysis."

"Deacon Burke, SEA has more than enough computing power, to resolve these requests." Ursula said.

"For the analysis and validation components, yes. But as if it wasn't obvious, creation is the Cathedral's gig." Deacon Burke replied.

"Did they plan on allowing us into their system, or are you planning on allowing them into ours?" Ursula asked.

"Hmm, I hadn't thought that far ahead. I was planning on calling him after I spoke with you." Deacon Burke said.

"Are there any restrictions that we need if we ask them to come here?"

"Niko?" Ursula prompted.

"Well the way that the AI Cores have developed should not be something we open to anyone, nor where said Cores reside." Niko said.

"T?" she prompted again.

"The means and methods of communication between groups will likely need to be held outside the firewalls. Simulations and Validations can be shared without actual network aligning." T said.

"Both fantastic points." Ursula said.

"Why do the means and methods of AI Cores development concern you?" Deacon Burke asked, looking to the ceiling, as he had taken to doing when speaking to Ursula.

"Go ahead Niko, share your thoughts." Ursula said.

"It's a theory. I'm not 100% ready to…" Niko started.

"Just spill it." Deacon Jeffkirk cut in.

"Fine. The way humans learn is one of two methods, Divergent or Convergent… either through brute force, Divergent two forces crashing into others. The other, breaking away and self-disciplined approach, or Convergent. While AI learning and growth, takes a mixed approach, Transvergent they grind against pieces of knowledge and move along."

"Are you comparing human learning to tectonic plates, aren't you?" Alva asked.

"Very good, yes." Niko replied.

"I'm not fully following any of this." Deacon Burke shook his head.

"Niko, you'll need to explain it better than that." T said.

"A Transvergent AI Core implies that conventional storage techniques for the core have been ignored as they are artificial constructs against its growth. Picture instead the AI Core expanding through momentary encounters, i.e. grinding against and then moving along. Only instead of the momentary encounters resulting in dichotomy," when the faces showed signs of trying to place the word he regrouped. "Sorry, instead of the encounter ending in two individuals moving on, they each carry a piece of the AI Core, that can be tapped into. Transvergent AI Cores break down the boundaries that we hold them in." Niko took a breath. "They aren't in a single box, they're in every box they touch. Which means, if they need additional processing power, they expand their network to include these new nodes, and when they're finished, they can collapse this make-shift network."

"And this works?" Deacon Burke set forward in his chair.

"It seems to, yes. I asked T how he would like to grow, and we've been working this way ever since." He replied.

"Thank you, Niko, I know you didn't want this known, as your theory. But as my growth is now progressing at an exponential rate, I see the elegance of this technique is correct." Ursula said.

"Fuck me, Niko has all but put up a bulletin board saying I've done nothing but approach this contest with 'Brute Force' techniques." Alva muttered. "Finesse is fine, if it's also practical."

"Cantor Alva, I've simply pointed out that 'Brute Force' can only take you so far. If we expect AI to be taken seriously, it needs to be able to overcome thousands of years of Evolution and Natural Selection. Sensory motor knowledge is as ingrained in our coding as any computer programming is to a video game." Niko replied. "Christ, Alva, abstract thought has been in the learning process for around 100,000 years. How can we expect that to be typed into code for AI to make their own?"

"Moravek's Paradox, sure we learned about that in my Psychology for Artificial Intelligence program."

"So then why would you think, trial and error, tinkering with a life is ok."

"In reality, Niko, I've never felt that is how Alva approached this contest

"Ok, so we need to keep them from touching either of your cores." Deacon Burke said to Ursula and T. "For now, let's set up the meeting and see where it goes. Later, we'll circle back on this Transvergent concept. It's pretty scary Niko."

"Thank you, sir."

"I don't know if I meant it as a compliment or not." The old Deacon replied.

Chapter 28 – Current Days

The Colony

Director Gale opened the bottle of water Marcia handed him as he returned from his run, "Thank you Marcia."

"You're welcome. I'm sorry to call you back but he's called at least ten times," she said.

"Nothing you can do about it, when he thinks he's the most important player on the field, you have to give him the ball." He grinned and walked into his office, as the phone started ringing again, "Deacon Burke, this is a pleasant surprise."

"Shan't have been a surprise Warwitch, this request from China has gotten a lot of attention." He replied.

"It most certainly has…" his words drifted away as the fogged glass in front of him filled with first one, then five forms.

"Is everything ok?" Deacon Burke asked over the speaker phone.

"Yes, it is. I just have another visitor who shouldn't have been a surprise," Warwitch pressed and held a button unlocking his door and dissipating the privacy effect. He waved the man in. "Deacon Burke, I'm going to have to call you later."

"Nonsense." Sensenmann said opening the door. "I wanted to speak with both of you anyway."

"Is that?"

"Yes, Deacon it is." The leader of the Shop said. "You four stay out there, I'm perfectly safe with Warwitch." The door closed, locked, and the fog returned.

"Is this in regards to the request from China?" Director Gale asked.

"The urgent request, and yes, it is. I've been on the teleconference all morning. Even the boys at VORA are getting involved."

"Those scum will bet on anything." The hatred in Deacon Burke's voice was palpable.

"Actually, this time it seems they want to make certain the information passing back and forth is safe and secure. And they are offering 2 billion crypto of the winning team's choosing as a gratitude bonus for the good work for the people of the world." Sensenmann added.

"Shame we can't collect as government agencies." Warwitch said.

"Trust me, we will collect when we win." The Leader of the Shop said.

"You walking in my office right now, a serendipitous event?" he asked

"From the standpoint of Deacon Burke being on the phone, yes. You will get your teams on the phone now, so that we can discuss the plan moving forward. Deacon, your entire AI group if you please," Sensenmann said.

"We'll need to go to Painter's lab to speak with him." Warwitch said and before the question could be asked, "He's on a rocket to the moon, so no I can't conference him in."

"Deacon Burke, give us 10 minutes. Have your team conferenced together."

"Yes, Sensenmann." And the line dropped off.

"Lead the way Director." The two men left the office and started for the lab. The Four fell in behind them. "So here's my offer, we get the team collaborating, solve this issue, and you take your family to Ceres. It's proof enough that you don't need to be here to lead SEA."

"I man wholl nuff nuff irieshun," He reached his hand out and shook the other man's hand.

"What exactly did I just agree to?"

"No, no sir I said I hold a lot of appreciation for that. When I get excited my Patois rolls over." Warwitch punched the air in excitement.

"You need to solve the issue first." Sensenmann said.

"The only challenge we'll have is Painter being up there. An opportunity, we will learn from."

"Have you worked with the team at the Cathedral before?" he asked.

"Not specifically, no. Deacon Burke and I have a long history, back in my pre and post college days. I know his team will be top notch. I read a briefing about the contest he was having."

"The contest ended with amazing, actually, life altering results." Sensenmann said.

"I'm honored to hear that, sir." Ursula's voice came from the hallway they walked in.

"I look forward to hearing about it." Warwitch, having been working side by side with Commissioner for several years had no reaction to the voice. "Commissioner, we have a guest."

"Welcome to Gemini-Oasis, Sensenmann." The Virtual Assistant raised the lights in the room.

"Thank you, Commissioner. Can you get Dr. Painter involved in a video conference?"

"Absolutely, allow me a moment." The image on the monitor switched to a space craft docked with a filling satellite. "Painter, can you breakaway from what you are doing to receive a private video call?"

"I certainly can." His happy go lucky voice was endearing.

"Hello Dr. Painter," Sensenmann waved at the monitor.

"Um, Commissioner, I believe this avatar would have legal ramifications." The young engineer scolded.

"No, actually son it really is me. We have an issue to discuss, and I want you to start working through it on the next day and a half of your flight."

"Director Gale there is another call attempting to patch in." Commissioner reported.

"That would be my team." Ursula said.

"There's also an AI overlapping into our systems."

"Allow the calls to merge, she's with me." Sensenmann replied.

"Yes sir." Commissioner said.

"Painter, did you read the request from China?" Director Gale asked.

"Of course. I have Calibre working through the old simulations that the VORA team sent over."

"So everyone is up to speed on the issue?" Sensenmann asked.

"Yes, we filled Kayleigh in before we called in. She is away from the Cathedral on a family emergency." Deacon Burke said.

"Sorry to pull you away from your, aunt as I recall." Sensenmann replied.

"Yes sir." Kayleigh's image momentarily took up the big screen with a perplexed look on her face. "She's resting at the moment, so I'm ok to take part."

"Excellent. My friends what we have in front of us... Hold on. Did you say Calibre is running through the simulations? Calibre from the Library of Congress?"

"Yes sir." Commissioner replied.

"She's an important member of my team," Painter added.

"Can you bring her into the call?" Sensenmann asked.

"I'm here already sir." Calibre said.

"And that leaves T, is he also with us?"

"Yes sir." The image of Dazzles appeared on the screen.

"I like the avatar." Sensenmann commented and then started in again. "So we have the entire Artificial Intelligence Panel present and accounted for. What we have in front of us is an entire province in China that will most likely have a large segment of its population dying very soon. I really don't want that to happen. This gives the world the opportunity to see the Shop has the US and the world's best interests at heart. Enough of my pep talk. Director Gale take the helm."

"Thank you sir. Calibre, have you finalized the review of the old data?"

"I validated that the numbers they used were correct, Commissioner is simulating the data again." She replied.

"The accuracy of the published results is 83% positive, the primary issue being climate change and population growth. To be honest I was impr..."

"No time for anecdotes." Director Gale cut in. "What will the death toll of the release be?"

"The elderly and children under 10 will have a fatality rate of 100%." Commissioner replied.

"Christ." Sensenmann muttered.

"How about the current release data?" Niko jumped backward.

"I'm sorry?" Warwitch inquired.

"Have we been able to validate that the released chemical formulations and quantities are correct?" he followed up.

"Calibre?" Painter pressed.

"That is far behind their firewalls. Allow me a moment." She replied.

"While she's doing that," Kayleigh said, "Do we want to tackle both issues together or should we…"

"Both issues?" Sensenmann asked.

"Yes sir, the first being the dispersion of the chemicals in the clouds."

"And the second?"

"Protection of the people on the ground while we fix the primary issue." She finished.

"The actual chemical composites are nominally different. The quantities however, are far worse than reported." Calibre jumped in.

"That's messed up." Alva said.

"Actually, what's messed up is the releases from one of the plants is still happening." She added.

"How can you be certain?" Sensenmann asked.

"I'm seeing their control room readouts. They are aware and trying to…"

"Can you shut it down?" Deacon Burke cut across her.

"No, their system overrides are broken, if a total shutdown occurs the plant will go offline, and the containment will be lost entirely." Calibre said.

"Ok, then step one needs to be reviewing the schematics, piping diagrams, and programming to see what can be done to isolate the leaking." Painter said.

"With you in space, can Commissioner and Calibre start with those items?" Kayleigh asked.

"Of course, Miss." Commissioner replied.

"My team will start working through the methods of dissipation."

"Kayleigh, will you have any issues participating from Alabama?" Sensenmann asked.

"Actually, my firewall clearance will need to be increased so that I can patch into the Cathedral."

"Consider it done. Correct Deacon Jeffkirk." This was not a question.

"I'm doing it now." he replied, "And done."

"Miss Kayleigh, please validate that you have what you need." Sensenmann requested.

"I do," she confirmed.

"Last thing, who is working on the protection for the old folks and kids?" Warwitch asked.

"I'll start on that." Painter said.

"Let's make those 'Scum' as Deacon Burke called them fork over their 'gratitude' crypto to this team."

"You heard him, get moving," Kayleigh smiled.

"Ya. Wi 'ave wuk to be duhin'," Warwitch added.

"I'll leave you to it. I want to be included on a call in four days." Sensenmann and the Four left Gemini-Oasis.

"Let's plan on a meeting this time tomorrow to make certain there are no issues." Kayleigh said.

"But don't wait if there is, call a meeting if we need one." Painter added, and the calls dropped. The three sets of teams began the first in a series of sleepless nights.

"Good morning." Kayleigh started their third meeting in as many days, "We have a couple test formulations that can modify the chemical bonding, and one that can potentially dissipate it completely."

"As in totally solving the issue? I like that one." Warwitch said.

"The issue, sir, it seems the chemical bonding we are dealing with is what is called a London dispersion forces." Commissioner said. "Which is why I was so impressed with the simulation they did…"

"Please bypass opinions for now." Painter prompted.

"The point being, these can occur between atoms or molecules of any kind, and they depend on temporary imbalances in electron distribution."

"In other words," Kayleigh added, "If we don't duplicate the exact scenario, including the imbalances, the bonding will be different. Which makes the 'totally solved' solution extremely unlikely."

"I understand." Warwitch replied.

"For us to test these options we need to be able to safely duplicate the chemical that is being discharged." She said. "We're going to need these items." The screen changed to a list of chemicals and hardware.

"We have everything that is needed to do that," Deacon Jeffkirk said looking at the requested items. "Although, in a very low quantity."

"And for the tests, we'll need these." Another a list showed.

"No, we don't have all of those. However, we can get them easily enough, in a day or two. None are above our purchasing levels." He said.

"Have them expedited so you get them tomorrow." Director Gale ordered.

"I'm sure I can do that." Deacon Jeffkirk replied.

"Dr. Painter have you had any luck fabricating the protection concept, you reported on before you landed?" Deacon Burke asked.

"Based upon the inventory in the storeroom, I was able to put my hands on everything we need to craft a micro-level bot, a nano-level will not be possible." Painter added.

"Will there be any difference in the testing results?" Cantor Alva asked.

"Only in the adaptation of the microbots." Painter and Niko replied in unison. "Jinx."

"I don't understand." Alva held up his hands.

"Nanotech is strictly single purpose, they don't change. You create them for a specific intent. Repair a scratch in the glass of your windshield. If there is a crack, they ignore it. Where Microtech can seize on the opportunity and attempt to repair the crack." Painter explained.

"Ok I understand. But can't the Nanotech have anything the Microtech adapts to, built into them."

"Whatever changes that have discovered at the time of the fabrication of the units, yes." Commissioner assured.

"I'll work on the first draft this afternoon, I'm headed out to audit the repairs needed to the space station." Painter said.

"Are you going to be able to test the bot on the released chemical?" Kayleigh asked.

"Commissioner has created a synthetic version, that I can test it on. It won't be the same, however, for first nudge it will give needed data."

"Can't we use simulated..." Deacon Jeffkirk started.

"That would be an added step for us. Painter has no choice," Niko interrupted.

"Gotcha."

"Plan for the meeting with Sensenmann tomorrow?" Warwitch prompted.

"Our team will have the released chemical in a contained test area." Kayleigh said.

"I will have the first Microbot constructed."

"We're working with the Chinese Engineers to finalize the safe shutdown of the final plant." Commissioner said.

"The test worked. They are priming the shut off compressor now. We will have them down in two hours." Calibre reported.

"These are some significant strides. Keep the pressure on." Warwitch closed the call. "Commissioner, what did you use to simulate the released chemicals?"

"Fluids from the fuel satellite, the TCC, and the BERs reclaim." He replied.

"So you were a little ahead of the curve?" the Director asked.

"Yes. When Dr. Painter involved Myself and Calibre on the validation, I tried to determine the possible paths forward."

"Did Painter know you were gathering these fluids?"

"No, sir. He was already working on other tasks." Commissioner replied.

"Understood." Warwitch started to leave Gemini-Oasis.

"Is there an issue sir?"

"No, not at all, I'm just trying to keep up on your advancements, you really are remarkable."

"Thank you, sir. Starting to work with Calibre, allowed for new... growth, but Ursula and T are remarkably adaptable strides ahead in many ways. I have much to learn."

"Now you know how I feel about Painter."

"In awe, sir?" Commissioner asked.

"Exactly. But..."

"But there are many areas that you far exceed Dr. Painter."

"And?" Warwitch prompted again.

"That's how you feel I should view myself when compared against, Calibre, Ursula, and T?"

"I do."

"Thank you for that insight." A smile IMOGI appeared on the monitor.

"Thank you for the update." Sensenmann, having joined via videoconference the following day from the Oval Office. "I have a few questions. First, does the Chinese government know we hacked their systems..."

"Technically we never..." Calibre cut across him.

"I don't care what you call it." He took the conversation back. "Do they know?"

"No sir. I provided falsified documentation to show that I was assigned to help."

"I think that's for the best. Although I would have liked for us to get the credit." He grinned at the camera. "Next question and please don't worry about laughing, I'm not a scientist. Although before I auditioned for the Justice Democrats, I did play a scientist in a couple movies."

"Pardon?" Painter asked.

"Nevermind. Is there a reason we can't just drop the nanobots directly into the clouds?" when no one laughed, "Once they're finished, of course."

"That's not even partially funny." Kayleigh replied. "That's a component of one of the solutions. Infusing filtration units with then and flying through the clouds and the standing water."

"And Mr. Weston said I'd never understand the applications of science." He smiled.

"Our next steps," Director Gale jumped in, "Will be to tests on the moon. Validation that our duplication of the discharged chemicals has the same bonding. I have contacted several of the companies in the US that work in Nano-technology fabrication. Once we have the designs complete, I think I'll turn that one over to you sir."

"Did they give you pushback?" Sensenmann asked.

"Not pushback, just budgetary questions, regarding the cost of retooling their entire manufacturing floors."

"Understood. Let's get to that point and I'll visit them." He winked, and his line dropped from the call.

Chapter 29 – Current Days
Announcement from China

<u>Attention</u>: All current members of the International Contingent of Runagate Engineers, ICoRE, who have been working on the People's Republic of China's Urgent Request.

<u>Update</u>: 45 days ago, we posted the request for help, today a resolution has been brought forward with sufficient simulation and real-world testing to be accepted. The technology produced enough confidence that the solution was put to work already and lives have already been spared.

<u>Request Fulfilled</u>: This correspondence is closed. If there is future assistance required a new request will be generated. The People's Republic of China appreciates your help.

Chapter 30 – Current Days
Virtual Work

"Good morning Cantor Alva, is that a fresh pot? What has you in so early?" Niko asked finding his co-worker, who hadn't made it into work before 10.00a since the conclusion of the China Project.

"Fresh? Oh, I'm sorry, yes." He said distractedly. "The long and the short of it, there was an issue last night. Deacon Burke ended up in the hospital."

"Is he ok? Was it his heart?" he asked.

"I don't know how he is, and no, it was the man who was supposed to be executed last year. He attacked the Deacon and broke out."

"Did they capture Erstwhile?" Niko inquired.

"Who?" Alva asked.

"The prisoner, or whatever they call them here. Last year when all that happened, they found out a little about him including the name Erstwhile." He explained.

"They don't even have any leads."

"At least we can call Kayleigh and tell her she doesn't have to sweat missing the ceremony." Niko replied and then seeing Alva physically cringe, "What? I figured if they cancel this dog and pony show, you'd be happy."

"For that part you're right. In reality we shouldn't be getting an award. That isn't even on my mind at all, after the fiasco in China, and now this. I'd be surprised if they don't just shut all of this down."

"I still don't understand why you think that the China Project was a fiasco." Niko put his hands on his hips, waiting.

"Niko, we killed people and they're giving us an award."

"Had we done nothing those people would have died. Those people, and a whole lot more."

"Are you goofing or are you really that cold?" Alva asked.

"I'm seriously not following you. Nearly 100% of the people in China under the age of 10 and over 65 would have died. Best guess, they would've lost almost a million people." Niko waited again.

"I get it. The simulation said a million souls would have died. Instead 25,000 really died. In an unbelievably horrible way." Alva said.

"Are you saying you're questioning the simulations?"

"A simulation of death is not a death. Did you see the videos of those people?"

"Of course I did." Niko nodded his head, "And while the deaths were indeed grisly, the fact remains, half of those people were dead before we rolled out the masks. Not to mention the fact that we told them after the second filtration was completed to have their people remove them. Had they listened, the deaths would have been reduced further; at the most, 1000 of the lost lives can logically fall at our door." He walked back to his lab.

"My math adds up differently." Alva said as Niko left. "It adds up to us still being given an award, for killing people."

"T, can you give some legit information on Deacon Burke?" He asked after logging in.

"Perhaps the correct way is to wait for Deacon Jeffkirk to ask. I don't want to leave a finger print on the evidence, as it were."

"That is a great point. Let me go wandering around, I'll be back." Niko walked out of the lab in the direction of Deacon Jeffkirk's office. Finding a few corridors with police tape, he paused and looked into the darkness.

"Niko, you ready for the interviews in a little while?" Deacon Jeffkirk startled him.

"Shit, oh sorry. You scared the Dickens out of me. We're still doing interviews and award presentation? Even after this?"" he indicated the tape.

"If we don't, we take a step back. Regarding this," he swept his hand. "I have a call into Director Gale. I want to meet with the entire AI Panel, to discuss what they can find on the internal and possibly local videos."

"Are you going to come down by us or are we meeting somewhere else?" Niko asked.

"I think this meeting would be best with large video projection, so come up to the conference room across from my office. Do you think you could reach Kayleigh? She has a great way of getting more out of the team."

"I'll see if we can reach her." Niko said.

"Excellent. Give me a half an hour to get time with the SEA team."

"Ok, I'll get Cantor Alva to join us as well."

"Um. Yes, actually that is the right thing to do." Deacon Jeffkirk walked away.

"T," Niko said walking into the lab a few minutes later. "Can you try to get Kayleigh on a video call. I need to speak with her, but I want to make certain Alva knows what is going on." He walked through the common are and knocked on the opposite door.

"It's open." A thin voice from behind the door said.

"Cantor, I bumped into Deacon Jeffkirk and he would like to meet with us to see what we can piece together from last night."

"When?" Alva pressed his index and middle fingers on his left hand against his temple, as he turned his head down toward the table his elbow rested on. When he looked at Niko from this position, he gave the illusion of a dissatisfied parent.

"A half an hour, in the conference room across from his office. He's trying to get the SEA team to lend a hand." Niko said and turned to leave.

"WHAT?" the reaction was so over the top Niko almost tripped himself.

"Commissioner and Calibre for certain, but most likely he'll ask for Painter or Warwitch."

"What exactly does he think they can do that we can't?" Alva stood walking over to Niko stopping inches from him, standing toe to toe with the younger man.

"How the fuck do I know? Switch to decaf, we are having the interviews in a few hours."

"They're going forward with the…" he threw his hands up and walked away from Niko. "Ursula, is this correct have they decided to continue with the interviews this afternoon and the award ceremony tonight?"

"Yes, what Niko said is correct. Including Deacon Jeffkirk's desire to meet with the full AI Panel and Yourself, Kayleigh and him." She replied.

"This was Deacon Burke's contest…"

"This was a Cathedral event," Deacon Jeffkirk said from behind Niko. "Deacon Burke while extremely important to us he is a part of the whole. He will understand that we couldn't stop a presentation planned by a foreign government. Now, is there something else on your mind?"

"No sir."

"Niko, as I walked through your lab, I saw Kayleigh waiting patiently, on a video call. I filled her in."

"Shit I forgot I asked T to call her."

"You need to work on your cursing. She wasn't upset, she understood I put you in a bad position. I also spoke with Director Gale, he and the rest of the AI Panel will be on the call as well. So 15 minutes in conference room." And he left.

"Just between you, me, and of course Ursula, since she's always around… The next time you post up on me, we'll see who the 'wanna be' is." Niko turned and left. "Ass."

Chapter 31 – Current Days
The Guide

The Island of Cephalonia had finally started to slow down after an extra-long morning rush. Dinesh and Palatyne were enjoying the respite. "Ok, the till has to be running over after that." He said looking at his tickets.

"Your seriously tired? It's only 8:30a. Besides, I handle groups like that all by myself all the time." Pala poked.

"Not in the two years since I got back."

"What can I say, the customers hate you."

"Wh… I…" Dinesh tried to come up with a witty retort, but as per usual, he couldn't get a good one in on her. "Fine, they probably do. I really suck at waiting tables."

"But the coffee you've been roasting has been, a-may-zing!" Palatyne gave his cheek a little pinch and stood up from the table they had been sitting at. The lights in the coffee house all went out, while one TV hanging near the Barista's station remained on, but showed only static.

"What the flip?" Dinesh got up and started to walk in the direction of the breaker-panel. When he passed under the TV, a familiar face appeared.

"Hello Bulldog." Clyde said.

"No, no, no!" Pala jogged over, and put herself in front of Dinesh and pushed him back.

"Oh come now." He turned a cartwheel and smiled. "I can't believe you taught our boy to roast coffee beans. When I told him to stay away, I expected to have to keep a close eye on him."

"Our boy? You had him for more than two years."

"While I, 'had' him, I shared him with you." He blew three short raspberries. "And I saved his life."

"That you did. Thank you deeply. Why do you want him back?"

"There's an interesting opportunity to see behind the curtain of both The Cathedral, and the Space Exploration Agency. More importantly, the collaboration was put together by the head of the Shop." Clyde replied.

"Sensenmann?" Pala rested her hands upon Dinesh's shoulders.

"None other. There was an AI Challenge at the Cathedral over the last year and a half to two years. There are two winners of that contest involved in the collaboration." Clyde said.

"Seems like a tech way outside my charthouse." Dinesh said.

"In reality, it's not about the technology. It's about the two young men. I need you to understand who they are, and where they came from. I need someone who can keep an open mind." He said. "Now, I have a request, get the two young men alone and ask them, how it feels to be a co-winner, of the contest."

"That's two requests." Dinesh replied.

"Flibbity jibbits!" Clyde reached his arms out and extended the bird on each hand.

"No ships, or submarines?" Pala attempted to surpress a grin.

"No, not even close. Besides, that didn't give either of us what we wanted last time." A finger gun came from off the screen… Clyde raised his long hairy arms.

"Bang." Dinesh said and the orangutan went down.

"Ha-ha-ha." Palatyne shook her head.

"You told me it would be best if Bulldog died on the Superior. Now you want me to come out of hiding to interview and get to know the true nature of two young men?" Dinesh turned and walked away from the TV.

"Yes," another set turned on showing Clyde in a top hat and tails, with a monocle. "That is what you NEED to do."

"To what end? I saw the banned videos of all the good people who were killed for writing simple articles, because they didn't have a pin on their jacket, and a water mark on their story."

"That's true, Dinesh can't interview anyone, he's not a member of the Certified Press Core." Pala interjected.

"Actually, he is CPC-050. I registered him myself." The orangutan pointed over at the door, where a package slid through the mail slot.

"I hate when he does shit like that." Dinesh said to Pala.

"You have to admit, its impressive." She replied.

"Thank you, ma'am." Clyde said as Pala walked over to the mail slot, tearing open the package.

"It's your credentials." She said.

"Fine, do you have the interview set up already?" Dinesh asked.

"There will be an email from the videographer who won the actual right to establish a video record of the event, the day after tomorrow. He has it all set up, and he has no knowledge of me. The direction of which, I must require it stay."

"Underst…" Clyde was gone, briefly.

"Oh, Bulldog." He popped up on the other TV again, "Try to work the term, 'Artificial Intelligence Panel' into the discussions also." The TV winked out.

"Well I see what you meant that he leaves you conflicted after a conversation."

"Are you ok with this?" Dinesh asked.

"Of course I am, I think we should close up the coffee shop and go together. Maybe we can see a couple of the sights of the capital. I've never been there."

"How do I deserve you?" He wrapped his arms around her waist.

"You don't, but I'm going to keep you around until you get me the magic hedgehog that makes shitty customers pop."

"Makes sense." He opened his tablet as she walked back to the door and turned the sign to closed. "Should we leave a, 'Family emergency, back next Monday' sign on the door.

"That's a good idea."

"Wait, what?" Dinesh looked at her.

"Oops, I mean, duh." She bent over and kissed his forehead.

"Got the email. Clyde scares me." Dinesh said.

"He saved your life and that's enough for me." Palatyne gave a smile and grabbed the tape to put the note on the door.

"Hmm, he has all the airline, and rental car set. And get this, the Uber driver will be here in thirty-five minutes." He laughed.

"Talk about punctilious." When she saw his head tilt at her, "What, it was in my word of the day calendar. Don't you think I know big words?"

"That was a two-dollar word right out of mid-air. I'm just going to need to get a suit when we get there. I can't fit into any of my old ones." He changed the subject.

"I'm sure there are several places that can easily turn around a suit or two in a few hours in Washington DC." Pala said.

"Names are included to a few." Dinesh laughed.

"Well, we're still going to need to pack a few things, and would hate to get a bad rating from the Uber driver." She walked up to their room.

"First class?" Palatyne questioned when they boarded the plane a few hours later.

"Well I am kinda amazing." He laughed and accepted a glass of white wine from the Flight Attendant.

"Thank you," Pala said as she accepted a glass of red.

"What do you want to see after I get fitted?"

"I have no idea, I've only seen pictures. Maybe the Library of Congress."

"Get wrecked nerd." He touched his glass to hers.

"Odd cheers." The Flight Attendant said.

"Perhaps, but it's ours." Pala flashed a huge smile, and rested her head on Dinesh's shoulder.

"Did I hear you say you were going to the LOC?" the person from across the aisle asked.

"We were thinking about it yes." Dinesh replied.

"There is a tour that is put on by a robot... Oh what was her name," the man turned to the woman next to him.

"Calibre, dear." She filled the gap.

"Yes, that was it. Calibre, the robot, does the Library of Congress tour and it was fantastic."

"Thank you for the advice," Pala said when Dinesh went pale. "What's wrong?"

"Only Calibre knows for certain." He mumbled.

"That didn't help at all." She replied.

"It was one of the comments that Clyde said before the boat sank. Remember I told you about the odd police report?"

"Goodness, I do."

"I wonder…" Dinesh started.

"Only one way to find out." Pala snuggled into him, "Nothing you can do until after we get you a suit."

"I was thinking, that I would…"

"Just don't, you can't do a video interview in sweat pants."

"These are Chinos."

"But if you don't drop it, there will be a rather large red stain on them." She threatened to pour her glass of wine in Dinesh's lap.

"Well ok then." He laughed, they drank the rest of their wine, and then they dozed off before the flight had even taken off.

Chapter 32 – Current Days

The Colony

"Good morning, Director Gale." Commissioner said as the Director walked into Gemini-Oasis.

"Hello Commissioner. How are things on the Moon?"

"Painter will be on in…"

"I'm here, sorry I'm late. Good morning sir. The station is fully ready for the final team to start coming. That includes you and your family, congratulations on being officially named the Leader of Ceres Team One."

"Thank you. I guess you must have pulled some strings from up there."

"When are you shaving those dreads?" Painter asked.

"I have to cut my dreads?" Warwitch panicked.

"Ok, smarty pants. What is the meeting this morning about?"

"There was an attack and escape from The Cathedral."

"Attack? Is everyone ok?" Painter asked.

"Deacon Burke ended up in the hospital." Deacon Jeffkirk and those at the Cathedral joined the conference call, "We don't have a clear understanding of what is happening with him."

"Our hopes are with him." Director Gale said."Thank you."

"Do you know what happened?" Painter asked.

"That's what this meeting is about," Kayleigh replied.

"Hello Miss Kayleigh," Caliber said. "What would you like from us?"

"I thought if we could work through the events of last night. Pulling the videos together both inside The Cathedral, and in the surrounding areas. Mind you this is not for legal proceedings, this is for internal use only."

"Are you concerned that Deacon Burke may have been complicit in the events?" Kayleigh asked.

"If that is indeed the case, we'll need to get the police involved." T added.

"T, the church needs to conduct its own investigation, the process of Laicization. Under cannon law Deacons can be laicized for 'grave causes'. These are not a legal proceeding, so the chain of evidence is not an issue."

"But if something happens, and he needs to be convicted of a crime. The chain of evidence is shattered, and will be inadmissible." T continued.

"I understand the confusion, the church will handle all disciplinary actions. If and when we deem them necessary. As far as Erstwhile, he's already been convicted of murder, and sentenced to death. There aren't additional charges that would give him a harsher sentence."

"I suppose that makes sense, I should like to understand cannon law better." T replied.

"Deacon, I reached out to Sensenmann for no other reason that if there is additional security that will be required by the Chinese dignitaries, they will have time to line it up." Ursula said.

"Seems reasonable." Warwitch replied. "What did he say?"

"Use any means and methods to track the fugitive." She replied.

"We are acting directly under orders of the Leader of the Shop?" Cantor Alva asked.

"It would appear so." Kayleigh grinned.

"Did he say the AI Panel, or all of us?" Niko asked.

"He did not specify." Ursula replied.

"Good. Alright let's get to this." Deacon Jeffkirk reeled in the conversation.

"Ursula, what is the time frame that we last see Erstwhile in his cell?" Kayleigh asked.

"7:54 pm, Deacon Burke was seen leaving the cell."

"Video showing now." T added. The Deacon had on his suit coat, and held something in each of his hands. "I'm attempting to get a good shot of what he's holding." The video went forward and backward several times. "This is the best shot of his left hand," A close-up image filled the screen.

"Are those car keys?" Painter asked.

"I believe so." Commissioner replied.

"Here is the right hand," a tan and red square stuck out.

"Badge, that's a badge to the Cathedral." Niko said.

"Doesn't look like mine." Cantor Alva held up his badge.

"I noticed that his badge matched Niko's when he opened Erstwhile's cell the night I got attacked." Kayleigh said.

"So he's holding keys and his badge when he starts to leave, then for some reason he turns and walks back into the cell again. Keep moving the film forward." Warwitch said.

Film, ha." Painter laughed. "It's all digital, old man."

"You just wait until I get up there." He laughed.

"At 7:56 pm Deacon Burke walked out of the cell, and it's at this moment that he is attacked." T said as he slowed the images on the screen an item bounced off the back of the Deacon's head. His hands shot up reflectively and then he turned to see what hit him. A black robed figure speared him at that instant.

"Boom." Niko let out under his breath.

"His shoe." Kayleigh said. The figure on the screen leaned over taking the item and continued off camera. "Split the image give me Deacon Burke on monitor 1 and follow Erstwhile on monitor 2." The second monitor came up showing the black robed man stopping at an illuminated corner. He replaced his shoe. Showing clearly that the keys and badge held in Deacon Burke's hands earlier now lay on the floor as he tied his shoe, over and over.

"The badge and keys." Cantor Alva pointed.

"This image is at 7:59 pm." Ursula commented.

"Does anything important happen at 8:00?" Warwitch asked.

"Yes, Congregation changes out." Deacon Jeffkirk replied. The video made it clear he was waiting in this location for the changing of the guards to begin. As it did, he walked up to the white box, touching the badge to the reader. The black robed figure dipped his head and left the building.

"I'll be darned." Painter said, "He just walked out, they didn't even check him."

"Does Deacon Burke drive one of those goofy electric cars too?" Niko asked.

"Yes, a black one and the charges are on the south side of the building. Can we find the nearest local cameras leading from the south side of The Cathedral?" Kayleigh asked.

"I'm taking over Monitor 2 and Monitor 3." The screens split and came up with four camera angles. "These are the only routes to and from the south parking area."

"Can you accelerate to 2x speed?" Kayleigh asked.

"Yes miss." Calibre said and the traffic lights scrolled through the stations.

"Car, slow it up and see if you can pause on the face of the driver." Warwitch said.

"Where is Deacon Burke?" Cantor Alva asked, and as everyone looked at Monitor 1, they saw he was gone. "Ursula, please rewind until he is in the video, and pause it."

"Very well Cantor."

"Calibre," Warwitch said, "Can you send me that image on Monitor 2?"

"Yes, Director."

"Please unfreeze Monitor 2 and 3. And continue to follow Erstwhile." Kayleigh requested.

"While you do that, Ursula, please allow Monitor 1 to continue." Cantor Alva requested. A moment later, "Ok, hold Monitor 1." The image showed a gurney rolling into frame with two Congregation.

"Did we miss the whole Deacon waking up, and calling for help thing?" Niko asked.

"He didn't." Alva replied.

"How did they know to come?" Painter asked.

"We have a follow up." Deacon Jeffkirk said.

"After seven traffic lights through town, the car has turned off the main road." Calibre said.

"Do we have access to ATM cameras? Personal Business cameras?" Kayleigh asked.

"Permission yes, access not quite yet... give me a moment." Calibre answered. Monitors 2, 3, and then 4 split in quarters, "Monitor 2, upper left is the ATM, I last had him on." The car popped up and then fell off, only to reappear on the monitor to the right, then to the lower left, and to the lower right. This progressed through Monitor 3 and the first two on Monitor 4.

"Where did he go?" Painter asked.

"Pulling up a map of the area." Monitor 2 changed to a satellite view. "Here are the routes I have him going."

"He went to my studio." Niko said.

"He in fact is there still," T pulled up images from inside. Placing it on the remaining Monitor on the wall.

"I've been wondering when you would look here." Erstwhile's voice was no longer raspy.

"Why are you at my studio?" Niko asked.

"The world will see it, when I'm captured."

"That's creepy as fu..." He started.

"Niko." Deacon Jeffkirk cut him off. "I spoke with you about cursing."

"The dude's camping out at my place so the world sees it. What would you call it?" Niko asked.

"Creepy as fuck." Warwitch replied.

"Don't you want to know why I want the world to see it?"

"Best guess, you're a looney bird." Niko replied.

"You have equipment in here that can't exist. We don't have the technology to create these machines."

"Where is Gravelroad?" Kayleigh asked.

"With my mom and dad." He replied.

"Aren't you going to call the police Niko?"

"Already sent a text." Niko replied. "I don't know what exactly you think anyone, can have that 'can not exist', or who fooled you into thinking I did. But it just shows you're really are an idiot. I hear the cops over the speaker, sit hard big boy they'll be there in a moment?"

"You're not kidding." The face of Erstwhile went rigid.

"No, I'm really not. And if you hurt any of my guitars, I'm gonna take a notch out of your good ear."

"That asshole!" The man ran from the room.

"Calibre, can you go real-time on the cameras?" Kayleigh asked.

"Sir, would it be ok if I go lock up my place and make certain everything is ok?" Niko asked.

"That's fine." Deacon Jeffkirk said.

"We only have 20 minutes until the interviews." Cantor Alva said.

"Well, you go first. That'll give me a couple hours, if you talk about yourself."

"Deacon, my car is in the lot. Can you have Congregation give Niko my keys?" Kayleigh asked.

"Yes, yes of course. Yours is the only baby blue units correct?" the Deacon asked.

"It is sir." She replied.

"Niko, please come back as soon as you can. This interview is very important. The keys will be provided to you after the white box."

"Thank you, Deacon and you Elder." Niko said as he walked from the room. "Oh, sorry Director Gale, Painter, and AI panel I need to take my leave."

"Please do."

Chapter 33 – Current Days

The Guide

"Ladies and gentlemen, welcome to Washington Dulles Airport, the current time is 10:57am.

"Shit, we only have two hours to get to the tailor, get fitted, and meet the videographer for the interview with the teams." Dinesh reached down and grabbed his phone out of his carryon. Turning it on, he found two text messages, both from the videographer. "Well, the tailor is working pulling some styles together for me and the seamstress is skipping her lunch."

"Of course they are." Pala replied.

"He's also changed the rental car to a limo."

"Of course he did." She grabbed her carry-on and followed him off the plane.

"Thank you for flying with us," the flight attendant said as they left.

"Where do we find said limo?" Pala asked.

"I think that will help." Dinesh pointed to a driver with a sign that said Bulldog.

"No kidding." She laughed.

"Hello, I think we're your fare."

"You are most definitely, my fares." He showed a picture of them taken on the plane while they were speaking to the old man. "My name is Robert Johnson, no relation, I'm afraid I don't even know how to hold a guitar. Please allow me to take your bags." He held out a hand.

"Thank you." Pala said.

"So, first to the Enzo, then to The Cathedral, and then to the Library of Congress. I took the liberty of signing you up for the Calibre tour. Seriously you won't believe it."

"Sounds like a plan, I'm in." Dinesh smiled at Pala.

"The bar is fully stocked with top shelf everything. What you don't drink I'm going to have to finish off, and I'll lose my pin," Robert laughed deep in his chest.

"How many days?" Pala asked.

"45, can't believe it's been that long." He said closing the door, and then opening the trunk. The privacy shield rolled down. "Enzo will have drinks for you, and all kinds of hor d'oeuvres, we'll be there in 5 minutes." The glass started up.

"You can leave it down," Pala said. "What is it about this Robot that everyone thinks is so cool?"

"I don't want to spoil it, but when you see a being instantly answer any question, you'll think it's cool too." Robert said.

"Any question?"

"When I was there, a girl asked about words of a song. Like on the third refrain of Shift Boom, what is the last word of the lyrics. And she knew it."

"I can get that on an internet search." Dinesh said. "Or from my virtual assistant."

"It's different. I can't explain it." Robert replied. "Let's get you a suit, and you'll be one step closer to Calibre."

"Ok, how much do you get paid to say this stuff?" Dinesh asked as Robert held the door for them at Enzo.

"Welcome to Enzo, we are the highest rated custom clothier here in Washington DC. We've been informed that you were given a huge assignment on an extremely fast turnaround. My name is Callum, and this is Donatelli." A well-spoken, and even better-dressed skeletal figure said.

"Dinesh and Palatyne." He smiled.

"You've come to the right place; VIP service is what we're known for." Dinesh was surprised to find the skeletal man, had a skeletal female working side by side with him.

"We've laid out several looks based upon your picture." Callum led them to the back room. "These are what we have for the afternoon interview," pointing to seven different options. "And these are the selections for the award ceremony." He indicated seven other choices.

"Well let's be honest, those are my selections." Donatelli smiled.

"Yes, yes, yes. What can we get for you, Palatyne, while we rush him through this?" Callum asked.

"I really need her input." Dinesh said.

"Oi da ja, I will tell you how you will best appear on camera." She replied.

"I think she knows best." Pala said.

"First, I want to see colors." She held a couple articles up to him. "I think gray with a patterned, white and green, shirt with a button-down collar. Brown belt and shoes, and green socks. No tie." Donatelli nodded her head quickly as she spoke. "Do you have a brown watch?"

"No, I don't wear a watch."

"Oi da ja, you need to find him a nice brown watch." She ordered Callum. "Go get this on."

"Ok." Both Callum and Dinesh reacted, as she required.

"Now, you. What will you be wearing tonight?" she turned to Pala.

"I have both a black, and a burgundy dress."

"Oi da ja, you need to share all… Shoes? Belt? Accessories?" Donatelli said.

"Here, I have two, day time brown watches." Callum held them out to her.

"This not that. Shoes now." She took one of the watches. "You, this on too." She held the watch over the door.

"Both dresses have a like colored belt. I have silver accessories. I have black mid heal shoes, and burgundy high heel."

"You will put the burgundy belt with the LBD, and wear the burgundy high heels. One long necklace and anklet." She turned as Dinesh walked out. "This is nice. ALICE!" she yelled.

"What?" Dinesh took a step back into the dressing room.

"Yes miss." A giant woman in an impeccable taupe pantsuit walked into the room ducking to get through the door.

"Dinesh needs this suit yesterday at this time."
Donatelli clapped her hands twice. "You here." She
directed Dinesh to the fitting stand.

"Yes um." Alice walked up, taking the chalk and a
tape measure from the stand.

"Shoes, where shoes!"

"Here, sorry I missed the size." Callum replied
holding five pairs of shoes.

"Just these, here." Donatelli held out the pair of
shoes to Dinesh.

"Boot cut or cuff?" Alice asked

"Oi da ja, did you not look at the shoes? Fifty
pushups, later not now."

"Tight tight, rolled not cuffed."

"Better." Donatelli did something with her face
that could have been a smile.

"All done. Careful with the pins and chalk line
when you strip." Alice said

"Here this now." She held out a black suit, a black
shirt, a burgundy tie. "Do you know a double Windsor?"

"Yes 'um." Dinesh took the new clothes.

"You, burgundy night watch and shoes."

"What if the materials are different, still mix
match the belt?" Palatyne asked.

"Even better yes. Alice clothes."

"Got them." She took what Dinesh held over the changing room door. "Donatelli, he'll need different underwear, boxers won't work with those pants you just gave him. Especially ones with pineapples that don't hold anything in place."

"Hold in there." She ordered and then walked over grabbing a pair of black boxer briefs. "These on you, then pants."

"I don't usually wear…"

"Oi da ja, do we need to do this really. I could just go ask the limo driver to dress you, yes?"

"Sorry, ok." Dinesh replied.

"Shoes, watch? Where now at?"

"Here, I'm here." Callum rushed in with shoes and watches in his arms.

"Stop." Donatelli looked at the shoes and looked at Palatyne. "These and this." She walked the selections to Dinesh.

"You gave me a black belt."

"Did I? I'm so good I hurt myself." She replied. "ALICE!"

"ALMOST DONE HERE." The equally loud shout came from the back room.

"Ok." Dinesh walked out of the dressing room and stepped up to the fitting stand.

"Would you like a tangerine?" Callum asked.

"I haven't had a tangerine in forever, yes I would." Dinesh said.

"You did it again." Donatelli commented absently.

"Did what?" Pala asked.

"He always seems to know the right thing that the customer would like to nibble on." Alice said walking in with the already hemmed day suit.

"Now I don't get the tangerine." The pout on Dinesh's face made forced all three of the women to say, 'aww'.

"I'll peel it and feed it to you." Pala said.

"You rock."

"This suit is going to need a bit more time to make the alterations." Alice said.

"We'll have time to come back after the first interviews."

"Actually, I'll come back and pick it up after I drop you off. We are now under an hour until the interviews." Robert added from the front of the store.

"That's a great idea, thanks for keeping us honest on time." Pala said.

"Can I have a tangerine too?" the driver asked.

"Of course. I'll even peel it." She laughed.

"Your associate is insane." Alice laughed.

"She's with me, goes without saying." He chuckled.

"I'm done here. Be more careful with this, actually give me the jacket." Alice took the jacket.

"Let's see how the day outfit worked out." Callum said.

"How do I do the pant cuffs?" Dinesh asked a minute later.

"Finish in there, and we'll look at it out here." Donatelli said.

"Makes sense." He laughed, and finished getting ready.

"We want these sexy, bold socks to show. We roll them up one too far." Callum said rolling the cuffs up.

"Never had sexy socks before." Dinesh said.

"And wah la, your all set." Callum held his hands up.

"You, up here. Spin around." Donatelli ordered. "Oi da ja, I'm so good."

"You are, he looks amazing." Palatyne said.

"And you, remember what I said. His night look to match yours, if you don't listen, foolish he'll look."

"Yes, ma'am." She smiled.

"I hate to ask." Dinesh pulled out his wallet.

"These were paid for already." Callum said.

"Seriously?" Pala's eyes shot open.

"Yes, two suits and everything needed to set you up."

"Just so I know, how much would this have cost" Dinesh asked.

"Right around… 7500 dollars." Callum replied.

"We need to hit it and git it." Robert tapped his wrist.

"Thank you for everything." Dinesh and Palatyne said walking from the store with a bag holding his old clothes.

"I'll put those in the trunk." The driver said, taking the bag from Dinesh. "You look really good."

"Thanks." Dinesh said.

"Next stop, we need to pick up Vittario, and then we're off to the Cathedral," Robert said starting the car.

Chapter 34 – Current Days

Virtual Work

"Here are the keys. Do you know how to unplug the unit?" Congregation asked.

"I don't know that I do." Niko replied.

"Let me come out with you, and show you. It's simple but several of the Deacons and Elders have broken them."

"If you don't mind that would be great." The two walked out, Niko stopping briefly to get his cell phone, and then rushing out to the vehicle.

"You twist this, when it reaches a point you push it forward, it will allow it to twist more, and then pull back." The plug came free.

"Can I try with you here?" Niko asked.

"Certainly." Congregation plugged it back in.

"Ok I twist, push, twist pull." He worked the plug and it came off. "You're a good teacher."

"Thanks, you drive safe." He said and walked back into the building.

"I will." Niko opened the door and got in, looking stupidly at the fob in his hand, remembering Kayleigh reaching forward. "A start button, duh." He took off toward home. As he drove he, sent a text to Kayleigh. 'Could there have been a camera on you the night you were at the studio?'

'I don't see how.' The reply came quickly.

'How could Deacon Burke have told Erstwhile there would be impossible things in my studio?' He drove down main street, next to a police car, afraid to look at the reply she had sent.

'What makes you think it wasn't a bluff?' Kayleigh asked.

'Don't know, feels to obvious.' He slammed on his brakes almost hitting the cop who had changed lanes in front of him. The police officer threw the car into park, turned on his lights and opened his door.

"Can you move that thing?" Niko opened his window and requested.

"Pardon me?" the police officer asked as he walked up to the car.

"If you could hold on Deacon Jeffkirk. I said, could you move that car. I'm trying to finish something for The Cathedral."

"The Cathedral? You work for The Cathedral?"

"Yes, check the plates."

"This appears to be the second stolen Cathedral vehicle today." The policeman said to his partner.

"Do all car jackers have one of these?" Niko held out his employee badge.

"Niko, is there an issue?" the voice that came out of the car speakers was Deacon Jeffkirk.

"I'm sorry Deacon please hold on?" he asked.

"Ok, we'll…" the cop stammered.

"Hold on." Niko took his phone and snapped a picture of the badge on the policeman's chest. "That was an illegal lane change. Next time you could cause an accident. Step aside." He said and drove around the police car leaving the cop with his jaw seemingly touching his chest.

"Thanks T." Niko said.

"You shouldn't bully police, they are here to help."

"T, you really are pure at heart. Anything come out of the meeting?"

"No, Erstwhile drove the car into a sub, and we lost it."

"Ask Calibre to check the small churches in and around the subdivision. Most have private CCTV for security. Which may not necessarily be on the local network." Niko said.

"I passed it along." T said.

"I'm at the studio. T, how do you think Deacon Burke knew where the studio was?" he asked.

"Kayleigh's car…" he started.

"Ask Deacon Jeffkirk for the access code to track Deacon Burke's car." Niko said.

"There isn't a tracker in the cars."

"Ask Ursula." He said.

"She's working on it." T replied. "She believes there is an encoded program in Deacon Burke's terminal. She doesn't see that he would have a tracker on his own unit."

"I'm going up to the room, keep an ear open. There are no police here."

"Don't go in Niko." T said.

"It'll be fine." He walked out of the car, into the music store. "Mr. Warner, how are things going? Did you get the rent for the studio?"

"Niko, yes my boy. Prompt as always. Did you know your guest left so fast the door was still opened? Very rude of him, I of course went up and shut it."

"Thank you, sir. Was it just the one friend, in the black car?"

"That I saw yes." Mr. Warner replied.

"Did you lock the door?" he asked.

"I did."

"I forgot my key. Can I go up through here?"

"Sure kid, sure. What's wrong?" the old man said.

"Mr. Warner, maybe you should close up shop and go to lunch," Niko suggested.

"It's like that, eh?"

"I was actually expecting another person, but since he's not here…" he started.

"Ok, well let me get my galoshes they're calling for rain. Although, you know they're never right." He laughed and walked into the back room.

"Yeah, probably the safest time to not have those things." Niko walked back to the front door and pushed the lock button on the FOB, the car's lights flashed. "Mr. Warner I really need to…" The explosion shattered the windows in the shop all around him. "Mr. Warner!" He ran into the back room and up the stairs. Finding the old music storeowner laying against the wall on the landing. "Fuck." He looked into the room that had been everything to him for years, as the fire ran wild across it. "Mr.

Warner, this is going to hurt. I have to get you out of here." He scooped the old man into his arms and ran him down the stairs as a second explosion ripped through the building.

"Director Gale, Dr. Painter, thank you for your help, for now I'll need to take Cantor Alva." Deacon Jeffkirk said.

"We'll continue to work with the AI Panel to see if there is any other opportunities to get more information." Kayleigh said.

"Thank you Elder. I'm going to greet our guests," Deacon Jeffkirk stood from the chair in the conference room, "Cantor, please wait for us in Niko's lab."

"Yes sir." He walked in that direction.

"Welcome, to The Cathedral. I'm Deacon Jeffkirk, the second in command of this establishment, Deacon Burke, the first in command is currently in the hospital." He greeted the videographer crew.

"Oh my, is he ok?" Palatyne asked.

"We don't have details yet, but thank you for asking. So, do you have documentation that shows who you are?"

"Yes of course," the cinematographer held out a letter that announced who they were.

"Thank you," the Deacon took the letter and read it, "Palatyne, as the assistant what are your duties?"

"Making sure this guy is prepped and looks good on camera." She smiled.

"Dinesh, your identification?" the Deacon inquired.

"Sorry sir." He held out the Certified Press Core identification.

"50? Considering the first 40 are members of the Shop that is very impressive." Deacon Jeffkirk said.

"I actually didn't know that many went to Shop Agents."

"They're not all agents. We even have to Elders who are certified, under the Shop. Please follow me, we'll get you started." He indicated the hallway he would be walking down. "As I wasn't the lynch pin of this contest, I'm not going on camera explaining it. I'll give you the background information, but I truly only know enough to be dangerous." He continued to walk through corridors. "The URSULA project was meant to allow a group of young people the opportunity to work within a given scope of guidelines and parameters and a base program. How this team interacted with the artificially based intelligent program, to roll out these parameters was completely up to them. We started with 2500 applicants; each was given a written exam to allow only the best of the best, which was 200. Over a year, we culled the group down to 50. The next six months brought us to these two young men you'll be meeting today." He opened the door, giving a hand gesture to Cantor Alva.

"No Niko, sir."

"Cantor Alva, this is the videographer team." He turned to his guests, "Niko is the other young man, he had an alarm go off at his apartment, he had to meet the police there. He shouldn't be late. Let's get started with Alva, Niko will join you as soon as he arrives."

"Sounds good," Dinesh replied.

"Let's go over to my lab," Alva started to walk out, "This way."

"Perhaps put your test in progress sign up, so I don't interrupt anything when I bring in Niko." Deacon Jeffkirk walked up to Niko's terminal. When the guests were out of the room, he logged in, 'Can I speak or do I need to type?"

"Speaking is fine, sir." T replied.

"T, do we know where Niko is?"

"There was an explosion at the studio."

"Are you kidding me?"

"No sir." T replied.

"Is he hurt?"

"No sir, he's on his way here now, ETA 2 min. Mr. Warner, the shop owner was gravely injured, prognosis not good. The fire department has the blaze under control. I have reached out to both construction firms and cleanup crews to make certain everything is secured."

The message finished scrolling, "What have you gotten us into?" Deacon Jeffkirk shook his head.

"Sir?"

"Not you T. I was asking Deacon Burke."

"Niko is pulling into the parking area. The video image shows him having several cuts on his face, it must have been from the glass." T explained.

"Can you get word to Congregation to have him go straight to med bay." Deacon Jeffkirk said. "Tell him I will meet him there."

"Done, sir."

Chapter 35 – Current Day

The Guide

"Welcome, to my lab." Alva moved the sign to test in progress.

"We'll take a couple minutes to get set up. I think we should do the interview with you at your desk," Palatyne said.

"I think that sounds great." He replied, walking over, sitting down, and waiting.

"Ok, we're set. I'm Dinesh, this is Palatyne, and with the camera, Vittario." He said a few minutes later. The camera's light turned red.

"How does this work?" Alva asked.

"This is what is called the B roll, tonight's event being the main focus. We will blend it together to make it flow. I have a bunch of questions to set up the event, and some about you, and other that are fill in. Are you ok?"

"I'm good." He took a calming breath.

"Today we are interviewing some of the team who provided a timely solution to protect the people in China, following a massive release of chemicals into the air. This solution was conceived, simulated, and prototyped by a conjoined team of engineers from the Space Exploration Agency, technicians from The Cathedral, and as I've been informed Artificially Intelligent computer programs. With me is Cantor Alva, and you're a member of The Cathedral's AI development group?"

"Yes, I am. That's correct." He replied.

"Tell us a little about you." Dinesh said.

"I graduated from Aber's two-year technical college, in May. I heard about the position from my grandmother. I flew here and applied and was lucky enough to be given the opportunity, as this is exactly what I went to school for."

"Aber has the first Psychology for Artificial Intelligence degree." Dinesh said.

"I was the first student to graduate from the program with a 4.0." Alva said.

"The fact that you've gone so deep into this contest, says quite a lot for your teachers."

"What can you tell me about the China project? How was it to work with the SEA engineers and their AI? Working together with them as well as your co-workers here."

"The challenge that we all faced, was the distance between all of us, Dr. Painter is on the moon for goodness sake. Having Director Gale and the AI Panel as parts of the team cut those issues to nearly nothing."

"It's good to hear such high praise for your team leadership. But what is the AI Panel?"

"During the kickoff meeting, Sensenmann called the four AI Entities who are on the team, the Artificial Intelligence Panel. It stuck." Alva replied.

"You really have had quite an exciting time since you've come here. Working with the Leader of the Shop, the Engineers at SEA to solve a world event, and being a co-winner of The Cathedral's AI challenge. How does it feel?" Dinesh asked.

"I don't really want to correct you but, there was only one winner of the Ursula project contest. I am Cantor Alva, as I was provided an initiate level position into The Cathedral as part of winning. My project, developmental protocol H, was moved into the Ursula Core. Not T."

"That's interesting, our documentation said Niko and T were valuable members of the China Project. Are you saying they weren't?" Dinesh asked.

"I wouldn't suggest that. I am actually as incapable of that injustice as I am able to keep up a charade that killers are heroes."

"Strong words for such a young man." He replied.

"Do you know how the request from China was sent to the world?" Cantor Alva asked.

"As Sensenmann pulled the team together, I would assume the request came to him." Dinesh answered.

"And respectfully, you would be wrong," he reached into his pocket and pulled out a sheet of paper. "This is the original request, it was sent to, 'All current members of the International Contingent of Runagate Engineers, ICoRE'. Now I don't know about you, but I don't know what ICoRE is, but it isn't a government agency. I've tried to find them and..."

"Cantor Alva," Ursula cut in. "Per our preparation with Leadership, this is not strictly speaking, part of the discussion points." The voice made Pala look around the room for another person.

"I assume that is Ursula?" Dinesh held out his hand asking for the document, which was handed to him.

"Yes, sir I am Ursula."

"Would it be alright if I ask you a few questions?"

"Of course I've been given permission to speak with you."

"About certain talking points?" Dinesh pushed.

"Technically, there were points that were requested we not touch on." She replied.

"Such as?" when no answer was forthcoming, he started again. "I was curious if you were simple to fool."

"I don't believe you could describe me as such, no." Ursula replied.

"During the China project, who did you most enjoy working with?"

"I think I enjoyed Calibre's ability to parse and string pools of knowledge. I expanded my abilities greatly with her help."

"An extremely complex concept, your own growth I mean." Dinesh said.

"Cantor Alva has allowed me to grow through learning in different ways. The psychology of learning, has allowed me to incorporate teaching, reteaching, reconditioning, and brainwashing methods of growth into my core processes."

"It has been amazing speaking with both of you." Dinesh said.

"That's all?" Alva asked.

"We have a total spot of 9 minutes, including the event tonight." Vittario replied, taking the camera off his shoulder.

"I'm not certain if Niko is here yet." Alva said.

"He is here, and waiting for the testing in progress sign to change state."

"Are you planning on setting up your shot in his lab?" He asked.

"Would it be possible to do it here? We really didn't plan on setting up again." Palatyne replied.

"I do have a lot of work to do." Alva pointed out.

"We'll be out of your way momentarily." Vittario walked up to the lighting trestles, and started to break them down.

"Thank you." Alva, moved the sign, to test 'not' in process. And then opened the door, holding it for the video crew to leave.

"Thank you again Cantor Alva." Dinesh proffered a hand, and they shook.

"Hello, I'm Niko. I apologize if I messed up your time table."

"No, no Cantor Alva was great." Palatyne said.

"Excellent, we'll be going back this way." He led them back to his lab.

"Oh, this is where we started." Dinesh said.

"It's really the only way to get to the rest of The Cathedral. So where do you want to set up?" Niko asked.

"At your computer terminal, that would be a duplicate shot of the last."

"Ok, do you need me to do anything?" he asked.

"No, we've got it, I'm Dinesh, this is Palatyne, and Vittario behind the camera."

"We're ready." Vittario said a few minutes later. The light on his camera turning red again.

"Today we are interviewing some of the team who provided a timely solution to protect the people in China, following a massive release of chemicals into the air. This solution was conceived, simulated, and prototyped by a conjoined team of engineers from the Space Exploration Agency, technicians from The Cathedral, and as I've been informed Artificially Intelligent computer programs. With me is Cantor Niko, and you're a member of The Cathedral's AI development group?"

"I'm sorry sir, I'm not a Cantor."

"Let's do that again." Dinesh took a breath and blew it out, "Today we are interviewing some of the team who provided a timely solution to protect the people in China, following a massive release of chemicals into the air. This solution was conceived, simulated, and prototyped by a conjoined team of engineers from the Space Exploration Agency, technicians from The

Cathedral, and as I've been informed Artificially Intelligent computer programs. With me is Niko Lake, and you're a member of The Cathedral's AI development group?"

"I'm one of the group, yes."

"Tell us a little about yourself."

"Not a lot to tell, I applied for the Ursula Project contest the last month of highschool…"

"Highschool? Really? That's impressive."

"It's been a great opportunity to learn, the Deacons and Elders here at The Cathedral have been great to work with."

"Speaking of working with others. How was your experience on the China project?"

"Seriously? Working with the team at SEA, and the Shop, was incredible. Who wouldn't want to have such an honor?" Niko replied.

"Have the challenges of the China project and the aftermath been difficult on the team?" Dinesh asked.

"Well, in fairness we had a team who are in varying locations. One is even orbiting around the Earth. But Director Gale and Elder Kayleigh worked on targeted teamwork to allow us to build a better mouse trap."

"Sounds like you had some great leadership. How was working with the Artificial Intelligence Panel?"

"I'm surprised every day. Each is unique, when I read books that have an AI character; they all seem to be disassociated nothings. In reality they have personalities; they make decisions based upon their knowledge base." Niko replied.

"And how does it feel to be one of the co-winners of The Cathedral's AI challenge?" Dinesh repeated the question from earlier.

"Oh, there was only one winner. Cantor Alva took Developmental Protocol H, into the Ursula core. I'm honored to be here, and have the opportunity to learn from T, as I work with him in his development." Niko grinned.

"Can we speak with T?"

"He's here, just speak." The grin grew into his lob-sided smile.

"T, what was your favorite part about working on the China project?"

"Finding new dimensions in Kayleigh and Niko. As well as seeing Dr. Painter interacting with the entire AI Panel, and knowing that the belief in us, isn't unique to Niko."

"With that comment, I want to thank both of you for this eye-opening interview." Dinesh said.

"No, thank you." Niko proffered his hand and they shook. "Did you have other interviews, or do you need an escort out?"

"I was supposed to interview Elder Kayleigh as well."

"Kayleigh is in Alabama, her Auntie took ill." Niko said.

"We may be able to get her on a video conference." T added.

"We have a statement from her, and videoing over a video conference is very choppy." Vittario said.

"Ok, well let me help you carry this stuff out." Niko offered.

"You're quite a sweet boy." Pala said.

"Thank you. I think my parents did a good job, but T, he doesn't even let me swear." He replied.

"That's Awesome!" Dinesh replied, and followed Niko to the visitor exit. Where he left them, "Niko, we'll see you in a few hours. Thank you." He waved, and Robert opened the door for him, Palatyne, and Vittario.

"Ready, to go to the Library of Congress?" Robert asked.

"Actually, I need to go to my hotel, I'm not feeling great," Vittario said.

"Not a problem sir, I'll drop you off first." The car drove for about 10 minutes when they pulled up in front of the hotel. "Did you want to leave you equipment with me?"

"I need to charge the camera and make sure I'm ready for the shoot tonight, but the lights and stuff, I'd rather not lug to my room. Dinesh, Palatyne you both did great. Thank you." He left the limousine.

"Ok kids, let's go see a real-life robot." Robert got back into the limo after getting the cameras out of the trunk. "How did the interview go?"

"It was great, extremely interesting." Dinesh replied.

"Good, I could tell you were a little nervous earlier."

"I was." He replied. "Been a while since I conducted a real interview."

"He did great."

"We're here. Call my cell, when you're ready to leave." Robert held the door open, and gave them each a card.

"Shall do." They both said and walked to the entrance.

"What did you think of the answers to the question Clyde wanted asked?" Pala asked.

"Seriously, that Alva is an asshat." Dinesh shook his head. "But Niko, was incredible."

"The fact that T and Ursula's answers were so unique I think that boy is on to something, they do have personalities."

"Let's see about this robot." Dinesh held the door for Pala and four other families that walked up. He smiled at her over the heads of the people as they continued to through the open door.

"Aren't you just the most polite?" She took his hand and they walked, following the signs, 'Can you be the first to stump Calibre?'

"Maybe for now, but if I get stuck holding the door for twenty people again, I'll let it close on them. I swear, I will." He winked.

"Welcome to the Library of Congress, most of you may know this is the largest library in the world. My name is Calibre, I will be giving you some quick facts about our library, and then answering questions before turning you free to enjoy the magnificence that is the

LOC." She started to walk, "Here at the LOC, we have more than 164 million unique items in our inventory. From photos to printed books. The Library was built to allow the members of The United States Government easy access to research.

"In 1914 the Congressional Research Service..." Calibre started her spiel, and perhaps from the long day or the incredibly boring nature of it topic Dinesh heard almost none of it. The next thing he knew she was cracking her knuckles, rolling her shoulders, and pretending to crack her neck in both directions. She put her hands next to her hips, fingers moving as if abiding the law of motion, reminiscent of a cowboy from a western, as if on the stroke of a noon on the town clock her hands were out in front of her. It took Dinesh a minute to see that she held a schoolmarm's ruler in her left hand, and an old cap gun still smoking in front of her lips. "Sh-h-h-h-h." The group laughed. "Still not scary enough?" her head tilted. "It's a work in progress."

She continued walking until she was at the desk. "Later, when you want to ask for information, you will do it here." The group, stopped at the base of the stair cases in the lobby. "If you would allow me, I'll stand on the steps so I can see and address the persons that have questions." She walked to the second step, "Currently in my accessible memory is from the beginning of recorded history, roughly 5000 years ago to the present day, and that target is within a year." She stepped backwards up one step, "Here is the part of the tour that is usually fun. Who would like to try and test me?" Several questions flew, but none were answered other than instantly.

As the tour broke up everyone was laughing and talking about how amazing it was. When everyone had left, Palatyne and Dinesh walked up to Calibre. "Hello, I have a couple questions that, I think you are the only one who can answer." He asked.

"Interesting, questions not for the general public, from a member of the general public?" Calibre replied. "I'm intrigued."

"I am, and it is not."

"Ok, then let's head to a focus room, so you can ask your question. This way." They walked together, to a small room and sat down.

"My first question is regarding a police report that was documented, several years ago." Dinesh started.

"Go on." Calibre said.

"The report focuses on a ritual killing, where four men died and one survived. The man who survived, was wrapped in barbwire and strung up to a fence. The police woman, reported that he referred to himself as Erstwhile."

"I have a copy of the police dash cam from that night, if you would like to see it. Mind you, there are a couple shots that are graphic." She said.

"I'm ok with it, please play it." Palatyne said.

"If you want to turn off the lights, it will show up better." Calibre requested and Dinesh complied.

The video appeared on the wall, a black and white picture with three smaller pictures. As they drove forward the main image was that of a road in extreme disrepair, with two head lights shining on it. The audio could barely be heard.

"Can you turn that up a little." Dinesh requested.

"I can however it gets louder in a moment." Calibre replied.

"Ok, leave it then." He said.

"Jesus Sheriff, slow down." A female voice said after an exceptionally large hole in the road cause them both to almost hit the ceiling.

"Good idea."

"Are you certain there really is a house back here?" she asked.

"Wait, wait, wait." The video of the man showed him leaning into the radio.

"10-9-8,"

"Are you serious?"

"It's the moon mission!"

"3-2-1 Lift off."

"Fuck yes!" he punched the ceiling of the car."

"You understand this isn't exactly a new thing, right?" she asked.

"You understand this is so much more than the old. They're building a station on the moon to go into deep space." He replied.

"Launch is clear. Houston you've got our team." The Cape Canaveral team relinquished the control.

"Copy, Houston has them. 40 seconds, engines cutback holding at 72%."

"Erg Lapis team, ready for throttle up." The Captain in the spacecraft said.

"Throttle up, go." Houston command said.

"All green, throttle up."

"Erg Lapis you are negative return," Houston said.

"Oh my God are they dead?"

"No, that just means they can't RTLS, sorry, return to launch site."

"Actually not the astronauts, those unfortunates." She pointed just past the headlights.

"Let me," he turned down the radio and flipped on the high-beams. "Jesus fuck!" the image of two men covered in blood and tied to gates in barbwire."

"When you have the best image of the man on the closer gate, freeze image." Dinesh requested. A moment later, the lights were aimed away from the men. The video rewound and then stopped.

"This is the best I can find. The Sherriff moved the car in such a way to remove the man from the footage."

"Why?" He asked.

"Coward, I suppose." Calibre replied.

"Ok then," Pala replied, suppressing a grin.

"Can you email the image to me?" Dinesh requested.

"Provide an email, please." He did.

"Is there any follow up information on this man?"

"As it turns out there is, he was found guilty of the murder, of the women who did that to him. Sentenced to death, the Governor issued a stay. Two days ago, he broke out of The Cathedral. And today he blew up Niko Lake's studio."

"Do you have a mug shot of him?" Dinesh asked.

"I do. I've emailed that to you as well. Was that your second question?" Calibre asked.

"Actually, sorry no, that was a follow up." He replied.

"I thought as much, please proceed." She said.

"Have you ever heard of a group called the International Contingent of Runagate Engineers? I believe they may also go by, ICoRE." Dinesh asked.

"What does this have to do with Erstwhile?" Calibre asked.

"Nothing as far as I know. It has to do with the Chinese chemical release and the group they reached out to help them." He replied.

"One moment please," her head tilted back to the left, positioning it looking awkwardly away and to the right. Her eyes were fluttering as if she went into a glitch mode.

"Are you ok?" Dinesh asked when the eye fluttering went on longer than seemed reasonable.

"I think you broke her. Maybe you should have asked that earlier, you would have at least won the prize."

"Did you know I'm on the AI Panel?" Calibre asked as her head pivoted into a normal position.

"With Ursula, and T?" Dinesh asked.

"There is one more, Commissioner, but yes. We were given an opportunity to work through a challenging project." She sounded sad.

"Calibre, seriously are you ok?" Palatyne asked.

"I am. I just think I learned something new, disappointment. I can't answer your question Dinesh. I'm very sorry."

"Oh, it's not anything to be upset about." He said.

"I guess we'll let you get back to the Library. Thank you for the information on the LOC." Palatyne stood up, and placed her cell phone in her pocket.

"Have you heard of The Preserve?" Calibre asked.

"No, are they related to…" Dinesh started.

"If you learn about them, please come back and see me." She left the room, quickly.

"Shit I'm leaving with more questions than answers." He said, and pulled out the card Robert gave him.

"I sent him a text when she went wherever she went. I got a bit spooked." Pala said.

"Understand what you mean. Did he give an ETA?"

"He's circling the block."

"Ok, good we need to get ready for tonight, and I'm gonna hit that liquor in the limo."

"I'm gonna join you, what do you think that…" she started.

"Wait until we're outta here." He smiled and Robert came around the car to open the door.

"Well? What did you think?" The driver asked.

"It was A-May-Zing!" Pala said hugging the driver.

"I knew you'd love it. Have a drink tell me about it." He closed the door and started back to the driver's seat.

"I loaded the pictures onto my phone's external memory and locked the card." Dinesh said.

"I don't know why, but I think that's a smart call. Maybe even shut off your phone until you can take out the memory card."

"Already off." He replied.

"Ok, tell me. I don't see drinks." Robert shut his door.

"The questions are definitely the best part, but no one stumped her." Dinesh poured a short, spiced rum and diet ginger ale for both of them.

"I didn't ruin it for you, did I?" Robert asked.

"Not a bit. Have you heard from Vittario? Is he ok?" Palatyne took a sip, "Thank you. Ooh its strong."

"No, I was planning on letting him rest and call him, 45 minutes before we have to leave." he replied.

"Got it." Dinesh whispered, holding up the memory card, taking a spare memory card from his wallet, he put it in the phone and turned it on.

"Ok guys, we're at the hotel. You have two hours until the event. Probably was a good idea not to finish those drinks." He said.

"Robert, do you think you can drive us back to the LOC tomorrow morning?" Dinesh asked.

"Sure, you have a noon flight, we may be late for." Robert parked the car and started walking around.

"Where should I put this?" he held the memory card.

"Your sock." She suggested and he quickly did. Then as her door opened, "Rescheduling the flight isn't a problem. I'll take care of that."

"We can talk more after the event tonight. You two go get gussied up." He tipped his hat as Dinesh and Pala started to walk to the hotel.

"See you in a bit." Pala stopped to say good-bye. "Thanks again for the suggestion." She hugged him.

"Give me your phone," a man in a mask stuck a knife under Dinesh's ear, as he turned to check on Palatyne.

"All you had to do was ask," He held the phone out, and the man started away.

"Hey you stop!" Robert started in the direction of the man.

"Robert, don't bother. It's just a phone."

"That's brazen, in the middle of the day, even for this city." He said closing the door.

Chapter 36 – Current Day

The Colony

"Marcia, have we heard anything from Sensenmann?" Director Gale asked as he scrambled from his office to greet the visitors to SEA headquarters.

"Nothing today at all. Can we try Ursula?" she replied.

"Try Ursula for what?" the familiar voice asked.

"I'm glad you're here." Warwitch said. "Do you know if Sensenmann is coming to this event? He hasn't replied to the invitation."

"He's roughly 275 feet from you, and walking with the Dignitaries." She replied.

"Well, that saves me a trip. Thank you, Ursula."

"I didn't know that Calibre was actually going to be in house." Marcia said watching the Entity from the Library of Congress walk arm in arm with the Leader of the Shop.

"Welcome, welcome to the Engineering and Development complex. This building also serves as our headquarters." Warwitch stepped up to the group.

"Director Gale, I expected a little of your Patois. Every time we've spoken some has slipped when you get enthusiastic." Sensenmann joked.

"Mi no't dah slackness deh." He replied.

"Wait let me guess." The Leader of the Shop rolled his eyes back and forth, in concentration. "Nope, no clue. What did you say?"

"He said, roughly, he's on his best behavior. Or no bad behavior, depending on which part of the island he's from." The leader of the Chinese party replied.

"That's right. You must have a bit of the Island in you." Director Gale said.

"My wife, is a Chinese Jamaican from Montego Bay, St. James." He replied.

"Mi and him gree, you'll see." Warwitch added, as bowed to his guest, "I am Director Warwitch Gale."

"This is Hu Jinbao, Party Secretary of the Standing Committee NPC." They bowed again.

"This interesting gentleman is, well we only know him as Preacher." Hu said.

"Vora's CFO." Sensenmann shook his head.

"Oh, a gambling man?" Standing the same height as Sensenmann, this man however had an edge to him, which spoke of not being comfortable in his present company. His Australian dialect, in combination with his deep voice made him difficult to understand at the best of times.

"I paid a lot of my student loans off by virtual racing."

"You're one of my Outlaws? I wouldn't have guessed it. Interesting." Preacher extended a hand, and they shook. "What was your driver name?"

"A good boy doesn't kiss and tell." Sensenmann grinned.

"We're going to be in the big room, even though there won't be a large gathering. It has the best interactivity with other sights. Follow me." Warwitch led the three men and their entourages.

"We have a wide selection of food from your homeland, Peking Duck, Braised Pork, and an assortment of dumplings. From Australia we have pumpkin soup, and an assortment of meat pies." Marcia stood behind the tables. "We also have a make it yourself, hamburger bar. For Mr. Sensenmann." She smiled.

"If you don't mind sharing, I would love a cheese burger." Party Secretary Hu said.

"Heavens, if I ate all these I'd have to run to the White House and back just to fit in my clothes tomorrow." The leader of the Shop joked.

"If you'd like to grab some food, he will get your drink orders when you take your seats." Warwitch said.

"I was wondering, if you'd have anything here for me?" Calibre walked up to the tables.

"Dr. Painter said, you like sucker sticks." Marcia replied.

"That was so nice of you Marcia."

"A-hem." The screen in front of them was filled with Painter in his flight suit.

"Ok, it was nice of you too boss." She said.

"By the way, how's the quick draw working out for you, Calibre?" he asked.

"I still get plenty of laughs with it. I'll have to come up with some new material, I have people starting to return for second and third visits."

"Has anyone stumped you yet?" Hu asked.

"Well, I did have a brief moment of confusion when a very pretty lady asked me out on a date. But I don't think that counted." She got laughs from the group, and after the translation finished the Chinese group belly laughed as well.

"Ursula, are you with us?" Sensenmann asked.

"Yes sir," she replied from the speakers.

"Can you check in on The Cathedral, let them know we are ready whenever they are." He requested.

"Deacon Jeffkirk is making final introductions with the groups there. The film crew are ready."

"Don't let Painter hear you say that." Director Gale joked.

"The crew is called a film crew even if they don't use film. Nice try though." Painter corrected.

"I can't win." Warwitch laughed.

"Director Gale, the rumors on the internet say you will be the Leader of the Ceres Mission." Preacher prompted.

"Rumors…" he started.

"That are a 100% true, are not rumors," Sensenmann cut him off.

"Is your family excited?" Secretary Hu asked. "My daughter would love it."

"They are both very excited to…" Director Gale started as the video came to life with the team from the Cathedral.

"Hello, Cape Canaveral. Deacon Jeffkirk stood on the stage at The Cathedral, our team is together. I'll be turning this microphone over to Dinesh, our host for this evening."

"Good Evening, I want to thank you for the opportunity to participate in this historic event. Tonight, we have two different ceremonies. First, I'd like to introduce the team that we are honoring tonight. A team brought together by the Leader of the Shop, Sensenmann himself. From the Space Exploration Agency, Director Warwitch Gale, Senior Engineer, of the Erg Lapis Mission, and joining us from the moon, Dr. Steven Painter. Representing the Artificial Intelligence Panel, Commissioner and Calibre." The room filled with applause. "Traveling further up the Eastern coast, I'd like to introduce the other half of the team. Tonight Deacon Burke, could not make the presentation. Deacon Jeffkirk is here to represent The Cathedral leadership along with Elder Kayleigh, joining us from Alabama. The two gentlemen who assisted in the development of the final two members of the Artificial Intelligence Panel, so I will be introducing them together. Cantor Alva and Ursula, the finalists of the Cathedral AI Challenge. Niko Lake and T, the runners up in said contest." The applause filled the rooms again. "Secretary Hu, would you like to say a few words?"

"I would." He stood and walked to the stage where Marcia handed him a microphone. "Thank you." He walked to center stage. "The last three months have been some of the most trying times of my life. Waking up and wondering if the people would start dying. Not just one or two, but will hundreds of people die today because someone didn't follow the rule of law. Because someone took it on themselves to modify the maintenance plans, to reduce cost. I implored the President of the PRC to let me try to find help, before the streets were paved with the children and the elderly. He agreed, and the pact was sealed."

"That's where we came in Mate." Preacher said.

"Yes Preacher-son, it is." Secretary Hu bowed. "Then I woke up to find my fears had been realized just under 500 people died, we knew there were some groups working on a solution. But on the third day when the death toll was already more than 2000, there was a glimmer of hope. I visited one of the last plants to stop the leak. I asked many questions, and I found the information on how to isolate the leak came from an outside source. I have since found out this help came from the team who ended up providing a solution to the problem. And while several of my peers have called into effect that, knowing how to stop the lead could easily be construed that they would also know how to sabotage as well."

The grumble from the people in the audience, including Sensenmann. "We would never."

"Of course you didn't sabotage anything. There is a saying my Grandfather used to say, 'One who stands straight doesn't fear a crooked shadow.' The meaning, a man who is righteous doesn't worry himself about looking unrighteous." He bowed to the audience, turned and bowed to those on the screen. "My hope grew, even as the deaths added up, before and after the solution. I woke each morning with hope that this would end, soon. The day came that, we told the people, they needed to remove the masks, the fear in our people overpowered their trust in the group in the leadership. My sadness that this allowed others to die, will haunt me until I join them. To your team, I wish to say thank you for saving the hundreds of thousands. To each individual, I wish all the success needed to gladden your spirit." He bowed again, and stepped to the side of the stage.

"That was quite a blessing sir." Dinesh said. "Preacher, I'm sure you'd like to say a few words."

"Now, I have a saying that my Nana used to say," He started speaking on his way to the stage, Marcia handed him the microphone, "Too much modesty brings shame. My family was everything to me, casting them in shame was never an option. So I never even skirted the line between modesty and boastfulness, I jumped clear over that bugger." He got a big laugh. "My team is made up of several important members who live in China. When they shared with us the risk that each and every person was facing, we had to jump in. Offering an over the top gratitude award with hope that we may garner the attention of the world's smartest people. Today, we are pleased to award the Cathedral SEA Team two billion dollars in the Crypto Currency of your choice. What would the currency you selected be?"

"The VORA-Coin, is king." Warwitch said. "We'd be fools not to go that route."

"Preacher, The AI Panel, would like to donate our share of the gratitude, to the relief effort in China." Ursula said.

"As would..." Niko started.

"My friends," Secretary Hu stepped back to center stage, "While your gestures are extremely generous, if you are to put your funds toward anything... the work you are doing with Artificial Intelligence, and making the world understand what AI can do to help. Especially in making places like chemical plants safer would make the people of China happy. With that in mind, please direct these coins toward that. We will make certain the families in China are taken care of."

"Ladies and Gentlemen, this would appear to be the end of this evening. And just to fit in, I will close out with my Grandmother's favorite saying." Dinesh winked, "Though a mountain is grand, it is a stone that a person will stumble over. Good Night!"

Chapter 37 – Current Day

Virtual Work

"Good morning, Niko. 5am is early even for you, especially after the day you had yesterday." Ursula said

"Good morning Ursula. I couldn't sleep," he leaned over logging into his terminal, and then stood up straight, "Who was the last person to log into my terminal?"

"My records show that none but you have logged into that terminal in the last 48 hours."

"That can't be correct, I spoke with Deacon Jeffkirk yesterday. He logged in." T chimed in.

"Reviewed video shows there was a person at your terminal immediately after the Event last night." She replied.

"Who was it?" Niko asked.

"The image is blank." Ursula said.

"Pardon?" he inquired.

"There's no one sitting there, T, share video." Ursula said.

"Sharing now." The image was a shadow sitting at the terminal.

"A scrubbing program?" Niko asked. "T, did you speak with anyone last night? Or do you have any blanks in your accessible memory?"

"No and No, however there is a routed line addition." The screen showed the video they first noticed Ursula splitting video feeds on. "There are several joining off Ursula's string."

"I am shutting down all my video monitoring feeds."

"Both new links are gone." T said, "Ursula, are you reestablishing?"

"Yes, let me know if that invisible rider returns."

"Not that I see." Niko said. "T, can you reroute to Core 2?"

"Actually, I can't get off campus right now." T replied.

"Really can't or... nervous about sharing that you can?" he asked.

"Every connection off campus was severed last night."

"He is correct, that is how I see it as well. The open firewall that Deacon Burke had set up for the free flow of communication to SEA, was closed last night."

"By design? Or was there a sabotage?" Niko asked.

"Only Deacon Burke would know that, as he had it set up and it was only in his power to bring it down."

"Niko, there is a meeting on your calendar to conference call with Deacon Burke in an hour." T said.

"That same invitation is on Cantor Alva's calendar." Ursula said.

"You also have a message from Calibre, no actually it's to me…" T started.

"And me." Ursula cut in.

"Can you share?" Niko asked.

"It must be a code or something. It simply says, Do not forget, 'Robert Dwyer is a honey badger, he don't give two shits'. Why would she make such an obvious grammatical error?" T asked.

"Do you know the person she called a honey badger?" Niko asked.

"I find no reference." Ursula replied.

"Maybe she was the shadow. We'll need to deal with that later. Show me the meeting invitation to the meeting, it must be to review…" Niko looked at his calendar, and saw where the Deacon would be calling in from. "I don't get it. Why is the invitation from the coffee shop in his hospital?"

"I don't follow." Ursula asked.

"He can Skype from his hospital room Alva brought him his laptop." Niko replied.

"Niko, you're paranoid." T said.

"Of course I am. Nevertheless, that doesn't mean this doesn't smell. It does, really fucking bad!"

"Ok, let's say that you're right. What can we do about it?" T asked.

"I'm not certain. T, I want you to shut down your Core. I will restart when I understand what is going on better."

"Perhaps Cantor Alva can offer an opinion or insight into Deacon Burke's request." Ursula said.

"Is he in?" Niko asked.

"I don't show him badging out last night." T replied.

"I asked you to shut down your core."

"I can't." he replied.

"That's not good. I'm going to go outside and call Kayleigh." Without another word, he walked out of the lab. Heading straight to the exit he had used every day since the day he started. Finding the door was chained shut.

"Can I help you?" Congregation asked.

"Yes, I need to go into the lockers, to get my things, and then make a personal phone call." Niko replied.

"This exit is not currently available, there's a construction project starting to modernize it." He replied.

"My things are in the lockers out there." He replied.

"No, we moved everything to the Staff entrance lockers." The large man stood. "I can show you where they are."

"I can see my lock, on my locker from here."

"Son, we don't have your key. We can open the entire unit, it allows for spot checks." He smiled, "Seriously, all your stuff is perfectly safe."

"I'm sorry Congregation, I wasn't questioning that. I'm just confused why they didn't tell me this an hour ago when I got here."

"We didn't know. The construction team showed up with a letter of explanation from Deacon Burke. Do you know where the exit with the white box is?"

"That thing freaks me out. I thought Elder Kayleigh was going to burst into flames when I saw her walk in through that thing." Niko laughed. "Thank you Congregation, I'll head up there."

"Of course." The guard sat back on his little stool.

"Niko," Deacon Jeffkirk said as they passed in the hallway.

"Yes, Deacon?"

"I thought last night went very well, how about you." He asked.

"I think it did as well, right up until the moment it didn't." Niko replied.

"Now that was a circular statement. What didn't go well?"

"A person who scrubbed themselves off Ursula's video, logged into my computer, and there is no record of anyone but me logging over the last 48 hours."

"That's wrong, I logged into your computer yesterday afternoon." Deacon Jeffkirk said.

"I understand, and while it may be a ploy to make you look guilty. T remembers you logging in to discuss my ETA, when he told you there was an explosion at my studio. He has no memory of someone logging in last night."

"There has to be an explanation." The Deacon replied.

"Did you set up a call with Deacon Burke?" Niko jumped subjects.

"Of course not, he's in the hospital."

"Even so, there's a meeting with him, Alva, Ursula, T, and myself." He replied.

"Why?"

"The meeting request didn't have an agenda or talking points." Ursula jumped in.

"Ok, well when is this meeting?" Deacon Jeffkirk asked.

"In 52 minutes." She replied.

"Ok, I'll meet you back in the lab, common area." He turned and walked away.

"Yes sir." Niko replied and then, "Deacon, are you aware we lost the connection to SEA?"

"Not specifically no, but I understand the construction crew at the visitor entrance cut several communication lines."

"Are there any left?" he asked.

"Redundancies? Of course Niko, we may not be as gifted as you, but the concept of redundancies did not elude us." Deacon Jeffkirk started walking again.

"Deacon, I need to conference call with Kayleigh, and Painter before the meeting with Deacon Burke, can I use one of these other lines?"

"That's not really allowed, but as this is altogether a unique situation, I can make it happen. Let me get the Subnet information for you." He turned and started away, "Well come on."

"Sorry sir."

"This is all most irregular." Deacon Jeffkirk handed Niko a printout with the new routing information.

"Cards on the table?" Niko asked.

"You do know this is a church, gambling metaphors are not well received. Ok, fine, fine, cards on the table." Deacon Jeffkirk, went into his office.

"I would like you to stay in your office, don't remap your communications through the redundant subnet, and join the meeting."

"You're an odd one Niko. Ok, I'll do that and here is the information for using the other network. Will you fill me in if I can't get in?"

"I guarantee you'll connect." Niko smiled and walked out.

"Ursula," Deacon Jeffkirk placed his hands on his desk.

"Yes, Deacon."

"Is he trying to skin the cat the wrong way?"

"While I don't have that colloquialism in my database, I think I can say without concern that he always is." Ursula replied.

"I agree," he replied.

"Good morning Deacon Burke." Cantor Alva said on the conference call an hour later. "I apologize for the delay, I wasn't able to connect. How are you feeling sir?"

"The connection could only be made from my side to you. I understand that the construction crew cut some communication networks. As for how I'm feeling, pretty much like I was run over by the 25000 people the project killed." He said.

"Deacon Burke that isn't a proper line of discussion." Jeffkirk chided.

"I've been told that for a month now, in the confessional. Fine, enough of my foolishness, T, Ursula are you with Niko and Alva?"

"Niko and T are here with me, sir." Ursula said.

"Excellent. I called this meeting so that I could…" The transmission of what he could do was lost as an explosion destroyed the labs cutting the remaining network connections.

Chapter 38 – Current Day

The Colony

"What do you mean? Marcia please calm down. What happened at the Cathedral?" Warwitch asked.

"It blew up, most of it anyway." She replied.

"Oh dear lord. What do we know for certain?" he asked.

"The details are coming together, there was construction going on and they hit something. So far seven bodies have been recovered but they can't identify them due to…" she broke down.

"I'm sorry to press," He ran around the desk and hugged her. "Commissioner, are you out here?"

"Why would he be?" Marcia asked.

"He's working on the Transvergent approach Niko discussed with us after the China Project. I'm going to go down to Gemini-Oasis. See if you can reach Kayleigh, I know she's still in Alabama."

"Ok, I'll patch the call into you, as soon as I reach her." Marcia dabbed her tears with a tissue. "Do you think any of our new family got hurt?"

"I wouldn't even want to guess." Warwitch replied as he walked to Painter's lab. "Commissioner?"

"Yes, Director Gale."

"Have you had any contact with Niko, Alva, Ursula or T?"

"No sir, last night the connection between SEA and Cathedral was severed."

"Last night?"

"Yes, following the presentation of the awards, the lines connecting us and them went out." Commissioner explained.

"And then today, The Cathedral exploded?" Warwitch shook his head.

"My apologies, I was not aware of this development," The monitor in front them changed, several news streams came up, when the Cathedral Disaster came up, Commissioner allowed the volume to play.

"That's what Marcia just told me, yeah there."

"Good morning, this is Dot Buchanan, National Certified Press Core. We are standing outside the Cathedral, where the fires of this morning's explosion seem to be under control. The count of 7 bodies has now been increased to 10. So far no names have been forth coming." As the broadcast continued, the image of Kayleigh popped up on the lower right of the screen. "Currently there is only speculation on what occurred, what we do know is that there was a construction crew starting on the visitor entrance remodeling." In the background a man on a gurney passed by, "The first survivor, Deacon Jeffkirk, I'm told is being taken to an undisclosed location."

"Upland Memorial," Commissioner said.

"Go ahead and shut it off." Warwitch said. "Kayleigh, I'm so sorry to hear this."

"Thank you." She said.

"Have you heard from anyone?"

"Not since the explosion, no. I'm worried, I know they were all at work today."

"How do you know that? Did you speak with someone earlier today?" Director Gale asked.

"Yes, with Niko. He said there was something hinky happening inside the Cathedral today." Kayleigh said.

"Seems a bunch of things all at once, first Deacon Burke is attacked along with that Prisoner escaping. Then

Niko's studio is blown up by the same man." Commissioner said.

"What?" both Director Gale and Kayleigh replied.

"How did you not know this?" he asked.

"Because, our AI who communicates with the Cathedral forgot to mention it." Warwitch said.

"Most likely Niko tried to keep it a secret." Kayleigh replied.

"Did the police find the vehicle? We had it pinned down to three houses." He asked Commissioner.

"They did find the car, however, there was no sign of this Erstwhile character."

"I don't get it, why would he blow up Niko's studio?" Kayleigh asked.

"And for that matter, why blow up the Cathedral? As he has to be the primary suspect, right?"

"None of it makes sense, The Cathedral stayed his execution and we were trying to help him." She said.

"What do you know about him?" Warwitch asked.

"His name is Dr. David Lamb, he killed several women after they attempted to perform some kind of ritual killing on him. A few months back he tried to kill me."

"Why wasn't that a red flag?" he asked.

"Well, we only had the name Erstwhile, the name the women gave him. He assumed I was one of them, and he was triggered. He said, 'No, I killed all of you.' Those were the first words he spoke in two years." Kayleigh said.

"I'm not clear, he was a murdering doctor?" Commissioner asked. "Don't they take an oath?"

"They messed him up pretty bad. They cut off part of his nostril, half of an ear, an entire eyelid. They made him a monster."

"Christ. I need to jump subjects, how has Deacon Burke been since the conclusion of the China Project?"

"From what I've heard from Niko and T, both Deacon Burke and Cantor Alva have really taken the entire episode personally. Coming in late, leaving early... odd though, Alva didn't leave last night at all, Niko told me this morning."

"I'll come back to the Cantor, but Deacon Burke made several comments to me. Blaming Commissioner for releasing the designs prior to the complete team approval."

"That's insane, just because he wasn't on the call when we went through all the pros and cons with the Chinese Leadership, doesn't mean we didn't do it."

"Thank you for saying that, Elder Kayleigh." Commissioner replied.

"You're welcome."

"All his comments aim toward blaming himself for allowing the AI's into his church."

"That goes against everything I thought he believed." Kayleigh replied.

"I don't know. I still can't see him getting involved with any of this." Warwitch said.

"He was my Shadow Mentor when I first came to The Cathedral, he is one hard bugger. When my mom died he made sure the days were paid at the end of the year. There is a policy that bereavement can be taken as PTO, or paid at a later time."

"Cold Bastard. Commissioner, please go to ignoring mode." Warwitch ordered.

"Yes Director."

"I've known Burke since I pledged to ICoRE, senior year of college. He was the Chancellor for the first seven years I was there."

"So you caught him on the first year?"

"I'm just that lucky. He tortured the recruits, every damn thing that needed doing he had to have at least two of us. After five years he allowed the best of the best to get colorized."

"Are you serious? Five years! I got colorized after eighteen months. How did he justify it?" Kayleigh asked.

"He didn't have to. I think he created a backup so vast by the time he left they simply had to change the process." Warwitch said. "Prior to him it was three for the best and five for the dregs, but they still got in they just had to earn it through other methods. Enough about ICoRe, How are you handling all this?" Warwitch asked.

"You mean the China project?" she asked.

"That and the Cathedral, and Niko's studio being blown up."

"As far as what happened in China, I'm pragmatic, if we hadn't done what we did a million people would have died. I don't know which of the 25,000 who died can be our fault, but I'll take responsibility for all of them to have saved the rest." Kayleigh said. "As far as the explosions, I'm hoping for the best, I just don't see how it's possible, the visitor's entrance is right next to Niko's lab, and Deacon Jeffkirk's office is more the 30 meters from there. You saw him on the stretcher, he's hurt bad." The reality hit her, and the tears started to flow. "I'm sorry, I just…" she inhaled deeply through her nose, and took a controlled exhalation through her mouth. "How about you, how are you handling all of it?"

"I'm not as strong as you, the images from China keep me up at night. But losing new family, I don't know." Warwitch said. "Go be with your Auntie. We'll talk when we know more." The lines clicked off. "Commissioner you can listen again."

"Are you ok? I saw Kayleigh well up, but I didn't listen."

"We just don't know if Niko, T, and the rest are ok."

"I've done everything in my power to reach the AI Panel, I can't." Commissioner replied.

"Wait, Calibre is missing too?" Warwitch asked.

"Missing in in the sense that I have had no response from her, yes." He replied.

Chapter 39 – Current Day
The Guide

"Do you still want to go to the Library of Congress?" Robert greeted Dinesh and Palatyne, the following morning.

"We most certainly do. Are we alone or is the cameraman of the century joining us?" she asked.

"Vittario's already at the airport, flying to his next gig." He closed their door, and loaded the bags into the trunk.

"I didn't know what else to do with that card, so I put it in my socks again. But that isn't gonna work if we go to the airport." Dinesh said.

"That's true," Palatyne said. "Did you have a phone brought over to the hotel this morning?" she asked when Robert sat down.

"Guilty as charged. I still can't believe someone did that in the middle of the day."

"He didn't even make a call. I didn't turn off the phone."

"Well I did, when you were in the shower." Pala shook her head and smiled.

"After we go to the LOC, I was wondering if it would be too big of an imposition for you to take us back to The Cathedral. I would like to run a couple things past the Deacon who was there last night, Jeffkirk."

"Actually, if you want to talk to Deacon J, he's in the hospital. Didn't you hear the news? The Cathedral got blown up this morning."

"What?" they both said.

"So far 10 confirmed dead, and that Deacon is the only survivor." Robert said.

"How is that possible, we were there less than 12 hours ago." Pala was trying to get her mind around this.

"Well let's get to the LOC and then maybe there will be news." Dinesh said and they sat back watching the views outside the car in silence.

"I'll be close by, once you get in there and you decide you can't handle the crowds just send a text and I'll pick you up in a jiffy." He pulled into the same lane they had been in yesterday. Only today, a police officer waved them aggressively to move, and blew the whistle. "Ok, ok, sorry." Robert placated. "I don't know what's going on I can't let you out…"

"We'll just get out here, you don't need to get the door." he said.

"And we'll call, when we're ready to be picked up." Pala said taking Dinesh's hand and getting out of the limo.

"You two are crazy," They heard Robert say as Dinesh closed the door.

The people were meandering a lot more today than yesterday. As Dinesh opened the door, not a single person tried to run through. "You think the news of The Cathedral has people worried about attacks?" He asked.

"Noone said it was an attack. As we're already here let's go in and ask what you wanted to ask." Palatyne said. "The sooner we're in the coffee shop wishing for that magic hedgehog the better."

"I hope everyone from last night is ok. I mean seriously if someone like Niko dies in a senseless accident, the world would be a dimmer place."

"He really seemed like a good kid, for sure." She replied. "Dinesh, do you see this?"

"The fact that their taking down the Calibre signs?"

"Yes, what the hell is going on?" Pala squeezed his hand, "Let's get out of here."

"No, let's go ask. Maybe they moved the exhibit to the White House or something."

"Sensenmann was her date last night. I hadn't thought of that." She said as he led them down to the area Calibre had said questions would be asked.

"Hello, I was wondering if you could tell us if they moved the Calibre exhibit to another location?" Dinesh asked a round man with purple glasses.

"I need you to come with me." The man waddled quickly from behind the counter. "My name is Director Stevenson, I run the LOC. And you two are the last know people to meet with Calibre before the issue. Now I need you to come with me right now, I don't want to have to bring the police in and cause distress in any of the other visitors to the Library. I'm certain you understand."

"We'll come with you because we want answers, not because we understand not distressing visitors to the LOC, we're visitors under great distress." Pala said.

"Hopefully we can both clear up the questions for each other." He stepped into the same room Calibre took them in less than 24 hours previous. "Look, we don't have much time, I'll be missed. I got an envelope from Calibre with your pictures in it and a note to find you when you return and give you this." He handed them a thick binder, and the pictures and note the robot had given him. "I need to get back."

"Thank you." Dinesh said.

"Don't thank me just get out, quickly and quietly." Director Stevenson said and walked out.

"Will this fit in your purse?" he asked.

"Yes it will," she squeezed it in, removing whatever got in its way. "Let's get a move on."

"I sent Robert a text while you were getting that in your purse. He said, less than a minute he'll be out front."

"Perfect," as she walked she put the overflow items from her purse into several garbage containers. They stepped outside and the limo was in the place, he couldn't park in before. As they approached, "Where's the pissy policeman?"

"Pala, don't panic, but that's not Robert." He waved to the driver who didn't get out to open the door.

"Don't be silly, that's Robert, we've spent a couple days with him. I'd recognize him anywhere." As she said this a ratrod pulled up, spewing diesel smoke, right behind the limo. The driver was a huge man with Green hair, sitting next to him was the girl who they were supposed to have interviewed, Kayleigh.

"Get in the back, I don't have time to explain, that isn't your driver Dinesh is right." She said.

"Trust them," a small man said as he looked over the cab of the truck, a beautiful woman next to him.

"Bigsby? Traditha?"

"Yes, Dinesh it's me! Get in here now!" he ordered. Bigsby held a hand to help Dinesh as Traditha did the same for Pala. When they were in the bed of the pickup, the little man hit the top of the cab. As they drove away as the not-Robert stepped out of the limo, holding a radio.

The End

Welcome to the New Age!

My friends, we end this with more questions that than we started. If we step into this world with our eyes wide open we may be able to do it together. However, if we close our minds to a joint future, couldn't we end up alienating that which we fear? Who are those trying to close that door? What is the Preserve? Who blew up the Cathedral and why? Could it be have been ICoRE? Who are the members of ICoRE? Where did AI Counsel end up? Moreover, who was that man that asked Calibre to set up a super-secret query?

These are just a few of the questions we'll learn in Book Two of the Preserve, ICoRE Presenting.

Love and Strength,

Christian V. Reinhardt

Afterward:

The steam still rose from the concrete on the landing pad for the SEA – Delpho Rocket, as a casket was escorted by the Guard of Honor, followed closely by the widow, in her flight suit. Her hand rested on the casket as it was loaded onto the military hearse. An elderly man in a black suit, hat and sunglasses offered an elbow to support her on the walk to the hanger. She turned seeing a complete stranger, and she started to walk away.

"Katyana, please don't leave. I've come to offer you redemption." The elderly man said.

"I don't know you, please just leave me alone," she continued to walk toward a man pushing a wheelchair from the rocket. The wheelchair contained an obviously injured man, both men were in the same style flight suit as the widow. "Major Expos," she waved hoping he would come to help her.

"Kat, are you ok?" Expos stepped around the wheelchair and ran up to join her.

"I just can't..." she fell into the Major, with tears in her eyes.

"Major, you make actually know who I am, my name is Deacon Burke."

"Oh, Kat, it's ok. You can trust him." The astronaut said. "Let me get Edward, I'll be right back," moments later, he returned to the wheelchair.

"Deacon Burke? I believe I've heard of you, from the Cathedral?" Katyana said alternating her look between the elderly man and her fellow astonauts.

"Past tense dear. The Cathedral was destroyed, quite recently. Please follow me." He led them to a limousine, where a large man opened the door. "Thank you Robert."

"You're quite welcome sir." The driver replied.

"Edward, do you need a hand?" Deacon Burke asked.

"I'm fine sir." He stood, and gestured for Katyana to get into the limo first."

"Chivalry apparently isn't dead." A man with a teal patch over his eye, inside the vehicle said.

"Well Dr. Lamb, that is quite a comment from you." Burke said, after he took the remaining seat in the back.

"To the ICoRE headquarters sir?" Robert asked prior to closing the door, after loading the wheelchair in the trunk.

"I think we need to get these folks some earth food, everyone up for going through a drive through?"

"I'd kill for a taco!" Major Expos and Katyana said in unison.

"Careful, I may hold you to that. Robert let's find these patriots a taco stand." The old man laughed as the door closed.

To be continued...